Sex in Public

A Black Lace short-story collection

Edited by Lindsay Gordon

Black Lace stories contain sexual fantasies.
In real life, always practise safe sex.

This edition published in 2007 by
Black Lace
Thames Wharf Studios
Rainville Road
London W6 9HA

Typeset by SetSystems Limited, Saffron Walden, Essex
Printed and bound by Mackays of Chatham PLC

ISBN 978 0 352 34089 4

Printed and bound in Great Britain by Clays Ltd, St Ives PLC

Sex in Public

A Black Lace erotic short-story collection

Look out for other themed Black Lace short-story collections

Already Published: *Sex in the Office, Sex on Holiday, Sex in Uniform, Sex in the Kitchen, Sex on the Move, Sex and Music, Sex and Shopping*

Published in May 07: *The Black Lace Book of Sex with Strangers*

Published August 07: *Black Lace – Paranormal Erotica* (short stories and fantasies)

Contents

Newsletter

Want to write short stories for Black Lace?

Please read the following. And keep checking our website for information on future editions.

- Your short story should be 4,000–6,000 words long and not published anywhere in the world – websites excepted.
- Thematically, it should be written with the Black Lace guidelines in mind.
- Ideally there should be a 'sting in the tale' and an element of dramatic tension, with oodles of erotic build-up.
- The story should be about more than 'some people having sex' – we want great characterisation too.
- Keep the explicit anatomical stuff to an absolute minimum.

We are obliged to select stories that are technically faultless and vibrant and original – as well as fitting in with the tone of the series: upbeat, dynamic, accent on pleasure etc. Our anthologies are a flagship for the series. We pride ourselves on selecting only the best-written erotica from the UK and USA. The key words are: diversity, surprises and faultless writing.

Competition rules will apply to short stories: you will hear back from us about your story *only* if it has been successful. We cannot give individual feedback on

short stories as we receive far too many for this to be possible.

For future collections check the Black Lace website.

If you want to find out more about Black Lace, check our website, where you will find our author guidelines and more information about short stories. It's at www.blacklace-books.co.uk

Alternatively, send a large SAE with a first-class British stamp to:

Black Lace Guidelines
Virgin Books Ltd
Thames Wharf Studios
Rainville Road
London W6 9HA

Bird's-eye View Mae Nixon

All men have a kink and I like to think I've seen them all. From the predictable (stockings, peephole bras) to the eyebrow-raising (spanking, exhibitionism) to the kind you have to visit a specialised establishment for, I pride myself that nothing shocks me. OK, I did once draw the line at allowing a lover to lick my eyeballs, but only because I was worried he might choke on my contact lenses.

Rob's kink comes somewhere towards the lower end of my sliding scale of perversity. Not as unusual as wanting to put on my underwear and be tickled with a feather duster, but a long way from the missionary position in the dark. He likes to do it in public.

Rob's little peccadillo has got us into quite a bit of trouble over the years. A homeowner once set his dog on us when he caught us shagging in his porch. We've been thrown off more public transport than I care to mention and we were even arrested last year when we were enjoying a quickie in a shop doorway and someone mistook us for burglars.

The police let us off with a caution in the end but they told us if they caught us again we'd be prosecuted. I went right off the idea of alfresco sex after that but, to Rob, it had seemed like a challenge and he began a one-man quest to come up with ever more inventive locations to get down and dirty. And dirty is just what we got more often than not; I've laid down in more muddy fields, damp beaches and building sites than I can even count.

Though it had never been my fantasy, after a while, I

began to get off on the excitement and danger just as much as Rob. Let's face it, most women have a touch of the exhibitionist inside us somewhere. Why else do we wear low-cut tops on a night out or worry whether our legs need waxing? We want to be looked at and admired. We like the idea of our bodies turning on men, even men we don't fancy in the slightest.

Once my inner exhibitionist had been unleashed I discovered I loved being looked at and, much to my surprise and delight, I also realised I adored the risk and danger involved in public sex. The fear of discovery and arrest and the idea that we might actually be exciting unseen watchers was thrilling and arousing. It always gave our public sessions a frisson of wickedness and shame that was more erotic than any aphrodisiac money can buy.

Rob's always thinking of new and exciting places to get horizontal. We've done it on the deck of a cross-channel ferry in a storm. Rain and wind lashed us as I held on to the railing at the prow, doing my best impersonation of Kate Winslet, while Rob gave me one from behind. We broke into the municipal bowling green and just managed to fit in a quickie on the rink before the security guard caught us.

We've tried swingers' clubs and dogging sites but, somehow, having permission seems to take all the excitement out of it. If there's no risk of discovery and no chance of outraging the public it just doesn't do it for us. Over the years, finding new places to express ourselves has become something of a crusade for Rob so, as my last birthday approached, I knew he'd have something extra special planned.

Though I didn't want to spoil the surprise, I've never had any talent for waiting. When I was a kid I wouldn't rest until I knew what was in every single one of my Christmas presents beneath the tree. Even if it meant creeping down in the middle of the night and picking off the Sellotape.

Rob was used to this and had grown skilled at outwitting me. He usually made all the arrangements from work, so there was never any paper trail for me to follow, short of breaking into his office. Which, believe me, I had considered, but I'd never been any good at picking locks and if it all went wrong nobody would have believed me and I didn't want to risk six months for breaking and entering. So all I could do was go through his pockets for any receipts he might have forgotten and eavesdrop on his telephone calls.

One evening I was coming downstairs after a shower when I overheard Rob on the phone talking about booking a flight for the night of my birthday. I stopped in my tracks and sat down on the stairs so he wouldn't be able to see me through the open door of the living room and strained my ears to listen to his conversation. I kept waiting for a destination to be mentioned, but all I heard was Rob giving his credit card details and then thanking them before hanging up. I crept back upstairs on my hands and knees, closed the bathroom door noisily then came back down again, as if for the first time.

I was in no doubt that Rob's plan was for us to head for the toilet mid-flight and join the Mile High Club. Then we'd go on to our destination for a weekend of pleasure and do the same thing on the flight home. It was one of the few places we'd never done it and, short of the space shuttle orbiting the Earth, the most exotic we could think of. And, with their safety record, even we weren't that reckless.

As my big day approached I grew more and more excited. I wondered what pretext Rob would use to get me to pack and go to the airport. Or perhaps he'd pack for me in secret, not wanting to spoil the surprise. On the day of my birthday I took a few hours off to get a haircut then went for a manicure, pedicure and a full leg wax. While on the couch, I asked the beautician for a full Brazilian on the spur of the moment, knowing that the unexpected sight of my naked pussy would surprise and excite Rob.

He picked me up after work, a taxi waiting outside, then took me to our favourite restaurant for a celebratory meal. Rob seemed to be in no hurry and I began to get a little worried about us making it to the airport in time. I still didn't want to spoil the surprise so I said nothing but he must have picked up on my anxiety because he began to give me funny looks and finally, during dessert, he said, 'Is there something wrong, Jenny?'

'Ummm, oh, not really . . .' I hoped I sounded more convincing than I felt.

'You're like a cat on hot bricks. Are you worried about something?'

'Err, no, not really. Only, I've got to admit I overheard you booking the flight and I'm just getting a little worried about us getting to the airport on time.'

Rob began to smile. Rob's smile had been one of the first things I noticed about him; his eyes crinkled, his cheeks formed into little round apples and a dimple appeared either side of his mouth. I still found it captivating and completely irresistible. It always made my nipples harden and my knickers grow damp and tonight was no exception.

He shook his head slowly from side to side, his smile growing ever wider until he gradually gave in to laughter. His shoulders were shaking and a little dark lock of hair over his forehead trembled.

'As usual, darling, your nosiness has led you in completely the wrong direction. We are taking a flight, but not in a plane.'

'What then? A hot air balloon? A helicopter?'

'You'll find out soon enough. Now eat your pudding before I do.'

Another thing I like about Rob – he loves chocolate and sweet stuff as much as I do. I hate it when you go out with a bloke and he turns up his nose at dessert as if he's Superman and you've just offered him Kryptonite. Nothing makes you feel guiltier about your sweet tooth or the size of your arse than a man who watches you eat a portion of sticky toffee pudding with an expression of pure disgust on his face. Rob tucks in with gusto and, often as not, asks for a second helping. And, you won't be surprised to know, he's got the same appetite in the bedroom. I like that in a man.

After dinner, we got into another taxi and Rob told the driver to take us to Waterloo station.

'Are we going on the Eurostar?'

The taxi snaked through the city traffic.

'What makes you think that?' Rob reached over and held my hand.

'It goes from Waterloo, doesn't it?'

'Does it?' He brought my hand to his lips and kissed it. 'Patience is a virtue.'

'Perhaps that's why I haven't got any.'

Rob smiled and the whole stomach-fluttering, nipple-hardening, knickers-dampening thing started again. He laid my hand over his crotch and put his own on top, holding it firmly in place. I stroked him through the fabric of his trousers and felt him grow hard.

At Waterloo, he paid the driver and led me off down the Embankment. I was completely mystified about our destination. London City airport was miles away and I knew that hot air balloons took off at dawn and dusk because the air conditions were at their best. And, anyway, balloons only flew in the countryside, didn't they? I'd grown up in the West Country where they were a common sight, drifting above the landscape like man-made clouds.

Then I noticed that we were drawing ever closer to the London Eye, its gleaming glass cars moving so slowly they seemed suspended in the air, and the penny dropped. Of course, a ride on the Eye was called a flight; that's what I had overheard him arranging. But there was no privacy in the cars; it wasn't like a train or a bus where you could always find a quiet corner. There was simply no way to do it that wouldn't attract attention and I wasn't that much of an exhibitionist even if Rob was.

'We're going on the Eye?' I smiled up at Rob.

'And coming on it, if I've got anything to do with it.'

As we approached the Eye we saw a long snake of people queuing to buy tickets. Rob took my hand and we swept past the queue and went straight to the fast-track window. As Rob checked us in for our flight, I looked up at the giant wheel. It was so enormous that I had to tip my head right back. The cars glinted in the light from the dying sun like giant soap bubbles. They seemed suspended in the air, not moving at all. I focused on the car at the top of the great wheel and tried to see it move, but the motion was so slow that I only succeeded in making myself dizzy.

'We've got priority boarding so it shouldn't take long. This way.' I allowed him to lead me by the hand. 'It's beautiful, isn't it?'

'It's spectacular.'

'If I've timed it right we should see the sun setting during our flight. They say it's really special.'

'Sounds lovely. But how are we going to . . .' I lowered my voice. A middle-aged couple beside us appeared to be engaged in a bout of competitive sulking and I didn't want them to overhear us. 'You know . . . I mean, there's nowhere to hide, is there?'

'Do I have to remind you about patience again?' Rob leant close and put his mouth next to my ear. 'There's no need for you to worry about anything. I've got it all organised. I'm going to fuck the arse off you when we get up there. I'm going to make you scream with pleasure. I'm going to fuck you so hard that your legs go all trembly and your heart beats like a drum.' I could feel his hot moist breath on my neck. Inside my bra my nipples had grown hard and sensitive. 'Now tell me ... isn't that worth waiting for?' I felt his mouth on my skin. He kissed my neck then nibbled on my ear lobe. A shiver of delicious pleasure slid along my spine.

When it was time to board we stepped into a car – or capsule as I'd learnt they were called. The experience was rather a non-event, a bit like boarding an escalator. Rob and I walked over to the far side of the glass enclosure and I waited for the other passengers to board but, instead, the door was closed behind us. I turned to Rob as realisation dawned and was rewarded with a wicked smile.

'The flight takes half an hour.' I could hear the excitement in Rob's voice. 'For decency's sake I think we need to wait until it's made a quarter-rotation before we get down to it. That way the people boarding the Eye on the ground won't be able to see us and we'll be out of the line of sight of anyone directly below or above us. We'll be visible to the cars on the other side of the wheel of course, but that'll just make things more exciting.'

'But they might dial nine-nine-nine. Everyone's got a mobile phone these days; they can call right from the car and the police will be waiting for us when we get off.' My voice grew higher in pitch as I spoke, and I sounded prudish and shocked even to myself but Rob just smiled and nodded as if the prospect of a night in the cells might be a price worth paying.

'I've got it all worked out. If we wait until it's done a quarter-rotation and then stop when it's halfway down the police won't actually see us at it. If we get off at the other end fully dressed and looking as if butter wouldn't melt there's not a lot they can do. That gives us fifteen minutes of action, which should be enough for you to have a couple of orgasms at least.' Rob was standing in front of me, casually rubbing the back of his fingers over my nipples. Even through my clothes the sensation caused a wave of shivery tingles up the nape of my neck.

'Has it occurred to you that people have cameras as well? They might take pictures of us – hard evidence, Rob.'

'Very hard.' He took my hand and pressed it against his swollen crotch.

We sat down on the central bench as the capsule ascended. As we rose higher we could see all the familiar landmarks of London spread out below us like one of those model villages my parents used to make us traipse around when we were kids. St Paul's and the Houses of Parliament in all its Gothic splendour, Tower Bridge and Nelson's Column. In the distance I could see the Albert Hall, gently domed like an enormous cake.

Between the ancient monuments and spires, modern architecture demanded attention: the BT Tower, the South Bank complex, Centrepoint and the Gherkin. Sunlight glinted on glass. Traffic moved through the streets like blood through arteries and the dark snake of the Thames bisected the city. As Rob had promised, the sun was beginning to dip, illuminating the sky with stripes of yellow and pink.

I was so absorbed in the view that I almost forgot what we were there for. But Rob had no intention of allowing me to forget.

'If we move over here –' Rob shuffled round to the far side of the bench, facing away from the capsules opposite '– nobody can see what we're up to. When we reach the apex we'll swap sides, that way they'll only ever be able to see our backs. Now, do you think you can slip your knickers off without attracting attention? I don't think anyone in the capsules opposite can see us unless they've got binoculars but we ought to be careful.' Rob's voice was thick with arousal.

'No need, I'm not wearing any. I thought it would save time.'

'Good, that will make things easier. Come and sit on my lap. If you lift your skirt up I should be able to get my hand underneath.'

I was wearing Rob's favourite dress. It was bright red with a tight bodice which emphasised my curves. I often wore it on our forays because the skirt was cut from a circle of fabric, making it so full and voluminous that it could be spread over both our laps, providing excellent camouflage.

I got up and sat sideways on his lap, lifting up the skirt of my dress so that it covered our legs like a tent. Rob slid his hand under the edge and I wrapped one arm around his neck, steadying myself so that I could open my legs wide enough to allow him access. I felt his fingers on my naked mound and he let out a little involuntary gasp of surprise and delight.

'No hair. I'll have to examine that in more detail later.' His voice was dreamy and soft.

His fingers slid down the length of my slit. I exhaled long and loud. The feeling of skin against skin as his fingertips stroked me was exotic and intimate. There was so much more sensation without the hair; it was all so much more slippery and intense. He easily found the groove between my lips, dipping his fingertips into the hot wetness.

I turned my head and kissed him, cupping his face with my free hand. His mouth was hot and wet and tasted of the coffee we had drunk after our meal. His stubble scratched my face. Rob's fingers were working my clit, circling it gently and every so often flicking across the sensitive tip, making me gasp. With his other hand, he held me on to his lap, wrapping his arm around my waist and pulling me close.

I could feel his hot breath on my face as we kissed. It seemed to hiss out of his nostrils like steam, reflecting the heat of his desire. He sucked and nibbled on my lower lip; his tongue explored my mouth.

My skin was covered in goose pimples. I was tingling all over. My crotch was aching and tense. Desire throbbed in my belly. I'd begun to sweat and my hair was damp against my back. Rob stopped kissing me and I felt as though I'd had my pocket picked.

'Have you any idea how uncomfortable it is inside my trousers now?' He wriggled his hips, grinding his crotch against me.

'It feels pretty comfortable to me. It's nice to have something firm to sit on. Do you want to undo them and give it its freedom?' I brushed Rob's hair away from his forehead.

'Not yet. It's got a mind of its own. If I liberate the thing it's going to want to get inside you straight away and I want to wait –' he rubbed his fingertips across my clit '– until you've come.'

'What a gentleman you are.'

He shrugged. 'Well, it's your birthday, I thought you deserved a treat.' He bent his head and began to nibble my neck. His mouth found the sensitive spot where jawline, ear and neck converge, making me shiver. His fingers worked my clit.

My nipples were rubbing uncomfortably against the bodice of my dress. Sweat filmed my upper lip and dampened my hair at the neckline and temples. Rob's strong arm pulled me fully on to his lap. Between my legs everything felt liquid and tingly.

There seemed to be some direct sensory connection between my crotch and my breasts. Every time Rob's fingers made contact with my clit there was a corresponding throb of pleasure in my nipples. A fiery ball of delicious tension had formed at the base of my belly, aching for release.

I bent my head and began to kiss Rob's neck. I nibbled on his ear lobe, nipping it hard with my teeth until he moaned. I traced my tongue down the side of his neck and kissed the base of his throat. His skin was salty and smooth. I could smell his cologne and his own familiar man smell.

Tension was building. Rob was working my clit directly now, rubbing his fingers slowly across the taut bud, bringing me to a pitch of arousal. I began to rock my hips, creating a rhythm which Rob quickly followed. I wrapped both my arms around his neck and held on, using his body for leverage.

The sound of our excited breathing seemed to fill the capsule. I was very conscious that we were suspended in the air. Though there was little sensation of movement, it felt alien and exotic, nothing like being in a room on the ground. There was a sense of separation and isolation and I could almost believe that Rob and I were alone in the universe, hanging above the Earth like astronauts in this gleaming glass egg.

My skin was damp and uncomfortable inside my dress. Strands of damp hair were clinging to my neck. A tear of sweat ran down my back. My nipples were stiff and sensitive. They stood out, fat and prominent under the thin material of my dress.

Rob's fingers were working their magic. I rocked my hips, using my thigh muscles so that my crotch rubbed against his hand. He stroked my clit, following my rhythm. Pleasure was building to a pitch. I was panting heavily, moaning and sobbing.

He ran his fingers down my slit and slid them slowly inside me. I gasped in pleasure and relief as they filled me, sliding past my muscles millimetre by millimetre. He stroked my clit with his thumb as he worked two fingers in and out of me.

I was trembling all over. Sweat trickled into my eyes. My fringe was plastered to my forehead. Rob began to mutter a running commentary of what he was doing. His eyes were closed and he seemed to be smiling to himself.

'I'm fucking your sweet cunt with my fingers. You're hot and wet and tight. Your clit's rigid. You're bucking against my hand like a bitch on heat.' He was talking to himself, I realised. More an expression of his pleasure than a desire to communicate. 'Your clit's dancing under my fingers, so I know you're close. Your body's all tense and wound up. You're holding on to me so tight you're hurting my neck.'

My belly was on fire with pleasure and tension. Blood was throbbing in my ears. My heart pounded. I was practically screaming now, a high, keening wail of helpless excitement.

'My cock's so hard now, it's hurting me. After you've come I'm going to put it in you and give you the fuck of your life. I'm going to fill you so full you'll scream for me to stop. But first I want you to come for me. Your pussy's all hot and slippery; I can feel it gripping my fingers. I know you're almost there. I want you to come for me.' He rotated his fingers inside me, pressing the tips against my G-spot as his thumb stroked my clit. It was all I needed to push me over the edge. 'Yes, yes, that's it. I can feel you coming.'

The dam burst. I held on to Rob and ground my crotch against his fingers. Jolts of electricity shot up my spine. My nipples tingled. I let my head fall back and I howled at the sky. The sound seemed to echo around inside the capsule, amplified and urgent.

I could hear Rob's excited breath hissing out between taut lips. My body was tense and trembling. Orgasm washed over me like waves crashing on to the shore, engulfing me and taking my breath away. His thumb circled my clit, coaxing the orgasm out of me. His fingers filled me.

Orgasm consumed me. I could feel it in every pore and particle, from the roots of my hair to the tips of my toes. Every nerve ending was alive and working overtime. My back arched. My nipples throbbed.

It seemed to go on forever, wave after wave, like the aftershocks which follow a big quake. My hair was sticking to my back and face. Sweat had melted my mascara, stinging my eyes. My mouth was parched and I was screaming so loud my throat hurt.

'Feels like a big one, Jenny. I bet they can hear you on the ground.' Rob used his free arm to stop me falling off his lap. 'I'm so hard it hurts. Can't wait to fuck you.'

I shuddered as the final jolt of orgasm pulsed through me. My body seemed to vibrate like a plucked guitar string. I was light headed and shivering even though it was a balmy summer night. My legs were trembling and weak. I wiped the sweat of my face, then laid my head on Rob's shoulder. He stroked my hair.

When I'd got my breath back he kissed me.

'Can we free the prisoner now, do you think? He's been on his best behaviour, surely it's time he was liberated?'

I rocked my hips, rubbing my crotch against his.

'I think I can feel him making a bid for freedom already.'

I slid off his lap.

'Look, we're nearly at the apex. Isn't it spectacular? I've never seen a sunset like it.' Rob stood up and led me over to the window.

The sky was the colour of purple silk, marbled with patches of dark and light. At the horizon there were bright slashes of orange, red, pink and yellow like light seeping through a curtain. The familiar skyline of the city was a silhouette of spires, domes and skyscrapers. The Houses of Parliament were illuminated and seemed to glow. It had always reminded me of a paper model lit from within and, from our vantage point, this impression was heightened, making it seem slightly unreal and mysterious.

'It's magical. Thanks for bringing me.'

Rob smiled. Silently he pulled me towards the bench. He sat down on the opposite side so that, when our capsule began to descend, we couldn't be seen by the passengers opposite. I watched as he unbuckled his belt and unzipped his flies. He slid his trousers and underwear down to his knees. His erection was rigid and purple tipped, pointing up at the sky as boldly and spectacularly as any of London's spires. Its tip seemed to gleam in the light and I could see a bead of moisture glistening at the eye. He looked at his watch.

'We've got about seven minutes. Turn your back to me and straddle my legs.'

I lifted up my skirts and lowered myself over his lap. I waited for him to position himself, then sat down slowly, allowing him to enter me. There's nothing like the first moment of penetration, when it slides past all those excited nerve endings, stretching, opening and filling me. Rob let out a long deep moan of satisfaction as he slid into me.

I spread my skirt over us both, concealing our secret. I was sitting on his lap with my legs astride his. Not an ideal position, in spite of how good it felt. It would be hard for me to get any leverage, as my feet didn't reach the floor even though I was wearing my highest heels. I felt Rob's fingers undoing the buttons at the top of my dress and gasped as he found my nipples.

He began to rock his hips back and forth, sliding inside me. I did the same but it quickly became obvious that my position wasn't stable enough. I spread my legs apart as wide as I could and managed to hook my ankles under his knees. By flexing my thigh muscles I was able to raise my bottom up and down, matching Rob's movements and causing delicious friction as he moved inside me.

Rob's fingers were rubbing my nipples, teasing them. We both knew that I wanted him to pinch them, to take them between thumb and forefinger and pinch them hard, pulling and twisting them. But he was a born tease; he loved making me wait so that, by the time he finally did what I wanted, I'd be wound up with arousal and hunger.

My crotch was tingling. Every movement of his cock inside me was ecstasy. It seemed to belong there and having it inside me was the only thing, in that moment, that made sense to me. Rob's legs were damp with sweat. I could feel his bunched clothes under my legs; I could hear him panting behind me. His hot damp breath tickled the back of my neck.

He was flicking my nipples with his thumbs now, brushing them across the tips. My breathing had grown rapid and loud. Having had one orgasm already, the next one would come easier. I felt the familiar burn of tension in my gut. My nipples were on fire. I leant back against Rob's chest and pressed my hands down on to my own thighs, steadying myself.

Rob rolled the tips of my nipples between his fingers. He bent his head and began to kiss my neck. His mouth was hot and wet and urgent. His tongue moved against my skin. I let my head fall back, allowing Rob's mouth full access to my neck. He licked my throat.

I used my feet for leverage and rocked my hips, following Rob's rhythm. The awkwardness of our position limited the depth of our thrusts. It was an entirely different sensation than normal, but incredibly intense. Limited by the range of movements available to us, we'd somehow achieved a sort of deep friction. I could feel pressure against my G-spot and every tiny movement of our hips stimulated my clit.

My hair was damp and stringy, trapped between Rob and I. It clung to my face and got in my eyes. He pinched my nipples hard, gradually increasing the pressure until I moaned. His mouth moved against my neck; hot, moist breath loud against my ear.

I was tingling all over. Hot pinpoints of pleasure radiated out from my nipples. Watery shivers slid up and down my spine. Heat burnt in my belly. We were moving as one now, my hips rocking up to meet his thrusts. The sound of our excited breathing seemed to fill the capsule. Outside the sky had darkened to navy and the dying sun made the dark water of the river gleam like fire.

'You feel like hot wet velvet.' Rob's voice was husky and deep. 'You're gripping me like you never want me to stop. Like it belongs there and you don't want to let it go. Doesn't it feel good?' He tensed his muscles, making his cock twitch inside me, for emphasis.

'It feels fantastic.' I was getting close again. My crotch felt electric, buzzing and alive with pleasure. He fingered my nipples, using just the right amount of pressure. My chest was heaving. Blood pounded in my ears. Sweat ran down my body.

'Can you see the view? Like a movie set or a painting. You can understand why Monet and Turner painted the river, can't you?' Rob spoke in short bursts, breaking up the sentences and timing each fragment with a jab of his hips. 'It's magical. Isn't it just the perfect backdrop to come to? I bet Turner went home when he'd finished and did exactly what we're doing now. It's the only way to celebrate its beauty; the only thing that does it justice.'

He pinched my nipples, pulling on them, stretching out my breasts. I began to moan and he kept on pinching them until I covered his hands with mine and moved them away. He laughed softly and kissed my neck. He wrapped his arms around my waist and pulled me close.

We were moving more urgently now. My crotch was grinding against his, providing delicious friction. Both of us were sweaty and damp; Rob's shirt was sticking to my naked back, his thighs beneath mine were slick and slippery. He had begun to grunt; a sure sign that he was close to orgasm.

He held me tight as we moved. Our hips rocked in rhythm, mine coming up to meet his downward thrusts, each motion co-ordinated perfectly. I was breathless and exhausted. Ruined make-up and sweat stung my eyes. The hairs on the back of my neck were standing on end. My skin was goosepimply and alive.

Rob repositioned his hands, sliding them under my skirt and placing a palm against each of my inner thighs and pulling me physically towards him each time his hips came up to thrust. The sensation was incredible; it ground my crotch against his and seemed to shift my arousal into a higher gear.

I gripped his wrists and matched his thrusts, using his arms as leverage. My nipples were burning and swollen. My breathing was frenzied and noisy. My crotch was a mass of pleasure, tingling, electric and overwhelming. I could no longer tell where he ended and I began.

Rob's grunting picked up speed. Under my fingers I could feel the rigid tendons and muscles in his arms. I was on the edge, riding that moment between arousal and orgasm. It was incredible, unbearable and I never wanted it to end. He had begun to make shorter thrusts, his fingers digging into my thighs as he pulled me on to him.

I was quivering all over. Electric jolts of pleasure shot up my spine and pumped through my bloodstream. Rob was lost in the moment. I could feel the tension in his body as he neared orgasm. The sound of his short staccato grunts seemed to get inside my head, as if I'd become possessed by his desire for me and his need to come.

Nothing existed except his body and mine and our combined hunger for orgasm. I ground my crotch against his, hips moving frantically. I was gasping for breath, rapid inhalations audible between moans. The sound mingled with Rob's more guttural noises.

I howled out loud as I began to come. My thigh muscles seemed possessed by an uncontrollable quiver. I held on to Rob's arms and arched my back, gazing up at the inky dark sky. His body was rigid against mine. He was grunting noisily through clenched teeth. He gave one final thrust and I felt him begin to tremble.

We were both coming. He pumped out sperm inside me. My feet were locked behind his knees, my hands gripping his arms. I could feel his taut muscles quivering as I rode him.

Rob panted behind me. I could feel his chest rising and falling. His fingers dug into my thighs. Sensation flooded through me. My scalp tingled, my toes curled. My belly was a pulsing core of pleasure. The capsule was filled with the sound of my urgent cries and Rob's staccato breathing.

As the peak subsided I leant back against his chest. With a shaky hand I pushed my hair away from my face. Rob's muscles began to soften and relax. He kissed my neck. He let go of my thighs and extricated his hands from beneath my skirt.

The sky had darkened to a velvet blackness, a few stars already visible. Lights were shining in many of the buildings beneath us, making the city look like fairy-land. It was a magical backdrop that seemed to belong to us alone.

'Do you know what it reminds me of?' I unwound my legs and stood up. Rob pulled up his trousers, still under the cover of my skirts. 'One of those snow globes of the city you can buy in the tourist shops, only we're on the inside of the globe.'

His clothing adjusted, Rob got to his feet. He put his hands on my waist and pulled me to him for a kiss.

'I hope I've given you a birthday to remember. We'll be back on land in five minutes or so.' He picked up my handbag and handed it to me. 'You might want to do something with your make-up.'

I sat down on the bench and got out my mirror. Smudged mascara was everywhere. My lipstick had smeared and spread.

'I see what you mean. I look like Alice Cooper after a heavy night. I think the only thing I can do is to take the whole lot off.' I fished in my handbag for a wet wipe. As I removed my make-up Rob took out his handkerchief and wiped his face and neck. He combed his hair with his fingers and instantly looked as well groomed and innocent as he had when we'd boarded the capsule.

A few minutes later, we arrived and stepped off on to solid ground again. As Rob had promised there was no delegation of angry passengers waiting for us and no police to arrest us. He took my hand and led me to the exit.

As we passed a group of camera-bedecked Japanese tourists they began to point at us and to talk excitedly to each other. Though neither of us was fluent in the language, we didn't need an interpreter to know that they were trying to let us know that they had seen us.

My stomach seemed to flip over inside me like a fish on the end of a hook. For a moment I feared arrest and humiliation but I gradually became to realise that they were just trying to express their appreciation.

They were smiling and nodding. Several of them were miming the act of clapping as if in applause. One of the younger members of the group gave us the thumbs-up sign and they all began to copy him, brandishing their stubby digits at us with broad smiles on their faces.

The young man who had initiated the thumbs-up frenzy stepped forwards and executed a small respectful bow.

'Nice one, mate.' In his accent, the colloquialism sounded both charming and absurd. He obviously thought so too as he began to laugh, covering his mouth with his hand as if suddenly embarrassed. The whole situation was so ridiculous that we started to laugh too and that seemed to start off the rest of them.

We walked away with the sound of laughter ringing in our ears and I knew that this was one birthday I'd never be able to forget.

Mae Nixon's first Black Lace novel, *Wing of Madness*, is published in April 2007. Her short stories have appeared in several Wicked Words collections.

Striptease A. D. R. Forte

Throughout her life she'd collected labels: visionary, romantic, rebel, slut. Others she didn't even remember. She wore them at various stages before tossing them off like cheap panties, not wanting to be stuck with some limited picture of what life should be. She always had plans and desires that demanded her to shrug off an old skin and slip into a new one. To find a new stage and a new role.

But the rebel she let out only behind closed doors. Only to a select few who might or might not tell stories. She wasn't worried about stories, and if she was in an adventurous frame of mind she would sometimes even kiss and tell. Kiss and show, however, remained out of the question. And for all that she did, there was one stone she'd left unturned.

From the time she could comprehend sex and the innuendo of late-night movies she shouldn't have been watching, she dreamt of being a stripper. Glitzy, painted late nights and high heels, shaking her ass for crumpled bills. Strange men's faces buried in the softness of her 34D tits. She could taste the sex, the attention, the lust. Taste the high.

But she harboured the doubt she wasn't tough enough, legit enough. What kind of street cred did a middle-class, suburban, Protestant girl have? Those who walked the walk would laugh at her attempts. And her mother would have been upset. That was the suburban girl: worried about making her mom cry. There alone was proof enough she didn't have any business on the wrong side of the titty bar.

So she flipped through vintage girlie mags and porno rags and even the damned Frederick's of Hollywood catalogue when nothing else would do. In college they swore she was a lesbian, so she fucked a few guys to prove she wasn't, and a few girls just to confuse everybody. But it all stayed behind dorm doors. And none of her lovers knew the real purpose for the magazines: that they simply served as replacement for the dream. The one role she didn't dare take.

Once, in a weak moment, she half-confessed to a college friend. 'So why not model then?' her friend had said, meaning it honestly and kindly. But she had shaken her head. Because the 34Ds came with hips and thighs to match and no way was she eating celery and doing power aerobics every day just to get her ass in a skin rag.

She'd stick with her magazines and her titty bar visits – and always on the proper side of the bar. The fully clothed side. No matter how much she longed to be on the stage, sweating under the lights, the pole like a cold, giant, stainless-steel dick between her legs . . .

Instead she found a reasonable compromise, one that worked for a girl like her. A marketing degree, a few dedicated years in the working world and a savvy business plan let her open the boutique downtown on 16th street carrying the best in fetish, leather and exotic dancewear and accessories. Her store was clean, she knew about treating customers right, and the boutique earned out in just two years. After that she sat back on her laurels and helped the girls who came to her store.

Often she helped them with more than clothes. The ones she knew didn't want to be in those spandex panties every night. She saw the loathing in their tired eyes when they looked at the patent leather pumps and her heart ached. It was so bassackwards. So unfair. She should have had their lives; she wanted it. But that wasn't ever how it worked. She just did the best she could and if anybody had asked her, 'Suppose you die tonight, can you say you got what you wanted?' she would have admitted the answer was no. But she had gotten damn close.

And then he showed up.

On a Friday afternoon he walked on to her stage and his gaze put her in the spotlight. Undressed her then and there. He was a friend of a friend and she met him across a dinner table in a swanky restaurant. And for the first five minutes she ignored him completely.

He had walked in and sat down still talking on his cellphone. She'd have forgiven him if she thought for a minute he really had to work. But this was a man who flaunted his French-made suit and cellphone along with his height and his soap-opera star looks. He knew women would stare. He dared them to. She didn't.

She ignored him even after he'd flipped the phone closed and flashed that perfect grin around the table. When her cousin introduced her, she shook hands and murmured something polite and aloof. She turned back to her own previous conversation, letting her gaze slide over him as if he was no more than an empty chair.

Even though she felt his gaze turned on her, making her sweat, putting her up on display for him to contemplate. She wanted to tell him, 'You don't have a chance in hell.'

But she knew and he knew that he damned well did.

He asked her for her number and she refused. So he got it from her cousin and called her the next day.

'Just let me send you flowers. I was a jerk and I'm sorry. I should have known you were smarter than to fall for my lame come-on.'

'And you should know I'm not falling for this act either,' she replied.

He fell silent, no doubt at a loss because this line had

always worked for him in the past. She smiled and waited to see what next, even though she didn't have much hope. His type was predictable.

After a half-minute, he laughed. 'OK you got me. I feel like an idiot. But I really enjoyed meeting you. You're a very attractive woman.'

'Thanks.' She paused, considering her next words. He had surprised her; she'd expected at least another five minutes of bravado and word games. 'Well, I have your number now. If there's ever . . . an opportunity for us to meet I'll call you.'

She hoped he got it; she found him classy in an uptown asshole way and she didn't want to spell it out in coarse terms.

'You're not serious?' he asked her after a long, long pause.

'Is it so surprising that I don't need strings attached? Or flowers or drinks first. I find *you* attractive. That's more than sufficient.'

Another long silence and then he laughed. 'I . . . um . . . well, hell, I'll be waiting for that call.'

She grinned. She loved the idea she could fluster a man like him. Oh yeah, she'd have him over and fuck him, all right. There was no question about that.

And then she didn't. She called him for coffee one afternoon. When he met her at the café, his cell was off and tucked out of sight and he smiled when he saw her.

'This wasn't what I was expecting.'

She smiled back as she gestured to the free seat beside her. 'Me neither, but I haven't been able to find the time for my original plan.'

Hse raised an eyebrow. 'That's no good. And I would offer to help you find the time, but you'd shoot me down in a heartbeat.'

She laughed at that and shrugged. 'You're right. But the only way you could help was to come over and help me clean my apartment. It's a wreck and I hate sex on a messy couch.'

He paused in the act of reaching for the menu card. 'You too?'

And while she laughed she thought that this was not going at all the way she had planned. She wondered too just where the hell it *was* going.

For the time, it went to her apartment. He came over on the weekend and she made dinner. She wasn't sure anything would happen, but after some consideration she donned silk garters and her sheerest stockings. Just in case.

He brought appetisers and dessert instead of wine, which pleased her. The man was full of surprises after all, and she realised that for years she'd been able to predict just about every turn of the game. So accustomed to it she didn't even think about it, and like the boiled frog she'd gotten comfortable in her boredom. He was turning up the flame under her. She liked it.

The potential of his choices – cheese puffs and mini-cheesecake bites and fresh mango slices – didn't escape her notice either. After dinner, she leant across the table and fed him slippery, juicy slivers of mango. He sucked on her fingers and used his tongue to catch all of the sweet trickles that ran down her wrist. The table stood next to the window and he cast a speculative glance at the twilight city beyond.

'Shall we open it?' he asked.

Blushing, she laughed and shook her head. 'Only if we let the curtains down first.'

'But that's no fun. That defeats the purpose.'

Oh, she wanted to open the window, sans curtains. She wanted to send the contents of the dinner table crashing to the floor so loud that neighbours and passers-by alike would hear the noise and look up to find the cause. But she didn't have the nerve.

'We don't need an audience,' she said.

Still holding her dessert-sticky hand, he stood and led her to the couch that she'd made at least some effort to neaten before he arrived, stacking the contents pell-mell on the shelves under the end tables. He sat with his knees apart and she stood between them, her hand still daintily held in his.

'I'll be your captive audience anyway,' he said softly.

He didn't know. Didn't know how close to home he'd hit with that casual flirtation. She wanted to perform for him, in front of a hundred other eyes, and have him know that she was his and his only when he chose. Now he was part of that dream. Her forbidden dream. But it was still only a dream.

Reality was staying behind these four walls; the stage she imagined only in her mind. But she would give him his performance nevertheless. She'd worn stilettos tonight along with the garters and the stockings. And she shed everything but those in slow motion. Turning for him as she did. Twisting. Caressing.

Loosening his tie, pulling his head forwards and burying his face in lace and perfume and silky feminine flesh. Feeling his tongue snake across her hard nipples. His teeth pull at her skin. That wasn't allowed; but here in private, because this stage wasn't real and they were alone, it didn't matter. The only downside: when there were no eyes watching it was hard to resist.

And they didn't.

He fondled her wet pussy while she writhed in his lap, her head thrown back in delight. Holding on to him while his tongue worked down her chest to her belly. Feeling his hands support her and hold her, and knowing that he wouldn't let her fall no matter how far back he bent her. Even when her hair brushed the floor and the blood rushed to her head and she thought she would pass out because as he held her like that his hot mouth closed over her clit.

Knowing he would be careful when he lowered her all the way to the ground and then joined her, shedding his shirt and his tie and his belt. When he spread her legs and held them wide to lick her calves and the backs of her knees, so that her stockings clung to her skin warm and wet and sexy wherever his mouth had touched.

She wrapped her legs around his neck and he started fucking her slow and hard. Called her a gorgeous cock-tease. Told her he'd wanted to do this to her from the first second he'd seen her and she'd blown him off. She smiled and between breaths told him he was an arrogant bastard with a big dick and why didn't he just shut up and use it. So he did.

Afterwards, he lay across her, one hand still holding the coffee table leg for dear life and told her she moved like a pro. She was incredible. She was beautiful. She lay under him, not believing a word of it but not caring either. Because it felt so good. And he could say all the sweet, insincere things he wanted just so long as he came to her and put her on stage with his intense blue-eyed gaze and fucked her brains out like that. Because she loved it.

She was so wrapped up in the aftershock of amazing lust that she didn't even notice the *National Geographic* lying on the coffee table until he left the next morning. He'd gone through the stash under one of the end tables and the pile was now neatly stacked end to end. But what got her attention was not the *Geographic* nor the neatness, but the magazine atop the pile. One of her porno mags. She hadn't known it was mixed in with the other stuff in the living room when she tidied. Normally she kept those particular items in the bedroom closet, just in case her mother or any other equally shockable relative showed up.

But this one had gotten away. And he'd seen it. Not that it mattered he knew she read porn. But he'd guessed or sensed so much of her desire. Like he'd passed an invisible barrier no one else ever had. And with this knowledge, with what had happened between them the night before . . .

She clutched her orange juice and frowned in the morning sunlight, her heart was beating a little too fast. Her mother would say that she 'had a feeling', a premonition. And she did. But she *was* just a little bit nervous about where it was going.

'Out of town?'

'Yes,' he replied. 'Just for a weekend. Please. I have a special treat.'

She laughed and rolled over on one hip. She leant on her arm propped against the pillows and played with the soft, thick jet-black strands of his hair. 'A treat huh?'

'Yes.'

'What kind of treat?'

He sighed and rolled his eyes. 'Obviously, I can't tell you.' He cupped one breast and tweaked her nipple. 'Just say you'll go. I promise you'll love it.' His hand released her and moved up to the back of her neck, pulled her down so that she lay chest to chest with him. He buried both hands in her hair and massaged her head, knowing how that made her silly and pliable just like a petted cat.

'Mmmm. You know how to get your way.'

'I do.' She felt his dick begin to stiffen under her thigh and his hands moved from her hair down her back. 'Say you'll go,' he coaxed.

She didn't answer, but as she slid one leg over him and reached down to wrap her fingers around his dick, he smiled. Smug bastard knew he'd won.

They drove out into the desert for half a day. She tried to figure out where it was they were headed. She pestered him with countless guesses. But he only smiled and shook his head at every try. 'Patience, darlin'. You'll see.'

The highway cut through miles of nothing. Sand-swept buttes and dry brush and pale sheaves of grass lining the road. She stared out at the endless vista and almost told him to stop the car. But another car might come by. A tiny risk, but a risk anyway. Would it be so bad if they did see? Not really. But it might be someone with kids. Or just someone who might get offended. So no, not today. Not here.

Was she just finding excuses?

He turned off the road on to a patch of dirt, hardly a track, and she raised an eyebrow but she guessed he knew where he was headed. Out here, although it seemed deserted, habitation thrived in trailer parks and on hidden ranches and towns so tiny you'd miss them if you blinked. She waited and tried to control her raging curiosity as they bumped from dirt track to dirt track and finally turned on to a gravelly, paved lot.

She looked at the back of the low-slung building before them as he circled the car around to the front, her gaze taking in the grey stained siding; the rusty green dumpster in a corner; the side door that he pulled up beside . . . and her mouth dropped open in shock.

He turned smiling. 'This is where you go in,' he said, tilting his head towards the door. 'Stage entrance.'

'No way!' she squeaked, staring at the door in abject terror. That was not a tingle of excitement in her stomach. It was fear and very proper disdain. 'I most certainly am not.'

He gave her a long look and simply shrugged as he drove forwards again. 'OK.'

'Don't "OK" me.'

'Why?' He laughed, steering the car around to the front of the building and pulling into what might have been once, long ago, marked with yellow paint as a parking space. 'I'm agreeing with you,' he said.

'No, you're not.' She stuck her tongue out at him and glanced with secret glee at the sign on the door: SUNFLOWERS.

So appropriately sleazy if you thought about it the right way.

'What are we doing here?' she asked as she crawled out of the car and hitched up her jeans.

He walked over to her and slid a macho arm around her waist, looked down at her over the tops of his shades and grinned. 'I'm puttin' you to work, little girl.'

'The hell you are.'

'Watch that mouth. I might have to teach you a lesson or two if you don't.'

She only snorted in reply and started walking towards the bar's front entrance, glancing back once over her shoulder with a look that told him to hurry up. And he followed.

Once out of the glare of the sun, he paused just short of opening the door and looked at her again. A serious, concerned look this time. 'Sure you're up to this?'

She took a deep breath. Still time to back out, but if she didn't . . . If she just took the plunge this time . . .

She nodded. 'Yes. Yes, I want to.'

The bouncer gave them a disdainful stare and sniffed. If a sentiment as genteel as disdain could be applied to someone wearing a John Deere cap and more tattoos than shirt. It was hard to stifle a giggle at the thought, to keep in character. But she did. Because this was her debut and her chance to refute the middle-class suburban girl who didn't dare. And she had no intention of screwing it up.

So she played it cool as they walked in. As if they had every right to be there. And when he stopped for a mumbled exchange with John Deere, she scoped out the premises with a jaded eye. Not hard to pull off since the place was no different from so many, many like it that she'd seen before.

Low chairs and worn tables pitted and marked from years of use: the impact of countless hands, stiletto heels and maybe the occasional knife or razor blade. The cramped bar. The stage lit in changing lights. Blues and greens fading to reds and pinks and yellow. And The Pole, of course. The phallic altar stone of this ritual gathering place.

She drank it in like a straight shot of bourbon on a hot night. Because it wasn't that places like this were special in and of themselves. It was all about context.

She flicked a heavy-lidded gaze back to the man at her side, with his arm heavy and warm on the bare skin between her baby-T and her jeans. He was context. Being here with him replaced ordinary with amazing. With insane-never-forget-this; I can't believe I'm doing this.

When Mr Deere pointed them to a door beyond the bar, she flashed him a grin and a kiss-pout. And then turned to head back with her heart beating a mile a minute and her feet all wobbly in her sandals. She wondered if she was going to be able to even stand up straight in heels.

He gave her hand a subtle squeeze before she followed Lacey, senior member of the performing staff, back to the dressing room.

'Later,' he said.

'Later.'

They looked at each other for one powerful glance, and then he headed back to the bar or outside or wherever he'd pass the time. And she turned and squeezed past Lacey's ample endowments, which took up half the doorway.

Lacey led her down the short hallway to a long

narrow room half the size of her own master bathroom at home. A long mirror ran down the counter on one side. A rack of costumes and a full-length mirror on the other side. Metal chairs with peeling paint scattered down the centre like pieces of an obstacle course. She loved it.

She saw Lacey looking at her, struggling to bite her tongue on what she wanted to say because the bartender/manager – a no-nonsense redhead as busty as Lacey herself – had made it clear the city folks were to be humoured. They were paying. And paying well.

She gave Lacey a helpless shrug. 'Yes, I'm exactly what you think I am. I'm one of *them*. And I'm parading around here trying on your life for one night before I go back home where it's safe.'

Lacey's expression went from sullen to surprised. And her face went a little red with embarrassment. 'I didn't ... I mean ...'

'Don't apologise,' she replied, smiling. 'It's OK and I'm not mad. But ...' And now it was her turn to go red. To splutter. 'But I really want to do this. And ...' She glanced back towards the closed door from whence they'd come, her blush deepening, and Lacey gave her a smile and an understanding nod.

'He's somethin' else. I don't blame you.'

They looked at each other for a few long, half-awkward, shame-faced moments where they understood each other perfectly. And then Lacey grinned. 'OK we're wastin' time. Let's find you something extra-special to wear.'

With Lacey's patronage, the two other girls who straggled in later tacitly accepted her presence. She got no friendly overtures, but no hostility either. 'Let the city bitch have her fun,' their glances said. Which suited her fine.

She was more worried about her costume. About how she was ever going to pull this off. About what he'd think ... would she live up to his expectations? Could she even live up to her own?

She brushed gloss over her vermillion-red lipstick and frowned at her appearance once more, searching for flaws. She'd expected it to feel strange, slipping on this skin: glitter on her cheeks, triple eyeliner, the threads of rhinestones covering her breasts and crotch that were her sole pretence to modesty. But it all felt right. She just hoped she wasn't wrong.

And then Lacey, coming back in flushed and sweaty from her act, breasts hanging free and her hands full of crumpled cash, tapped her on the shoulder. One of the other girls, Dee, was already on her way out, heels clicking away down the hall. It was showtime.

The hardest part was the inch of shadowed stage between the red curtain hanging at the back and the glaze of lights ahead. Right there, the lights acted as a multi-hued barrier between her and her audience. One more step and there wouldn't be any turning back. She'd have to see it through. All the way.

She took a deep breath. And one platform-stiletto-step forwards.

He sat in the front row. Right smack-dab up against the stage. She could make out the width of his shoulders. That shock of dark hair. And ... oh hell, she could see the shapes of a dozen other patrons. All waiting. All wanting. She had her wish at last.

Guitars screamed from the giant speakers, bass vibrated through her heels and into her belly. And there was The Pole, like a steel lighthouse in a storm of light and heat and cigarette smoke. The pole was supposed to be the easiest thing for beginners to wet their feet, and other parts, with. So, much as she wanted to make her way straight to its thick metallic safety, she refused to even look at it. She didn't have night after night to perfect her technique slow and steady.

All she got was one chance to steal the show.

Deep breath. Feel the beat of the music. Feel the sweat. Be Venus, be a slutgarden goddess, a painted diva. Be just who she was deep inside.

Smoke hissed and slithered out around her ankles, her cue. No more time to hesitate. Hands on hips, lips pouted in tempting defiance, she tossed her hair over one shoulder and sauntered forwards.

She might have done this all her life. It came to her as easily as breathing, although her legs protested just a little at the extra demands being placed on them. This wasn't Pilates on the exercise mat before the TV after all. No, it wasn't by a long shot.

But if she kept the brightness of the spotlight in her vision, if she let it turn the crowd of dark figures to one faceless, silent shadow, she could forget the panicky voice that whispered, 'What are you doing here?'

She could abandon herself to the sensation of her own hands sliding over her skin, over the rhinestones. Rubbing the metal and plastic against her flesh until her tits were hot and heavy, her nipples tingling almost painfully, her pussy lips sensitive and wet with need.

And all the while, the music pulsed under her skin. Her hips moved in rolling, twisting, explicit rhythm. She twirled and shimmied. Arched on the glitter-strewn floor of the stage.

And even if she couldn't see them, she could feel the eyes on her. Watching her unhook and peel the rhinestones away from her tits. Watching and wanting the dream of feminine pleasure. And then the thrill as she remembered that was her, really her. Not some android in synthetic skin, dancing for them. This was *her* stage.

She tore off that middle-class label with the bra-top.

She left it lying somewhere near the pole as she cupped her breasts and sashayed to the edge of the stage. As she ran her fingernails down unfamiliar faces rough with unshaven beards and stained with tobacco. Or smooth with eager, lustful youth. As strange hands fumbled at her waist trying to snatch an extra second of contact with her skin, as money crinkled with the relentless motion of her hips.

And like a drug shot straight to her bloodstream, the knowledge that he watched. Watched her dance and tease and captivate her audience. She could work a room at a party of social-climbing suburbanites. She had charmed church socials of would-be pillars of society. She'd handled banking executives in their own boardrooms and talked down penny-pinching suppliers, beating them at their own game.

These men staring at her in wordless, heated, animal fascination were putty in her manicured hands.

He waited his turn until the others had moved on. Then he claimed her without even rising from his seat. He looked at her and she lifted her chin, tossed her sweat-damp hair. She made her way down the stage steps and to his chair. Behind her, Dee took over centre stage and attention shifted to the new temptation. But there were still enough eyes on them. Enough to witness this sacred blasphemy.

She straddled his lap and cradled his head with both her hands, burying them in that thick hair, so familiar to her and yet so strange in this dim smoky place where nothing was quite the same. She ran a finger over his lips and his chest and his crotch. Of course he was hard. There hadn't been any question about that.

But until now she hadn't been quite sure how brave she'd be. How much she'd dare. How far she'd go. Now she knew. The knowledge made her grin.

She wriggled his zipper down while he pressed the

twenty into her G-string and his eyes widened. He hadn't expected that either. Good. Just where she wanted him.

In one fluid twirl, she spun to press her ass against his exposed dick. She writhed just as she knew he liked it and felt him hold his breath, saw his hands grip the sides of the chair, knuckles straining, body tense. Oh yeah. Yeah, this was perfection. A whole new meaning to captive audience.

She ground harder and he groaned into her hair as she leant her head back on his shoulder. She spun again to slide her belly down his shaft. Then her tits. Then just the tip of her chin, her lips a millimetre from touching his dick. And he was in pure hell. An inch from losing control he couldn't afford to lose and she'd never been so high before.

The music rose to a crescendo, the singer screaming anger or ecstasy. Up on stage Dee scraped her nails down the pole. Heat from aroused, sweating bodies rose, charged the atmosphere with the electric thrill of unfulfilled desire. Everyone watching them knew what she was doing. Everyone saw his torment. Everyone took vicious pleasure in it.

She was the consummate entertainer.

She brought him to the edge, facing him. Her tits in his face; her crotch grinding his, rhinestone G-string bruising his dick. Her hands on his shoulders. Her lips surreptitiously brushing his neck. Playing him like her puppet until sweet spasms ran through and through her clit and her thighs and her ass. Knowing every watching eye saw her come. And loving it.

And then when he was almost there, when she felt his body weakening, she pressed her lips to his ear. Whispered, 'Do you want to come?' and laughed at his strangled, 'Oh God . . .'

'I know you do. You're dying to,' she said. 'But you can't touch me.'

She pulled away, laughing, and saw him bite down on his lower lip. She'd have bet money he'd drawn blood. She ran her hands through her hair and blew him a kiss while she made sure her weak legs wouldn't simply give out from under her. She gave him a long, long look as he sat there, one hand half-covering his abused erection, his eyes worshipping her. Then she smiled and turned to head for the dressing room.

Exeunt. Stage right.

She left the cash she'd earned in a pile on the dressing-room counter where the others could take it without shame after she'd left. Then she got dressed and found Lacey smoking out back.

'Thanks.'

Lacey nodded. 'You're a real job, you know that?'

She grinned. 'Yeah. So they tell me.'

'But you pulled it off.'

It was as close to a compliment on her performance as she'd ever get. Smiling, she shrugged.

Lacey took another drag on her cigarette and looked upwards. Out here the stars were bright and sharp, unsmothered by smog and light. 'You'll hang on to him won't you?'

It wasn't a question. She looked at the older woman with her profile scarred from years of a life on the wrong side of the bar. She frowned. 'I don't know. Maybe.'

Lacey turned and only gave her a small shake of the head, as if to tell her she was a fool.

Lights punctured the darkness as the car rounded the side of the building and slowed.

She hesitated. 'Maybe,' she said again and this time Lacey nodded and smiled.

'Don't do nothin' I wouldn't.'

Laughing, she told Lacey goodbye and then walked to

the car where he waited for her, behind doors that didn't need to be closed any more.

Curtain.

A. D. R. Forte has had several short stories published in themed Wicked Words anthologies.

Derailed Cal Jago

We had been waiting inside the tunnel for almost ten minutes. The carriage was heaving as usual – it was rush hour after all – and people were being their usual tetchy selves when it came to rail disruption. The air was full of tuts and sighs and commuters dramatically checked their watches or stood mute, frowning, with the odd 'can you believe it?' eye roll thrown in for good measure. The situation wasn't helped by the heat. A young man dressed casually in jeans and a T-shirt, who looked far too sleepy to be setting out for the day, pressed his right cheek against the door in an attempt to find some coolness. He had been standing like that, stooped and heavy lidded, for the past five stops.

I stood sideways on to the set of doors opposite Sleepy, my back against the glass separating me from the seated passengers, my briefcase held neatly in front of my knees. Just in front of me a woman with a rucksack bearing the slogan 'Designers are Crazy Bastards' was looking from the crumpled tube map in her hand to the map on the wall above the door and back again. To my right, a middle-aged man frowned into a book whose title claimed to be able to teach him Italian in seven days. I was sceptical.

The person who interested me most, however, was leaning against the doors to my left. Thick dark hair emphasised the blueness of his eyes and full lips pouted from a shadow of stubble. He held a rolled-up copy of *Q* magazine but clearly wasn't interested in it as he hadn't looked at it all the time he'd been on the train. Out of the corner of my eye I noticed him smile as the driver made a garbled announcement, indecipherable due to persistent crackling.

And then the lights went out.

Well, that really pissed them all off. As I listened to people complain and try to outdo each other by being more in a rush than everyone else – because their life was busier than anyone else's – I simply smiled and saw the situation for what it was: an opportunity.

The heat seemed to swell the moment we were plunged into darkness. An uneasy hush fell upon the carriage as the lights failed to immediately come back on as expected. I stood perfectly still for a few seconds as anticipation shot through my body like an electric force. My eyes gradually became accustomed to the lack of light and I began to make out the silhouettes of my fellow commuters. Bizarrely, Crazy Bastard still appeared to be hunched over her map, holding the paper up to her eyes in a desperate attempt to activate her see-in-the-dark super powers.

I cleared my throat and slowly reached down and placed my briefcase on the floor. As I straightened up, I turned my body so that I stood directly in front of Q. My skin tingled. In the eerily silent carriage the roar of my blood rushing in my ears was deafening. Then, ever so slowly, I took a small step backwards with my left foot and failed to suppress a sigh, which escaped from my lips and hung in the silent blackness, as my arse made contact with Q's thigh.

I shifted my weight from one foot to the other, the movement positioning my buttocks over his groin. I smiled. I knew he was smiling too; I could feel it on the back of my neck. I hovered there for a few seconds relishing the anticipation of the moment. Then, keeping the rest of my body absolutely still, I pushed my arse out slightly and finally made the contact with him that I craved. I remained still allowing him to feel the pressure of me against him. Then I gently swung my hips from side to side, exhilarated by the sensation of his excitement pushing against me. As I leant back into him more firmly every nerve ending in my body buzzed. This was going to be a good one, I could feel it.

Perfect timing then for the lights to flash back on and the train to lurch to life. Thrown off balance I reached up to grab the overhead handrail and in that split second the contact between his body and mine was lost. Feeling suddenly light headed, I gripped the handrail tighter as we approached the next station. I quickly looked around to see any obvious signs of my behaviour having been spotted. Crazy Bastard was now tracing a route along her map with her finger and Sleepy's eyes remained half shut. Elsewhere, the return of light had put reading and make-up application back on the agenda. No one appeared to have noticed mine and Q's small but significant indiscretion. As we roared to a stop at the next station, my tight chest and damp knickers and the presence of Q again nudging against my arse made it clear what I absolutely needed to do. As the doors whooshed open, I scooped up my briefcase, spun on my heels and flung myself on to the crowded platform.

I was swept along for a few frantic seconds, caught up in the wildebeest-esque herd of commuters until, at the mouth to the exit, the mass bottlenecked causing a jam. We stood packed together, all trying to pigeon-step our way forwards. Anxiety bubbled in my chest as I waited. I darted into a small gap and pushed my way up the steps, no doubt annoying everyone around me. But I had to get out. I had to breathe.

Once outside, I took a deep breath, filling my lungs with exhaust fumes and passing cigarette smoke and taking comfort in the roar of traffic. I looked at my watch and sighed as I began the long walk to the office.

My underground – and, for that matter, overground – train adventures could fill a book. Illicit liaisons with strangers in packed public places – what could be more delicious? There are times when the only thing that's got me through my working day is knowing that I'll soon be stepping into a new carriage, a new playground. Trains are my thing. I have lost count of the number of men and women I have teased, groped and generally been filthy with around the national rail network.

And yet, here I am having alighted four stops too soon about to walk the rest of the way to the office. So why have I just walked out on a great hit? Have I had a bad experience? Did I target the wrong person? Was I caught on camera and forcibly removed from a train and banned forever by Transport for London? No. Basically, I'm just trying to amend my ways. For the past three months I've been officially sort of 'seeing someone' and I figured that, early days or not, curbing my public-transport groping ways is probably the least I can do. But my God it's a struggle.

Dan and I met at a work thing. He had coveted the best art director award at a magazine do and so, when I found myself standing next him at the bar later, I offered him my congratulations. We already knew each other vaguely – same publishing house, different magazines – but our relationship up until that point had barely stretched beyond 'good mornings' and the odd eye roll in mundane meetings. But something must have happened that night as we celebrated with canapés and strawberry bellinis because a few days later, when he appeared in my office with offerings of a mocha and a muffin and asked me if I fancied going for dinner sometime, I said yes. I think he may have caught me off guard. Nevertheless, dinner the following evening had been a triumph and what followed that night back at my place, even more so.

A few months later all was going surprisingly well. And that made me slightly nervous. Not that Dan and I were serious. It was all just very light and fun and casual. And sexual. It's just that I'm very good at being single. I like to do my own thing, play by my rules and come whenever I like with whomever I like. And that's why I had almost gone into meltdown about Brighton.

'I've got to go to that conference next weekend,' he had told me through a mouthful of linguine one night.

I pulled a face. 'Lucky you. The agenda looks truly scintillating.'

'You're not going then?'

'Nope.' I had topped up our glasses with Shiraz and smiled. 'Budget cuts. They've almost halved the number of delegates and managing editors have been given the chop.' I took a gulp of wine. 'Damn shame. At least you'll be by the sea.'

'Come with me,' he'd said.

I had laughed. 'Are you asking me or telling me?'

He'd smiled. 'I'm asking you. But of course you have to say yes.'

I'd fallen suddenly serious. 'I'm not invited, remember?'

'I'm inviting you – as my guest in the hotel room. You can shop your way around the Lanes during the day, then we can do something in the evening. We could even make a weekend of it.'

I'd frowned. 'A weekend away?' I'd asked. 'Together?'

'Christ, Kate. I'm not asking you to marry me! I just want to take you to a hotel for a couple of days so we can quaff champagne and fuck each other senseless.'

Well, when he put it like that, nothing about the suggestion seemed to contravene any of my relationship-phobic sensibilities. So Brighton was on.

By the time I made it to my office I was almost an hour late and had already missed the start of a meeting. Natalie, my assistant, raised an eyebrow as I rushed in.

'Trains,' I said simply by way of explanation and headed for the meeting room. And despite my good intentions, flashbacks to Q and the possibilities of the journey home were already all I could think of.

The week passed quickly. Work was hectic and, besides meetings, I felt that I barely saw or spoke to anyone. At home on the Thursday evening I put on a CD and sank into my favourite chair, exhausted after another manic day during which I felt I had hardly achieved anything important due to the hours spent responding to constant emails. I was in the middle of convincing myself to never turn my computer on again when my front door buzzed and there was Dan.

'Brighton's tomorrow, isn't it?' I said rather abruptly.

He laughed. 'Yes. But it's not actually a crime to see each other on consecutive days.'

I wondered if perhaps it should be, but let him in all the same.

You know how you sometimes have evenings where you didn't set out to want to do anything or see anyone or make any effort at all and then before you know it something happens and you're having a good time? Or how you think to yourself, a quiet evening in, an early night, perhaps one glass of wine but that's it. And then you find yourself whooping and shrieking and laughing into the early hours convinced that you'll never come down for long enough to ever be able to sleep again? Well, that's how it came to be that Dan and I were both sitting on the floor of my lounge, smashed on an ancient bottle of tequila that Dan had found in my kitchen and sharing intimate thoughts and anecdotes with each other at four in the morning.

Through the highbrow medium of drinking games, I had learnt all sorts of personal details about Dan and had made a fair few revelations myself. The tequila, my tiredness, the intimacy and the varied sexual confessions had a potent effect on me; before I knew that I was even considering saying it, I heard myself boldly confess my most secret hobby.

'So I've touched all these men,' I was saying. 'And quite a few women. And I touch them until they lose all control and all they can think about is coming. People who would never think they were capable of such behaviour. But they do it for me, surrounded by all those people, because suddenly the only thing that matters to them is that I don't take my hand away.'

It was the first time I had ever confessed to it and once I started I couldn't stop. On and on I went, explaining how it felt, trying so hard to convey the absolute thrill of it. I was wet just talking about it. But it was a while before I realised that Dan had been silent for some minutes.

'What a dark horse you are,' he said when he finally spoke. He gave me a sideways look. 'Who'd have thought it, eh?'

'Have I shocked you?' I giggled and leant towards him to kiss him. I really wanted him then. I really wanted us to go to bed.

'A bit,' he said seriously as my mouth was just a fraction from his.

I hovered where I was for a moment before moving to sit back down again. I frowned. 'I don't even know why I just told you that,' I said lightly. 'It's really not a big deal.' But the awkward silence between us told me it was too late.

Dan cleared his throat and slowly stood up. 'I'd better get going or I won't be in any fit state tomorrow.'

'You can stay if you like?' I said casually. 'It's late.'

He shook his head. 'No, I need to get home tonight.' He kissed me lightly on the top of my head. 'See you tomorrow.'

'Six o'clock at Victoria?'

He looked at me blankly for a moment.

'Brighton?'

He smiled and nodded and then he was gone.

Standing by the coffee cart at Victoria station the following evening could have been very *Brief Encounter* but, as it happened, it wasn't. Dan was nowhere to be seen. I tried to look nonchalant as I sipped my cappuccino and I attempted to shake the feeling that I must have looked like I'd been stood up. Or perhaps, the feeling that I really couldn't shake was that, actually, I probably had been stood up.

I hadn't heard from Dan since my revelation the previous evening and the more I thought about it, the more cross I was with myself for blabbing and the more clearly I recalled the serious expression on his face. Part of me believed that it was his problem if he wasn't able to deal with a small sexual peccadillo but I also felt embarrassed by my clumsy confession.

I still felt twitchy. Even if I was being paranoid and Dan was on his way he was cutting it fine. There were five minutes to go before departure.

My phone beeped signalling a new text.

'Held up at work. You've got your ticket anyway so might as well just meet you at the hotel. Dan.'

I reread the message. It hardly sounded enthusiastic. Was this my cue to go home? Was its formal tone Dan's way of telling me not to bother? Or was I simply misinterpreting his message because I already felt on edge?

'For fuck's sake,' I muttered and then I tossed my empty coffee cup into the nearby litter bin and strode across the concourse towards my platform.

I glanced at my ticket; typically, my seat was in the farthest carriage. I hopped on board as lithely as one can when carrying a suitcase and wearing high heels. As the door was slammed shut behind me I stood wedged between it and the back of the man who had got on just before me. In front of him stood a queue of people, each shuffling forwards on a mission to find a seat. I gripped my ticket impatiently and sighed as I resigned myself to the fact that there was no point in trying to barge through to my seat. I would just have to wait.

On the opposite side of the vestibule area a man had already taken his chances, opting out of the shuffle simply to secure a decent standing space. He pressed himself back against the door behind him to allow the shufflers to move past him more easily. As the crowds began to disperse and I had progressed to standing in front of him, it struck me how perfect he looked. How absolutely my type. Approaching forty, he was dressed in a plain dark suit – Armani, I noticed, from the label inside the jacket, which was revealed when he removed it and slung it over one arm. His fairish hair was greying slightly and he had some fine lines around his pale-blue eyes. He looked a little quiet. Shy perhaps. Like I said: perfect. Even shy people need to let themselves go sometimes and when they do it's nice to be around to witness it.

As commuters began to move along the carriage I watched Armani gradually relax as more space opened up around him and I suddenly felt an overwhelming sense of longing. Apart from short instances of surreptitious train friction, I had been a very well-behaved girl over the past few months. No teasing, no grinding, no touching. And, oh, how I'd missed it. And now Dan was being an arse, my libido had gone into overdrive and here I was standing near the perfect Armani. Could I really be blamed if I were to seize this opportunity? Wouldn't it serve Dan right? And, more to the point, wouldn't it feel good to regain a sense of my old single self again?

Ahead of me a woman with four children and twice as many Hamleys bags was battling to get all her party along the aisle and safely into her reserved seats in the next carriage. She blocked the space entirely as she struggled. As I stood, lust momentarily gave way to irritation. I was irritated by the harassed mother for travelling with her brood during rush hour. I was irritated by her whiny children who continued to grizzle despite clearly having been bought half the contents of the world's most famous toy shop. I was irritated by my fellow commuters who did nothing to help her but simply exacerbated the crush by puffing their chests out and huffing loudly. I was irritated by the presence of Armani and the niggling thought that even though I wanted him I really shouldn't do anything about it although I tingled to my very core. But, of course, no prizes for guessing who I was most irritated with at that moment in time.

It was very appropriate, therefore, that on that thought the object of my fury came into view. The woman had managed to seat herself, the children grim and the numerous bags, so the crowd began to disperse. As I moved through the carriage and the crowd thinned as people found seats, my view cleared. And that is when I saw Dan sitting in his reserved seat reading a copy of *The Times*. I stopped suddenly and stared at him, amazed.

What the fuck was he playing at? He leaves me standing on my own looking like a social reject then annoys me with a grumpy text and all the time he was sitting on the train reading the paper? I frowned as I contemplated what to do. I was furious but I suppose it was petulant to make a point of standing all the way to Brighton on my own. And even if I did do that, what would things be like when we got there? Pissed off or not, I didn't want a weekend of awkward silences.

I sighed and started to move forwards but as I walked towards him a woman approached him and asked if the seat beside him was free. He looked up from his newspaper and smiled. Then, unbelievably, I noticed him glance fleetingly at me before telling her that it was indeed free as his travelling companion had missed the train. I stopped abruptly and stood still, incredulous. As the woman collapsed thankfully into the seat – *my* seat – Dan looked at me with a sly grin and an arched eyebrow before returning to his newspaper.

Shocked, I decided the best course of action was to retreat and gather my thoughts. Dan continued to stare at his newspaper but I could tell he wasn't reading anything on the page. I backed up until I was in the vestibule area again. Armani was now alone in the space. He looked up as I rejoined him.

'It's packed down there,' I said unnecessarily.

He smiled.

I snuck a peek at Dan as the door separating the vestibule from the carriage closed. Irritation had given way to curiosity now. I frowned slightly as I stared at him through the glass and tried to work out what he was up to. This was obviously a game. But quite what game we were playing I wasn't sure.

Armani had opened a book and begun to read. I was struck again by how attractive he was. There was something intense about him that I was drawn to; I liked the concentration on his face as he read. He was stockier than I had initially thought. He had a thick neck and strong forearms but I noticed that the hands which held his book steady were soft, his fingers on the book's spine, long and slim with perfectly smooth square fingernails.

A small train judder was required, I decided. A sudden lurch or a particularly bumpy stretch of track; all these factors that make a journey more uncomfortable for other passengers were things that I positively welcomed. After all, a girl has to reach out to steady herself if she feels herself falling. So I willed the train to jolt with all my might. And that's when a man with shoulders far too broad for public transport strolled through the door, forcing me closer to Armani in order to save myself from getting my ears knocked off. He lumbered through our space, pausing for a few moments to unwrap a sandwich. As he battled with the packaging, I made an effort to look terribly helpful and leant closer towards Armani to give Shoulders and his BLT more room to manoeuvre.

I smiled apologetically at Armani. 'Sorry,' I whispered as my chest made contact with his.

I was sure he blushed slightly as he smiled back. 'No problem.'

And then I slid my thigh between his legs.

Armani cleared his throat and shifted his weight slightly. I knew that the redness in his cheeks would have deepened but I didn't check to see. And I suspect that if I had looked at his face he would not have met my gaze. So instead I look at Shoulders who had accessed the sandwich but continued to look around in front of him, bemused.

'Here,' I said and reached across a little way and pressed the button to open the door.

He grinned and shook his head. 'Sorry. Thought it was automatic. Thanks.'

I increased the pressure of my thigh against Armani's crotch. Something was definitely stirring. 'You're welcome,' I said lightly.

As Shoulders disappeared through the door leaving Armani and I alone again, I did not move immediately. When I did finally, slowly, turn around, I saw Dan through the glass looking at me, his newspaper neatly folded in half on the table in front of him. He winked mischievously and, when I casually edged backwards so that my heels kissed Armani's toes, and his hardening cock grazed my arse, I knew that the game had begun. I just really hoped no one was planning on going to the buffet car any time soon.

I rocked against Armani firmly but slowly, resisting

the temptation to grind like a harlot. My desperate desire to just grab him and fuck him there and then shocked me. But the reality was that playing in this sort of public situation you had to be as discreet as you could force yourself to be. Although the pair of us were alone for now, we were only separated from the crowds by a couple of sliding glass doors. The thought of that alone made me squirm in delight. But it was also a reminder that something a little more subtle than a full-on fuck in a vestibule was required.

I moved my hips slowly but rhythmically, keeping the pressure against him constant. His left hand moved to rest on the back of my thigh, the touch so hesitant, so gentle that it was barely perceptible. But I felt it like a flame burning through my skin. And feeling it confirmed that the games had commenced. The confirmation signal, whether it was a moan, a touch or a stonking great erection straining against my arse, was always a relief. Even if you are totally convinced that you've picked well – and that kind of complete conviction is rare – only when you've felt or heard or seen undisputable proof can you totally relax and really begin to enjoy the encounter.

His breathing became heavier as I increased the friction. As I moved, constantly aware of him pushing against my flesh, I imagined how he would look if I stepped away from him now and turned to face him. I pictured his face – flushed skin, muscles tight – and, turning my attention lower, I imagined the impressive bulge in his trousers begging for release. Sometimes I abandoned them then, that image of utter desire and complete helplessness frozen in my memory as I left them in the carriage and lost myself in the crowd on the platform. But this time I was sure I wasn't going anywhere prematurely.

Armani's hand disappeared for a moment before reappearing on the back of my thigh, this time underneath my skirt. I held my breath as his hand rode a little higher, his touch still butterfly light. His fingers fluttered around the tops of my stockings. He skimmed the lace and pressed himself against my buttocks more forcefully. I did like a man who appreciated expensive hosiery. He felt harder all of a sudden as I felt his ridge pressing against the cleft of my arse.

I leant forwards a little, then reached back and ran the palm of my hand across the front of his trousers. A blast of hot breath prickled the back of my neck as I couldn't resist any longer and squeezed along his length. And that's when Dan stood up.

I continued to touch Armani as Dan edged out of his seat and began to move his way along the carriage, heading towards us. He gripped his newspaper tightly in his hand, the crossword page flapping open in front of him as he walked. He stared at me hard and I struggled not to squirm as Armani's fingers pressed more insistently into my flesh. Excitement caught in my chest as I wondered whether I had gone too far. Dan's expression was unreadable as he came closer but he walked with purpose, his gaze never leaving mine. I probably should have played it safe and stopped doing what I was doing. Stroking a stranger's cock when the man you're sort of seeing is approaching is probably, on the whole, unwise. But I couldn't stop myself. I couldn't let him go. I had waited months for this and the knowledge that Dan knew what I was doing and knew that he had been watching turned me on even more.

Dan hesitated just as he arrived at the other side of the door and that's when he let his newspaper fall to his side and I saw that I didn't need to worry about having gone too far. It was very clear that he had enjoyed the show. Only then did I realise that Armani obviously had no idea that Dan was there and that we could be seen. I assumed that Armani had his eyes shut. Obviously, he was not used to playing in public. Closing one's eyes in such a situation was potentially dangerous, as he was about to find out.

As the door whooshed open, Armani's body froze in an instant – apart from his hand which rocketed out from under my skirt and then rested limply at his side. Dan moved into our space and then stopped. My right hand still held Armani's cock but I had become still too. Dan did not look at either of us at all, but straightened his newspaper up and then folded it and turned it over so that he was looking at the top half of the back page. Sport. Not Dan's thing at all but then I didn't believe for one second that he was reading it. I realised that, standing behind me, Armani would not have been able to see Dan's obvious arousal. As far as he was concerned, this was a stranger who had walked in on our indiscretion – whether he had seen everything or not he wasn't sure – so probably the best thing to do in his mind was to shrink into the background. I had other plans though. I couldn't let Armani be too mortified or scared. More to the point, I couldn't have that cock of his go to waste.

So I slowly reached back and touched him again, my gaze never once leaving Dan who I am sure, out of the corner of his eye, could see that play had resumed. I couldn't help but breathe a small sigh of relief when I gripped Armani again and found he was still hard. His entire body was tense, however, so the possibility of him losing his nerve and taking flight was still very real. We had to play this absolutely right or we would lose him.

I continued to squeeze along his length, gently but firmly. I kept my body movement minimal so that Armani could see that I was still being discreet but still his body felt tense behind me. Gripping him firmly, I began to rub him through his trousers, strokes as long and smooth as I could get them through the material and from the difficult angle I was working from. Then I worked my hand lower and reached back between his legs. He felt heavy in my hand, his balls cupped in my palm. I squeezed them before returning to stroke his shaft again. Bingo. Despite his severe reservations he was relaxing. His body wanted this as much as mine did.

I noticed Dan quickly glance around checking that no one was coming through either door. He took a couple of steps closer towards us and then, as he looked down at the sports page again, he pushed his right hand up the front of my skirt and slid his fingers over my underwear. Taken by surprise, I barely stifled a moan. I bit down on my bottom lip, painfully aware of how wet the material was on his fingertips. I continued to watch his face as he continued to stare at the newspaper. He was good; an expression of pure concentration, apparently focused on the sports report, remained on his face while his fingers roamed over my underwear, lingering maddeningly but never staying in one place for quite long enough. Divine frustration. I wondered whether Armani's eyes were open now and, if so, whether he could see where Dan's hand was. Did he know that he was part of our game? Or was he blissfully ignorant to everything around him because all he could focus on was whether he was going to come in his trousers?

Dan's fingers began to rub rhythmically back and forth right where I needed it most. I opened my eyes wide in alarm to try to tell him that it was too much, that I wouldn't last another minute if he did that, but he still wasn't looking at me. I concentrated on trying to make the scenario last but Dan had his own way of moving the action forwards.

'Pull her knickers down,' he said quietly, all the while looking somewhere to the side of us into the middle distance.

It was the most I could do not to come right there and then the moment I heard those words.

Armani was silent and still. I wondered whether he

had heard Dan's instruction and I knew that Dan was holding his breath in anticipation, just as I was. Then both Armani's hands were holding my arse, gently kneading the flesh for a few seconds, before he hooked his fingers under my knickers and eased them over my buttocks and hips so that they came to rest halfway down my thighs. Without a moment's hesitation, Dan's fingers were inside me, filling my wetness, pushing himself deep.

I vaguely heard Armani murmur something close to my ear and then his hands were back on me, gliding over my stockings, caressing my arse, squeezing the hot flesh. And then I felt fuller still as another finger pushed inside me from behind. Together, Dan and Armani found a synchronicity that blew my mind.

I pushed myself back on Armani's fingers forcing him deeper and imagined each man's fingers touching the other's inside me, sliding through my wetness and over each other's skin as they fucked me. And that naturally led me to imagining the pair of them fucking me for real like this, their hard cocks rubbing against each other inside me. I bit my lower lip hard as Dan's thumb flicked across my clitoris, his fingers still buried deep. He held his thumb across the swelling, rocking the tip of his thumb firmly, causing exquisite stimulation.

Armani was breathing hard behind me. As I tried to hang on for just a little while longer I felt him nudge me away slightly. His fingers remained inside me but I felt his other hand move behind my arse. The movement was followed by the barely audible yet unmistakable sound of a zip unfastening. Armani's hand knocked against my arse as he worked himself to further excitement. I imagined him pulling hard, his face taut with tension, his cock ready to explode. His speed increased and the contact of his fist against my buttock became more forceful and I looked at Dan just as he withdrew his fingers from inside me and pinched my clitoris hard.

A sharp spasm of pleasure raged between my thighs and I came with such intensity that I'm sure I would have fallen down had the two men not been standing either side of me. And after a few more sporadic movements, Armani caught his breath and then became suddenly still before his body relaxed behind me.

Dan, flushed and still hard, stepped to the other side of the vestibule and breathed deeply. Armani cleared his throat and straightened his clothes. Rather touchingly, he rearranged my clothes too. I wasn't used to this post-fumble awkwardness – I never hung around that long.

The silence was broken by the train manager announcing our imminent arrival at the next station. Perfect timing. A couple of minutes sooner and we'd have had a stream of people traipsing through our little display. And perfect timing also because, when we came to a halt and a woman on the platform opened the door, my suitcase was conveniently beside me on the floor whereas Dan's was right the other end of the carriage.

'Excuse me,' I said in my sweetest voice and I picked up my luggage, pushed past an astounded Dan and stepped off the train.

I couldn't help but grin as I marched along the platform. For a moment I half expected Dan to suddenly appear beside me, panting after running to catch me up. But I knew I had been too fast for him to have realised what was happening, sped to the other end of the carriage, located his luggage and got himself off the train. I knew I had won.

I left the station and headed for the taxi rank. A taxi fare for the remainder of the journey wouldn't be cheap but seeing Dan's shocked expression had been worth it. I wondered what would be going through his mind now, stuck in the vestibule with Armani, but I didn't have the heart to be too cruel to the man who had done his utmost to accommodate my favourite kink. As I slid into the back of a cab and gave the driver the name of the Brighton hotel I sent Dan a text: 'Hope you didn't mind me getting off?'

His reply came through in seconds. 'Not at all ... so long as I'm next.'

I relaxed into my seat and smiled. I could hardly wait.

Cal Jago's short stories have been featured in numerous Wicked Words collections.

The View From on High

Heather Towne

I looked up the forest fire tower, way up. The steel ladder that ran between the green steel support legs seemed to go on forever: a stairway to heaven for some park ranger, a stairway to hell for me.

But I was 21 years old, starting yesterday, as good a time as any to start conquering some of my many, many childish phobias, this particular one being the fear of heights. Let's put it this way, if I'd grown up over five feet, I would've been scared to death long ago.

I glanced around at the sun-drenched forest. My best friend Carrie, who'd suggested the hiking trip (to celebrate my birthday and help me overcome my fear of dust, dirt and bugs) was somewhere off in the bushes, her kind, but nauseating, words of encouragement out of earshot. I was all alone on the rocky clearing, just little old me and my nerves and that giant Eiffel Tower of the Park Service.

I swallowed hard, ducked in underneath the structure, touched the steel ladder. A chill ran through me, chased by a dry heave. The metal was almost cool, despite the midsummer heat; cool like the grave.

The fingers of my left hand closed over the fifth rung up. Then my right hand was there on the steel too, fingers curling over the rounded metal. I stared at my hands, not daring to look up now. The key was to focus on the task itself, literally take it one step at a time. My daring plan was to ascend as high as I could before my heart stopped.

A warm gentle breeze caressed by, lifting my blonde hair, leaving me ice cold and cursing, telling it to bugger off. Hot shafts of sunlight struck my bare arms and legs, weighing me down, heating me up not a bit. One step at a time, I told myself. And my feet started to move.

One hiking boot on the first rung, the second boot, two feet off the ground. I clung close to the ladder like a hunchback to a gargoyle, palms sweating up a storm. I sucked in some pine-scented air and lifted my left arm, placed my left hand on the sixth rung, my right foot on the second.

Insects buzzed all around, but I hardly heard them, the roaring in my ears was so loud. I stared straight ahead, hands throttling the rungs, body coursing with adrenaline, climbing, knowing just how Sir Edmund felt.

I swallowed again, but no spit came this time. Not at this altitude. I'd lost track of the number of rungs, scaling the ladder like a cat coming down from a tree. My mind was blank. I just moved, with the resolve and speed of an arthritic turtle. One hand, one foot, other hand, other foot, rung after rung after rung.

Then I looked down, and froze solid. I gripped the ladder like Kirstie Alley gripped the last piece of cheesecake. I was at least twenty to one hundred feet off the ground, the freefall to hard Canadian Shield below dizzying. My head spun and my eyes swam with tears, my limbs trembled with a life of their own. I full-body pressed against the slim slippery metal that had far too many open spaces and shivered hysteria.

What seemed like hours later, I tried to open my mouth to call out to Carrie, but my jaws only cracked, the terror not allowing me to form words. My knuckles blazed white on the metal, my knees dug in for the long haul.

Yogi and little Boo Boo would find me here, a skeleton still clinging to the ladder, twenty rungs up from Earth with no way down. Park Ranger Smith would have to cut me off his tease of a tower with a blowtorch, or a bone saw, bury me with my section of steel.

'Goin' up or down?' someone asked, jolting me.

I slowly, painfully tilted my head downwards, neck bones snapping like twigs.

There was a man on the ground, a big man, staring up at me. He had a wide grin on his sun-browned, black-stubbled face, the black hair on his head thick and tousled, eyes shining. He was wearing a dirty white T-shirt and a faded pair of jeans, and he had his hands on his hips, his bare muscular arms covered with hair that rustled in the breeze. Clarity comes to those about to die.

He must have glimpsed the panic in my eyes, because he started climbing, coming after me. The ladder shook with his weight, and I desperately clutched my body to it, an animal whimpering escaping from between my cold dead lips.

Then the giant was on top of me, all over me, his huge warm body pressing against my bloodless, foetal form. His words came hot and spicy in my ears, talking me down. But he'd have to do a lot more than talking to get this girl down. And he did.

He grasped me around the waist with a big hairy arm and tore me off the rungs. I clawed frantically after them as they spun out of sight, but he held me away easily, an arm around my middle, a hand on the ladder. We went down, way down, until I collapsed to my knees when at last a dangling foot touched blessed terra firma.

He helped me up, and I spontaneously hugged him, grateful and giddy, my strength returning in a heady rush just ahead of my fears. Then he kissed me, hard, on the mouth.

'Hey, you big ape!' I gasped, shoving him back, my face burning hot as the sun. One of my other phobias, you see, is public displays of affection.

* * *

His name was Ken Kane, and he lived in a small cabin in the forest, operated a small sawmill. He invited Carrie and me back to his place, not the least bit put off by my indignant rejection. She accepted, and we sat around his rough-hewn kitchen table drinking his home-made wine.

He was a big, physical, no-nonsense kind of guy who'd never even heard of mind games. Rough and ready, with untroubled brown eyes and teeth as even and white as fence pickets. He laughed loud and hearty, coming from deep in his chest, as I briefly recited my litany of fears, explaining why he'd found me making love to that steel ladder.

'Me and you'll get along just fine,' he said with a laugh, clapping a heavy hand down on my bare knee and squeezing.

'I'll just bet you two will,' Carrie added, grinning at me and his hand.

He was large enough to swallow me whole, old enough to be my father when I looked at his seamed, unshaven face up close. But he did have a raw, ultra-masculine appeal that was a furry far cry from the emaciated office boys I was used to. I wrenched my knee free of his paw, but I was smiling a little, too.

He insisted on giving us a tour of the area around his cabin. So we trekked through the forest, Ken pointing out flowers and plants and birds' nests, streams and beaver dams and deer droppings. Then he led us up a hill that overlooked the surrounding woods, green stretching out as far as the eye could see.

'You're not afraid of this little hill, huh?' he said, beaming down at me. He grasped my hand, clasping me in warmth and reassurance.

I quickly slipped my hand free, afraid Carrie would see. 'Well, no. But there's lots of room up here, and the slope of the hill is nice and gentle, and –'

He shut off my gibberish by bending down and

kissing me, thick red lips sinking into mine, softer than before.

I jerked my head back like before. 'Hey, Carrie will see us!'

He grinned. 'So what?'

I looked around, couldn't spot the girl, and relaxed just a bit. But things were still happening way too fast for my go-slow comfort zone – the elevation and the kissing and all.

Ken kissed me again, bold as the bright-blue sky, expressing his affection like a giant sloppy puppy dog. And I didn't pull back this time, the outdoorsman's lips feeling so very good on mine, his self-assurance filling me with assurance.

He crushed me in his bearlike arms, our lips together, moving together. All out in the open on that sunny hilltop in the middle of that pristine wilderness. I flooded with a thick heavy heat, my breath catching in my throat, my arms finding their way around Ken's bulky shoulders.

His tongue shot into my mouth, aggressive and insistent and playful all at the same time. I moaned with excitement. We entwined our tongues together, Ken's huge hands capturing my little bottom and kneading the taut flesh.

I dropped my own hands lower, on to his broad muscled back, clutching as much as I could. He groaned into my mouth, his voice rumbling through me, setting my body to vibrating. The wind swirled hot air around our melded forms, the unblinking sun burning down on us. But I took little notice of the elements, just like I was taking little notice of the fact that Ken and I and our spontaneous combustion was exposed out there on that hilltop for any wandering hiker or fisherman or chipmunk to see. I was swept up in the fire of our passion, fears scorched by lust.

Until I heard a giggle come from behind Ken's bulk. I

broke away from the woodsman's mouth and craned my neck around his trunk. And there was the missing Carrie, in Ken's shadow, grinning at me.

'Get a room,' she quipped.

I flushed redder than my four-alarm sunburn, plucking Ken's mitts off my bum and hastily backing away like Bambi from a bumblebee.

The next outing we went on, we left Carrie in the city.

I'd been thinking about the backwoods hunk all week, reliving our lusty, sunshiny time together within the cold sterile confines of my cubicle. The feel of his hot massive body pressing against mine, the gamey taste of him, the sharp bristle of his whiskers against my cheeks and lips, the wild tingling sensation of his meaty hands on my needful flesh.

He was twice the man of any men I'd ever met before. He did something to me, mentally, as well as physically. His whole powerful persona instilled in me the confidence to face my fears, the insight to see just how foolish they really were, and the willpower to actually lick them. And that was only after spending one sweaty afternoon with the guy.

The fact was, of course, that I wanted to change, and he was the locomotive catalyst pushing me in the right direction. So when the weekend finally rolled around, I drove the sixty miles out to his cabin in the woods in total ignorance of the posted speed limits.

'Ever been on the swinging bridge over the Sturgeon River chasm?' he asked, after we'd exchanged a few heated greeting kisses inside his log home.

'I ... I've heard about it,' I mumbled, the very word 'chasm' sending shivers down my malleable spine. 'It's pretty ... high up, isn't it?'

He grinned, teeth and eyes gleaming like an animal's in the darkness of the cabin. 'So what?'

He bit into my throat, bear paws latching on to my

backside and squeezing, the animal. He was dressed in a plaid shirt with the sleeves ripped off and a pair of once-blue jeans, and I pressed my tiny body against his colossal frame, drawing strength from his strength.

'Yeah, s-so what?' I exhaled, clutching his unruly hair as he chewed on my neck.

The 'so what?' stuck in my throat like a chicken bone when we stepped out on to the long, narrow, sagging wooden and wire bridge that spanned the raging Sturgeon River below. Like a thousand feet or so below.

The entire length of the bridge shook in my damp hands as I tentatively walked out on to its planks. I struggled to get my balance, the bridge quivering even more than me. I risked a glance down at the white water, the crashing of the rapids filling my ears with horror stories. I took two steps back for the one I'd just taken forwards.

And ran into Ken. He was right behind me, big body pressing into mine, dissipating some of my chill.

'One step at a time!' he roared over the tumult. Then he kissed my neck, propelled me ahead with what I could only assume was the hard outline of his cock in his jeans. Either that or he'd packed one heck of a roll of Lifesavers.

I lifted a hiking boot, brought it down. Repeated the process with my other foot. The bridge swayed. I prayed for a quick and painless death, preparing for my nose-dive sunset. But then the bridge steadied, something stronger taking hold.

'I got your back!' Ken bellowed.

I slowly cranked my head to the side, tendons straining, and grimly smiled. I rotated my head square again and watched my boot lift up and out, sink down on what surely had to be the cheapest and flimsiest of balsam woods. I was moving.

I smothered the guy wires in white-knuckle sandwiches and tortuously crept forwards, Ken close behind me, urging, cheering me on. I moved a little more quickly, baby to toddler steps.

The bridge was stable, the blazing sun bathing me in warmth, mist from the thundering rapids drifting up to coolly lick at my bare legs. It felt good, it felt exciting. I could do this, was doing it. I set my steely sights on the opposite shore and strode forwards, taking control of myself and the bridge.

Ken stopped me halfway across. I'd been sure all along that the big galoot was going to shake the bridge like the giant his beanstalk, really rock and rattle me and my nerves. But I didn't know him well enough, then.

He gripped my shoulders and spun me around, somehow keeping the unstable bridge stable with his tree-trunk legs. 'Time for a breather,' he said, tilting my chin up, and dipped his lips into mine.

I backtracked like a skittish pony. 'Hey!' I protested. 'We're on the middle of a public bridge here – over a ch-chasm. All those people we passed on the trail are going to be here any second.'

'So what?' Man Mountain replied, the two easiest, most liberating words in the world.

I stared at him, at his hard-rock physique and handsome sun-lined face, his laughing, challenging eyes. So what, indeed.

I flung myself at him, mashing my mouth into his. The height and the sight were no longer my concern. Fear had been steamrollered by lust, the strongest emotion a repressed young woman is capable of.

We kissed deeply, hungrily, out there in the over-exposed tree-rimmed sunshine, hanging high over that dangerous stretch of water. I painted the fullness of Ken's lips with my eager tongue, then darted my tongue in between his lips and shoved into his tongue.

He held on to the wire railings as we swirled our slippery tongues together, holding us and the bridge securely in place. I took advantage of the situation to uncoil my arms from around his tree-stump neck and run my hands down his swollen chest. Down to his wide leather belt, and below the belt.

''Member where we are?' he asked with a laugh. Then he stopped laughing when my fingers drifted on to the hard slab of meat bulging the front of his second-skin jeans.

'So what?' I breathed, brushing my fingertips over his massive erection, delightfully feeling it swell even further at my warm gentle touch.

He shuddered with the erotic impact of the soft balls of my fingers tracing, teasing his pulsing manhood. I glided back up, swirling my fingertips around the bulbous head of his yearning need.

He grabbed my wrist, and the bridge shook. 'Two can play that game, Fay,' he growled, collapsing to his knees, jarring me and the bridge.

I grabbed on to the waist-high wires and tried to calm things down. I'd had no intention of going overboard, not really, not there, at least. But if you pull the tail, expect to get the claws. The animal yanked my shorts down, exposing my white cotton panties with the prominent wet spot at the crotch.

I gaped at the wild man on his knees before me, hardly believing even he was bold enough to try something like this. I scanned the brush on either side of the bridge, scoured the water below. No one – at least not at the moment. Then I felt hands on my bum, roughly gripping and squeezing the hot pliable flesh, powerful fingers pushing under the elasticised outskirts of my panties and digging in.

I moaned, and Ken smiled up at me, licking his lips with his thick wet tongue. Then he stuck that tongue out to its full ridiculous length and poked my panties with the tip of it, pussy level.

'God,' I groaned, my knees and the bridge buckling.

His tongue surged against my cottoned soft spot, sending a wicked tingling sensation shimmering throughout me. The bridge quivered as my arms quivered, Ken's flattened tongue wagging back and forth across my panties, my pulsating pussy.

The horny outdoorsman locked my trembling butt cheeks in his iron grasp and dipped his head down, dragged his heavy, beaded tongue up and over my thinly veiled sex, starting from deep in between my legs and ending all the way up at my waistband, coating me in electric wetness. Over and over.

The wind blew and trees swayed and the bridge rocked and the sun bore down, as Ken licked me in my most sensitive of places. Again and again, lapping at my pantied pussy with his velvet sandpaper tongue, his shaggy head bobbing in between my legs, fingernails biting into my bum. I bit my lip and whimpered, coursing with a raw, red-hot need in rhythm to Ken's tongue, frivolous fears of heights and public affection lost in the erotic maelstrom.

Each long, lingering, pressurised lick dragged me closer and closer to the edge. And I was dangling directly over the gaping abyss of all-out orgasm, two tantalising tongue strokes away from blistering open-air ecstasy, when a pack of cub scouts jerked me back from the brink.

'Look, that guy's biting that lady!' a boy yelled.

My eyes flew open and I stared at the chubby lead scout at the edge of the bridge. He was pointing at Ken and me, guiding his onrushing troop as they boiled over the top of the trail.

I shoved the licking man back and raced for cover, showing the boys my fluffy white tail as I made frantic tracks for the far side of the bridge, Ken's hearty laughter hot on my trail.

'I hate the city,' Ken grumbled. He wrinkled his nose, staring sullenly at the traffic grinding by my first-floor apartment. We were out on the patio, sipping some more of his wine. 'Too much noise and smog and concrete. Too many people.'

I smiled, happy to have the rugged man on my own turf for a change. 'Well . . . I just might know a place where we can get some peace and quiet and fresh air.'

He looked at me. 'Let's go.'

I took his hand and led him out of the apartment, into the elevator I'd never had the courage to use before. We stepped out on the 25th floor, and I followed the signs, guiding the lug through some halls, up some stairs, and out on to the roof of the high-rise.

The wind caught me and pushed me back. But there was Ken, to grab on to and steady me.

We crunched our way across the compacted gravel to the very edge of the building, a three-foot-high concrete lip that mouthed the word 'Jump!' But Ken's supportive hands and my new mindset held everything in check.

'Nice up here, isn't it?' I commented, spinning around in Ken's arms and kissing him. 'Far from the madding crowd.'

The big guy was all citified for my benefit, looking mighty uncomfortable in a tight white shirt and a pair of black slacks. I helped relieve some of his clothing discomfort by unbuttoning his shirt and sliding my hands inside, over the top of his huge hairy pecs. They jumped up and down in my hands for my amusement, Ken pressing his lips into mine, excitedly kissing me.

I pinched his sun-browned nipples between my fingers, rolling the rigid rubbery protuberances, and he groaned into my open mouth. Our tongues slid together in a flash of silver, and Ken worked the buttons free on the back of my dress, as I squeezed his thick nipples, then my mouth caught and briefly sucked on his restless tongue.

He yanked my summer dress down and caught up my bare breasts in his wide-span hands. 'Yes,' I moaned, as his strong warm hands squeezed my soft charged flesh.

He bent his head down and flicked his tongue at one of my swelling nipples, then the other, teasing the pink buds harder and higher. I ran my fingers through his ruffled hair, holding him close, trembling with desire.

He swirled his tongue around and around my aching nipples, bathing them in hot saliva, as his heavy hands groped my pale breasts. He took a blossomed nipple into the wet hot cauldron of his mouth and sucked on it, and I cried out with delight.

We were all alone on the windswept, sun-flooded rooftop, the city bustling far down below, but there were office towers and other high-rise apartment buildings within easy eyeshot. Not that I cared. I was flaunting my new-found fearlessness, high up and on public display, putting on a show of my achievement for any curious, elevated citizen who wanted to see.

Ken bit into one of my nipples and I arched my back, my body brimming with erotic energy. He bounced his bushy head back and forth between my tits, feeding on the buzzing tips, mauling the electrified meat.

Not until my heaving chest shone with his ardour did he finally pull his head back and rip away the rest of my dress, leaving me madly naked except for my sandals. I watched the flimsy garment sail over the edge of the building, worrying just a bit about the cost, but wondering not at all about what lay beyond.

Ken tore off his shirt and pants and spread them out on the pebbles for our comfort. Then he tried to spread me out on top of them. But I fought him off, shaking my head and laughing. I was in charge now. This was my environment, my day in the sky-high, community sun.

I pushed him down on to the clothing, got him to stretch out on his back, his huge hairy body filling my eyes. Then I helped him wiggle out of his underwear, and his big thick cock flopped out into the open, bedding down straight and twitching on the fur of his groin and stomach.

I straddled him, squatting over the top of his member, resting my slickened pussy lips on the throbbing shaft of the monster. I rubbed back and forth, christening his manhood in the name of my sticky lust.

He grunted and grabbed up his erection and parted my swollen pink petals with its mushroomed hood. He thrust his hips up, slamming inside of me, filling me up, jolting my pussy and body with fifty thousand volts of raw, juicy sexual electricity.

'Fuck me! Fuck me, you animal!' I screamed, grabbing on to his matted chest hair.

He clutched my waist and churned his hips, pistoning inside me. I sagged to my knees and hung on for the ride, cowgirl-style, my mouth seeking and finding his. I bounced my bum up and down in rhythm to his powerful thrusting, the sharp, wet smack of our bodies coming together filling the buzzing air.

My entire being went molten, melding with the wild man as he pounded his huge stake into my tiny opening, as I desperately rode his cock. He stroked back and forth inside of me, stoking and stoking me, the wet hot friction igniting my pussy until I burst into flames, burning ecstasy sweeping all through me.

'Oh, God! Yes!' I wailed, shaking out of control, an epic orgasm searing my soul.

Ken gritted his teeth and fucked even harder, ploughing my gushing pussy with reckless abandon, powering through my liquid joy until he, too, jerked with all-out release.

It was in the sweaty, cuddly aftermath of our thin-air, open-house frenzy, when the blood had stopped pounding in our ears, that we finally heard the news chopper hovering overhead. Ken roared with anger and reared up on his hind legs, shaking his fist at the noisy whirlybird, his glistening cock jumping delightfully. I just lay back and smiled, totally mentally and physically content for the very first time in my life.

Later on, Ken had to fight his way through the crowd gathered at the bottom of the building, while I got a satisfied chuckle out of one of the news channel tickers, which read: 'It Was Beauty Drilled The Beast!'

Heather Towne's short stories have appeared in numerous Wicked Words collections.

Housebound Nikki Magennis

It's been five months since I was last outside. A steel door separates me from the rest of the world, keeps me locked in here, circling. Counting the hours I spend alone waiting for him.

The flat is a calm landscape during the day. The sheets on the bed are smooth and clean. The blinds are raised open to let in sunlight. The little red light on the DVD player blinks a silent warning pulse. I tiptoe around, restless, tempted to pull out one of his lurid porn mags from under the bed and steal a frantic orgasm lying spreadeagled on the kitchen floor. But I manage only to bite my lip and dig my nails further into my palms.

Save it, I hear his voice in my head. *Don't break the spell.*

And I know it's all part of the game, so I wait and feel the anticipation gathering inside me like thunderclouds building in the scorched summer sky outside.

I look out the window without getting too close. We're high up here, the fourteenth floor, and I have an old fear of heights. I like watching the clouds pass, but I don't look down. Everything's so small and far away. It's easier to keep my gaze inside, running over the contents of the flat, learning everything in detail. The walls are twenty paces apart. The ceiling is just a little further than I can reach when I stretch up towards it, pressing my body flat against the wall. A skyscraper with a low ceiling – what an irony. But it is a luxurious space, full of light and polished wood floors. He's made it beautiful for me. Filled it with expensive furniture and big pictures. The vast iron bedstead – though that's not just for aesthetics. It provides a good anchor for cuffs or ropes. I know it well. Every inch.

In the house we are free to explore the darkest reaches of our desires. It's utterly private, utterly intimate. The two of us orbit each other like moons caught in a gravitational embrace, the house being the planet around which we turn. A cupboard full of cords, whips and secrets. A fridge full of ice cubes, cream and camera film. We have a little darkroom, even, for developing prints that would get us arrested in the local chemist. Shelves stacked with the stories of other obsessive lovers: Nin, Bataille, Miller. Films he's brought me, which we watch together in fascinated silence. We've travelled to the furthest edges of our imagination together, finding inner landscapes that are dark and expansive. Beautiful corners.

Trapped for so long in this most civilised of cages, you might think I'd be losing my mind. But then the mind is a strange creature. Hard to pin down. Desire can become twisted into unrecognisable shapes, like a creature in a nightmare shifting from one form to another. The particular taste of the dream remains in your mouth, the sharp flavour of it. But the forms it takes become ever stranger, till you find yourself looking at a bizarre, unfamiliar picture. Like this one.

This arrangement. Our peculiar set-up. The lengths he goes to to keep me fed and healthy. And what's happening to me as I circle the rooms, pacing quietly from bedroom to kitchen to living room and back. How my world has shrunk and changed, from a wide-open, bright and busy adventure, to a certain, square, enclosed space. Nothing to see except the interior. Nobody to see except him, at night. And all through the day, pictures of him that haunt me like erotic demons and keep me simmering. Tense. Ripe.

I woke up this morning at the sound of the door slamming when he left, and lay in bed remembering the boys I never fucked. When I was a teenage girl, all the crushes and the fantastic terrors – the questions that zipped through my mind at the speed of light. Would he hold my hand? Would he brush up against me? There's something perfect about those non-existent relationships, old memories of – God, such slightness. A look, a certain smiling in the eyes. Or even the way my first would-be boyfriend would studiously avoid looking at me. We'd spend hours drinking coffee and smoking cigs till we choked. Talking inconsequential crap, trying to be funny. Aware of the screamingly small distance between us, that gap of air so thick I could feel it. And yet never reach across and touch.

Because then the whole damn thing would start, the crazy world of sex and maybe even love. Which these days is a well-worn path, but back then was a trip into uncharted territory. Everything we did not know then was a huge force, like gravity, that pulled you inexorably towards someone, but repelled you at the same time.

What would happen? How would it feel? Would his skin be strange against yours, would it hurt? What if it took you to the brink of where you lost control, wasn't that what happened? You'd somehow be split open, scattered, dissolved in the night air, left drifting in the firmament with all the hard, glittering, foreign stars.

And now, since I've been housebound these past months, I get the same feeling. Trepidation. I can spend all day imagining my lover's body, the unexpected reactions of his cock, hands, mouth. The sleeping strength in his gracefully curved biceps, the long lines of sinew and the slim hips. There's nothing soft in his body. It's all strength, the form and matter of it fused into animal force, charged with intent and certainty. Part of him will always be a stranger to me, no matter how well I know him.

That assuredness, when he looks at me it's like arrows, pointing straight to my innermost secrets. He knows the hidden places of me, perhaps even better than I do myself. He explores there, silently, observing how I move. Ebb and flow. He keeps a chart of the moon above the bed, so he can tell me – *first quarter, this is what is happening now. Inside you. A slippery channel, a warming of the flesh. Your legs are weaker, your clit will respond faster. When I touch you.*

More than that, he knows the movement of my emotions. My moods.

Now, you want to be held gently, he says. And he does.

Spoons me, kisses me so lightly it's like a whisper along my spine. A feather against the back of my neck. Licks me like an ice cream, makes me shiver with opulent pleasure.

Other times he'll hold me down, wordlessly, and fuck me hard.

Pin me to the mattress, keep me splayed open and immovable while he charges into me. Reaching that place inside that is untouchable by any other means, the very darkest reach of my soul that can only be taken by a brutal rutting.

My thoughts move slower these days, focus sharper on the small things. While at first I railed at the situation, like a moth battering its wings against a bare light bulb, I am now finding surprising changes taking place.

For example, my body has grown huge. I have expanded – and I don't just mean that physically. Sure, the lines of my figure have grown looser, wider, softer. There's not much exercise to be had in a four-room flat. But at the same time, I've never been so conscious of my living, breathing self. I'm the only thing moving around in here, bar the occasional wasp or bluebottle that finds its way in through the open window and spends an hour throwing itself at the glass, trying to escape. So I've become almost spellbound by my body, curious to the point of obsession.

The way he looks at me, those hungry eyes feasting on my naked self when I'm bound and stretched open, burrowing into the soft parts, makes me wonder.

I find myself examining the curves, the folds, the smooth expanses and wet spots of this pale and unfathomable object. Stroking, prodding, rubbing. Absently, I can wander round tweaking on a nipple, massaging the swell of my breast. There's no one to see. My world is utterly private. If I meander around, half dressed, pleasuring myself, it's like an exercise in meditation.

Even the way that my clothes restrict me, nip me, wrap me up, has become entrancing. In the afternoon I can stand in front of the mirror, tracing the red indentations across my thighs, waist, back and breasts. The lines where I have bound myself, buttoned into tight skirts, heeled shoes, underwired bras.

The rituals. Washing the dishes has become almost transcendental. When your world is reduced to such simple elements, every action is important. The movement of my wrist. The pressure of the sink against my solar plexus. Warm frothy water sloshing against my arms to the elbow, spilling over the edge, running down my legs, pooling at my feet. Likewise, I can wash my own body for hours, standing under the shower head and feeling the water drum on the crown of my head, careful to clean between my legs with the special rose-oil soap, so that I smell good for him later.

So this is how I pass my days, watching, feeling, waiting.

The evening, when the light turns from hard white to softer yellows and greens, is when he gets back.

Loaded with buttoned collars, briefcases, the smell of the city and exhaust smoke. A roar of intensity that crashes into the still space of the house, that has been waiting for him. And me, here, with my slowly ballooning flesh, becoming paler and more sensitive by the day.

Tonight I'm shaking a little, at the sound of him, the knowledge that he will be wound up and hungry after a long day out there. My palms sweat.

What will he bring tonight? Another film, a toy?

He looks at me and his face is sharp with intent.

You know how you dare each other. Up the ante, bit by bit. You need to go a little further each time. A little harder, a little hotter. Like marking lines on a stick as the waters rise, we watch each other's moves, try to predict the next twist.

But I could never have predicted this.

I thought we were lost in our own dark universe, weaving ourselves together with spit and sperm to glue our bodies closer, limbs intertwining, minds meshing.

Only *you need an element of surprise*, he said.

To keep it fresh, to get that banging of the heart and the racing pulse, you need to keep changing the rules. So he's brought us here. Brought me here.

Outside.

The corridor, the sharp scent of pine disinfectant. The lift, the lurch in my stomach as we descend. His dark presence next to me, holding on to me. My white knuckles, the twitching of my shoulders as I try to breathe. The sliding doors, which move apart soundlessly, impassively, like they aren't at all concerned with the momentous occasion of my release. And now I see a glimpse of the wild, reckless world outside. It looks so – cool, and strange and different. The air tastes so sweet it makes me want to weep, and I'm ready to fall down on my knees and feel the new ground beneath me. But he doesn't pause, he keeps pulling me steadily towards the car, parked just yards away and waiting.

After twenty weeks of smooth floorboards underfoot, my steps meet the hot gravel and it's like walking over coals. The sky – the sky stretches above us like an unimaginably huge blue vault. The city is alive in every direction, full of inquisitive eyes and fast movement. Kids and shopkeepers and traffic swerving across roads, flashing lights and brash signs in neon that dazzle me.

His hand holds mine, cool and firm. Gripping. He leads me. Into the car, which seems at first a safe haven, a little familiar box where our breath will mingle in comfortable warmth. Until I realise where we are going.

Out of the city, past all the acres of houses and streets and little lives that I have no idea about. We start climbing the hill to the south, winding upwards at a steep incline. In a low gear, the engine strains, as though the car is as reluctant as I to reach our destination.

The Car Park in the Sky. Sounds kind of romantic, doesn't it? I'd thought so when I first heard it, until I was told that the local boy racers used it for their trysts. It's certainly a wonderful view from up here – the whole of the city spread out below you, like so much grey rubble. At night the lights are mesmerising.

But the guys – the guys in cars with the windows rolled up tight, smoking grass and stealing fumbling, sordid gropes from the girls they pick up in town. Leaving beer cans and used condoms strewn over the tarmac, covering the grass with the greasy pall of their exhaust smoke. It's an elevated shithole, a dustbin with a beautiful name.

They watch with that idle curiosity in their eyes as we arrive. Two cars, one a black Merc that just has to be borrowed, because the guy in the driver's seat looks barely eighteen. Greased hair. Baseball cap. Unless he's a drug dealer, there's no way he owns such a flash car.

Maybe he stole it. Either way, the boys wait up there like predators, intrigued by the sight of us arriving. Obviously out of place.

The engine is still running. He knows what I'm feeling right now, just how much I'm shaking. He turns the key and silence rushes in.

'Get out.'

His voice is calm, like a gun pointed right at me with a steady hand. I look at his lap and, right enough, his cock is hard and bulging in his lap. He's not touching it though, knowing it's ready, liking the tension. One more minute passes.

'Babe. Trust me.' He says, and leans over to open my door, letting his arm press hard against my chest as he does so, pulling the back of his hand across my nipples as he sits back in his seat. I look at him and see the universe stretching between us, realising he's setting me free.

In his own way.

Like I'm in a trance, I get out and walk round to sit on the bonnet, where the hot metal warms my ass through the thin fabric of my skirt. I don't usually dress very carefully these days, as it's only he and I who'll see me, so I'm wearing one of my rather bedraggled, risqué outfits. A slip that should be a nightgown, but I like the silky feel of it so I wear it round the house. Thin straps. No bra, so my tits are nearly exposed, shaking with the sudden shock of feeling the cool evening air against my skin. A lace skirt, with a rip in the side. It's nearly see-through anyway, and the rip shows the curve of my thigh, high up, near my ass. I'd put on make-up this morning, one of the things I do when I'm whiling away the hours till he gets home, but now it's kind of smudged, so I guess I'm sitting there perched on the bonnet like a delicate version of Courtney Love, undone, shivering, barely clothed.

The boys in the cars don't, as I feared, roll down their

windows and shout obscenities at me. Perhaps they're just as confused as I am, or more so, because they don't know what the plan is. They're sitting there, smoking, watching me quite calmly but with unwavering attention.

Then it strikes me that they may be used to this.

Things go on in car parks, don't they? The country gets more sordid and wilder by the day, and it seems from the stories in the papers that everyone out there is caught up in some kind of scandalous orgy. Far more colourful and glamorous than the hidden games that he and I play behind closed doors.

But I'm torn from my thoughts by the sound of the car door, and the footsteps as my lover approaches me. He stands in front, eyes betraying no flicker of emotion. All his movements are quiet and smooth as he leans forwards and pulls my knees apart.

No knickers, of course. I like the feel of air against my skin, and it keeps me kind of half wet all day, just the friction and the sense of being naked under my skirt. So when he parts my thighs, my pussy is bared to the world, a crumpled, wet flower that he opens with one finger, just lightly touching me. To check I'm slippery.

And I am, of course, despite the burning shame of being laid out on a car in front of these strangers. I'm turned on. He just has to think about fucking me and I'm ready for it, my body answering his desire instantly.

While he rubs slowly at my clit, working his fingers a little further into me like he's digging into watermelon, looking for seeds, I keep my eyes focused straight on his face. I do not look at the cars beside us, I do not meet the gaze of the men occupying them. There's no noise up here, just birds calling in high whistling notes. And the sound of people watching, that tense song of complicity as I am being prepared to fuck.

Then he does it. Unzips his fly with a quick movement,

takes out his familiar and beautiful cock, and sinks it into my cunt.

There's a collective pause, while we all feel the sensation of him sliding into me, hilt deep and lying heavy against my chest. I let myself melt a little, let his cock fill me.

As his hips start swinging back, drawing the length of his prick out of me, I realise that we are performing, with a small but rapt audience and no intention of stopping. He's fucking me with a delicious bravado, and I know he's proud of the fact that it's him up here with the girl on the car. Showing off to the guys, letting them see just how much his cock makes me gasp, bumping into me to give me the full force of his thrusts, making me rock against the car like it's a machine designed for just this purpose, a cradle to lay me down and fuck me on.

I'm gripped, suddenly, with a desire to see what the other boys are doing, what they think of this display of ours. Because it has been so long, after all, since I had any contact with other people, and I want to know what they think of me. Are they laughing? Do they think we're some deranged swingers, desperate to squeeze every possible thrill out of our lives, never mind how many taboos we break?

I swivel my head round, to see what the audience are doing behind their rolled-down windows.

And the sight makes me spin with arousal. The guy on his own, I can see him jerking off. His arm is bouncing up and down as he watches us, and I know he's holding his cock tight. The other car, the Merc, now, that is something I never thought I'd see. The driver has turned to his passenger and buried his head in his lap. I can guess he's sucking him off, while the guy murmurs under his breath, watching us, eyelids half closed. Maybe telling him what we're doing.

Charged up with this display of mutual arousal, I decide to give them all more fuel, another flash of depravity. I shake my shoulders, let the straps fall and show my tits to the world. It doesn't take a second before my left breast is taken in his mouth and he's sucking hard, without losing a stroke, still fucking me into a frenzy.

I need a couple of buttons to be pressed before I'm in sight of an orgasm, but having one nipple chewed on while his cock drives into me is usually enough. The added thrill of having three guys chasing their own pleasure right next to us brings me close to the edge, and I ride the wave just as everything starts to speed up – the movement of the cock inside me and the frantic jerks of the guy in the faraway car, the blow-job merchant and his shotgun lover. We're all pounding out that rhythm, the silent, intense beat of bodies striving for white-hot oblivion. All eyes fixed on me, on my face as it flushes scarlet, as I take on that expression I know means I'm coming – I've watched it in the mirror, half shock, half delight.

Mouths falling open, animal sounds forced from deep in the belly, a few hard shoves – again, once more . . .

Bliss.

The occupants of the Car Park in the Sky convulse into their own private nirvanas, suddenly oblivious to each other, rocking with silent ecstasy. My lover and I, we fall against each other and hold on tight, because this is the moment we get to come as close to each other as is possible while trapped in our human bodies. The time when we let the orgasm take over, obliterate thought and render us nothing more than liquid heat.

It's something like flying or floating, I imagine, and as I career about the sky in heavenly freefall, cunt pulsing and fireworks going off inside me, I think of the guys who'd cheered us on with their own version of audience participation. I think of the Merc driver, his own hard-on aching as his buddy comes in his mouth, and the solitary guy squeezing an explosion out of his fist, holding tight to the steering wheel with his other hand. We are all of us trapped in the chase, stuck in the moment. Hooked on bliss.

I squeeze his hips between my thighs, letting him know that I've sailed over the rainbow. Thanking him, for his perverse little scheme. And for pushing me to go further than I'd ever have dared. He knows how to frighten me, it's true. But he knows how to make it feel good too.

I kiss him, and feel suddenly shy again, stealing another look at the cars next to us. As though fucking in front of them were one thing, but sharing an intimate kiss was really crossing the line.

I needn't have worried. After such an intense experience, it's strange how the faces of the guys seem to change. They look kind of goofy, playful. Rather than the sinister predators I'd taken them for when we arrived. And as I slide off the bonnet, pulling my skirt down in a too-little-too-late gesture of modesty, I sense the wide-open sky above me break open like a blessing. The birdsong sounds exuberant, like a cascade of applause. As though everything were a stage, and we were the players now relaxing after our show. I resist the ridiculous urge to take a bow, and instead walk slowly back to the open car door. It seems kind of sad to leave our new friends so soon after our shared revelations, but the night is falling and I know it's time to head back. I shut myself into the car with a mix of relief and regret, and take a last look at the boys.

They seem as dreamy as cupids, even wave as we leave, tipping the brim of their baseball caps with one hand as they reach for the Rizlas to roll a post-coital joint.

Driving back downhill, still sticky with sex and

humming from the shag, I'm moved to open the window a crack, just to let in some of that air. It blows over my face like freedom, and I close my eyes while the engine soothes me back towards home.

'You OK?' he asks gently.

I nod without opening my eyes. We're going back, to the walls that surround me, the cage that closes me in day after day. Tonight was a brief mouthful of freedom, and it's left me with a sweet taste in my mouth.

I want more.

He senses this, I know, just as he senses all my moods since we grew into one inseparable whole. Pre-empts what I'm going to think, guesses all my feelings.

'It's OK, honey. We'll fix this.'

I turn to him then and open my eyes, look at his face and meet his sweet blue gaze as he tries to reassure me. It's hard for him too, having a girlfriend who can't leave the house. Who's scared of the outside world. Who has to lock herself in just to feel safe, and demands he tie her to the bed every night. Asks him to hold her down and draw out the demons that torment her.

Maybe in time he'll entice me back out, into the big wide playground that is the rest of the world. Show me what there is out there to enjoy. Until then, we're going home, holding hands tight across the gap between us. Side by side.

Nikki Magennis is the author of the Black Lace novel *Circus Excite*.

Seeing Double Monica Belle

I spoke to Evangelina de Sevilla once.

The bitch.

It's true what they say about her, all of it. Well, nearly all of it. She really does fly her dogs first class, and she did demand that the US government make the sky above her Florida beach hut a no-fly zone. Everybody really does have to call her Miss de Sevilla, and when she stays in a hotel she insists that the rooms to either side of hers are empty, and she won't go in unless there's a red carpet laid out for her with a row of pink candles to either side. I mean, really, red and pink together!

The only thing that isn't true is the rumour about her being a kinky sex fiend, or at least, I don't think it is.

I always knew she looked like me, or rather, that I looked like her, because every irritating, smarmy creep who tries to chat me up uses it as his opening line. It's always, 'Hey, you know, you could pass for Evangelina de Sevilla?', or from the ones who're liars too, 'Hi, Evangelina, what are ... oh, I thought you were my friend Evangelina de Sevilla.' Then there are the ones who suggest I ought to work as her body double, as if I ought to be flattered, and they always think they're so fucking original, like they're the first person ever to spot the resemblance.

They're not, because I have worked as her body double, and I wouldn't do it again for a hundred thousand pounds. I'd joined an agency, you see, to try and pick up some work while I was at uni. At the time she wasn't so well known, and I'd never even heard of her, but when I went for my interview they snapped me up immediately, and included two pics of me done up like her in my portfolio.

I didn't think anything of it, not then. It was just part of my job. I'd do things like pretend to be her at the opening of some new club and, while the groans of disappointment when they found out I was me and not her were a pain, it was no big deal. I was getting paid. Then the silly cow decided she was an actress.

They always do that, don't they? If they're an actress they want to be a pop star, or if they're a pop star they want to be a top model, or if they're a top model they want to be an actress. The result has been some of the most dire crap in all three fields, so you'd think they'd learn, but they don't. Certainly Evangelina de Sevilla didn't. She thought she was going to be the biggest thing since Monroe, but of course she wasn't. What was the film she made again: *Straight to Video*?

Anyway, if you see *Straight to Video* ... OK, *Stairway to Vegas*, and you notice the scene where Missy Marmalade or whatever she's called is just pulling her knickers down when six heavies come into the room? Well, that's not Evangelina de Sevilla's bum, it's mine. That's right, I was her bottom double.

Oh, and the bit where she does a back flip through the open window and dives eight floors into a swimming pool, that's not her either. That's was done on a computer.

My bum is flesh and blood though, and the reason I'm showing it off on camera for an audience of maybe as many as five or six people, is that Miss Prissy-Pants Evangelina de Sevilla has a clause in her contract stating that she never has to go nude, so muggins here had to do it instead. Not that I mind going nude. I mean, what's the big deal? But there's nude and there's being Evangelina de Sevilla's bottom double.

It was a nightmare from the minute my agency rang

me up, sounding as if I'd just won the lottery. All they told me was that I was needed on the film set for *Stairway to Vegas* that same day. It was a done deal, and if I didn't accept I was out. So off I went, to Ealing, and back, and to Ealing again the next day, and back, and to Ealing again . . .

Five days later I was finally admitted on to the set, without a word of apology or any explanation at all for what was going on. I was still trying to be friendly, and walked in with a big naïve smile, to a mocked-up hotel room in the middle of a huge studio, in which a woman who looked strangely familiar from my reflection was having a hissy fit because the director wanted to use the same brand of knickers for both of us. Apparently they were by somebody called Lauren, and only she was allowed to wear Lauren's knickers, or something like that. Then she saw me, and she spoke to me.

'Oh my God, it's got my face. Take it away.'

So they did. I had never felt so small in my entire life, but it got worse. Once I'd been hidden behind a backdrop of New York at sunset while she was helped away to finish her hissy fit in her trailer, I was once more ushered into the mocked-up hotel room, where I was, in order, told off for upsetting Evangelina de Sevilla, made to wait, told to show the director my bum, made to wait, told to change in front of everybody, made to wait, told to show everybody my bum. I still remember the assistant director's words, so kind, so tactful, so gentlemanly.

'OK. You, take your panties down.'

I did, in front of the director, both his assistants, six actors, three cameramen and two sound engineers, assorted technicians and make-up artists, various people with no apparent function, an enormously fat man, who for all I know may have wandered in off the street for a good lech, and the girl who made the tea. Fair enough, I don't care who sees my bum and I knew I had to go bare. What I didn't know was that I'd have go bare 27 times in quick succession.

It wasn't even my fault. They seemed happy with my knicker-lowering technique, but the six heavies couldn't get it right. First it was the big fat one, whose cloth cap wouldn't stay on his head. Then it was the little one who looked like a ferret, whose big silver kipper tie was catching the light at the wrong angle. Next it was the tall skinny one, who was sneering too much, or the sort of ordinary-looking one, who wasn't sneering enough. And all the while my knickers were going up and down like a yo-yo.

You can imagine the shot too, which showed the door from between my open legs as the heavies came in, so that the camera was more or less stuck up my bum. I wasn't at all sure just how much he could see when I was bare, and what with that and the endless knicker dropping I was beginning to wonder if it was humanly possibly to feel more humiliated. It was. Oh, it was.

They were about to do take 28, by which time I had it down pat. I stood with my thumbs in the waistband of my knickers and, when I saw the door handle move, down they came and in rushed the six heavies. Only this time it wasn't the six heavies who came in, it was Evangelina de Sevilla. I remember her words with perfect clarity.

'Oh my God! She can't be me, she's fat! Look at her fucking thighs, you fucktard asshats! She's fat, fat, fat, fat, fat!'

And she left, followed by the director, both his assistants, six actors, three cameramen and two sound engineers, assorted technicians and make-up artists, various people with no apparent function, an enormously fat man, who for all I know may have wandered in off the street for a good lech, and the girl who made the tea. I left too, only instead of chasing after her I just left.

* * *

And that, dear reader, should have been that. They used the shot, take fifteen I think, and I even got paid eventually, despite a note to my agent complaining about my inappropriate attitude. I continued to work as an extra and as a model, which kept me out of debt until I'd finished uni, won the right to wear a thing like a medieval monk's habit but with a fetching pink hood, and got a job trading commodities in the City.

Evangelina de Sevilla, meanwhile, had gone from strength to strength. After brilliantly managing to blame the failure of *Stairway to Vegas* on the director, both his assistants, six actors, three cameramen and two sound engineers, assorted technicians and make-up artists, various people with no apparent function, and the girl who made the tea, she married the enormously fat man who I thought had wandered in off the street for a good lech, but was actually some Hollywood big shot.

Two years later they divorced, leaving her richer and more famous than ever, with both her modelling career and her extravagant behaviour rising to such dizzy heights that hardened paparazzi had been known to drool like babies at the mere thought of getting a picture of her. Not that they succeeded very often, as she was more determined than any other celebrity to keep it all under control.

Which was why she was in London last June. I knew, I admit, because the way the pictures of her getting off the plane were splashed across the papers it was as if somebody genuinely important was visiting. What I didn't know was where she was or what she was doing. I had other things on my mind, notably the launch for Rio Dorado zinc. By the end of the day I'd put seventeen per cent on the value of my portfolio and my floor manager had given me an open tab at Champers and Oysters. So I went.

I had a bottle of Krug with the other traders, then a bottle of Cristal for good measure. I had a bottle of La

Grande Dame with a money broker from the floor below me and a bottle of Dom with some guy from the New York building. I had a large Hine with the director of a Japanese bank and an even larger Zubrowka with some footballers who rescued me from the Japanese guy. Then I went outside.

It was just getting dark, and there still a few people about, so I went to sit in the little park opposite the bar and watched the world go by. I was feeling happy and I was feeling horny, and vaguely wondering about one of the guys who'd been chatting to me while I drank my vodka. He was an arrogant git, but he was all muscle and he'd had a very prominent bulge, which I was sure was just for me.

I was just about to go back in when a man spoke to me, one inevitable word.

'Evangelina?'

He really meant it, or I'd have told him where to go right there. As it was I was still searching for a more worthwhile put-down when I realised just how good-looking he was. Adonis had nothing on him, and Narcissus would have drowned himself in despair. I just stared for maybe half a second, then patted the bench next to me.

'It is you, isn't it?' he asked.

His accent was all-American, Boston and Harvard, but with a twang that spoke of the South, just like hers did, only less annoying, much less annoying. He was that type too, tall and dark and with a lot of muscle, like Superman only not with his underpants on the outside. His eyes were the palest blue I'd ever seen.

I couldn't help but fancy him, and once I hadn't denied I was her I was too shy to put him straight. He spoke about school, how he'd known her in the eleventh grade when she was in the ninth. It didn't mean much to me, but I smiled and nodded and he seemed happy. He asked why I was alone and I spun him a line about needing to get away, which he swallowed, fake accent and all, and that was when I saw the camera in the bushes.

Well what could I do? The American guy was leaning close and I knew what he wanted. I was willing, more than willing, and the drink had left me full of mischief. When he asked for a kiss for old times' sake I let him, and I let my mouth open, and I let him take me in his arms. I knew we were being photographed, and I was thinking of how she'd treated me, a little, but mostly I was thinking of him, and of how much I wanted him.

He wasn't passing up a good chance, and nor was I. The park was empty now, or so he thought, and lit only by streetlights. Nobody could see us in our little alcove with the bench behind the fountain, nobody but the man in the bushes, the man spying on our intimate moment as a hand made a tentative move to my chest. I was hoping the man had a good camera.

It had been so, so long since anyone had touched me like that in public, and maybe I'm just a bad girl, but it felt so good, not just the touch of his fingers through my blouse and my bra, but the thrill of being in the park, of knowing we were being watched, and who he thought I was. As his lips broke away from mine he muttered something about high school, but I barely heard. He'd pushed my hair back and started to kiss my neck, while his fingers had gone to the buttons of my blouse.

I couldn't stop him. I couldn't stop myself. Each button that came undone was like an electric shock, and so was each touch of his lips to my neck. I was holding on to him, my eyes shut and my head thrown back, the shivers running right through my body as bit by bit my breasts came bare, and I wondered how far he'd take it.

The answer was all the way, and still I couldn't stop him, not when he opened the last button of my blouse to let it fall wide, not when his hand slipped behind my back to tweak my bra open, not when he lifted my cups to get me bare, bare in public. His mouth moved lower, and I knew he was going to kiss my breasts, but all I could do was stroke his hair as his lips pressed to my skin, and I couldn't restrain a gasp as he began to suck a nipple.

I was lost, full of naughty thoughts and full of mischief. He had my blouse right open, my bra right up, my breasts fully bare to the cool night air and to his mouth. I knew the cameraman was still there, and I was getting more daring, more dirty. So was my man, now with one bare breast in each hand, like he was considering which orange to buy out of two, then licking my nipples, turn and turn about, and kissing them before he spoke.

'Do what you used to do, Angel, spank the monkey.'

I had to ask. 'What monkey?'

'You kidder.'

He laughed, and moved my hand to his cock. It was rock hard, and big, but I wasn't ready, not for that. I wanted him to play with me a little more. I wanted to be sure the cameraman had something really, really good for his papers, and my randy American had just given me the most wonderful idea, something so utterly humiliating that maybe, just maybe, Evangelina de Sevilla would know something of how I'd felt in that studio.

'Never mind the monkey. Why don't you spank me?'

'Spank you?'

'Yeah, you know, smack my bottom like I'm a naughty girl. Come on, pretty please?'

He blew his breath out. 'You were never like this!'

'Just do it. Spank my naughty bottom, right here in the park.'

He nodded and I kissed him before draping myself over his knee, bottom up and breasts dangling down, such an undignified position to be in and, if the truth be told, really rather a nice one. I was smiling as he put his arm around my waist to hold me in place, a big happy grin, which grew bigger and happier as his hand settled on the seat of my office skirt and he began to spank me.

It was ever so gentle, really just pats and a lot of groping in between, so that I was forced to wriggle and gasp to encourage him. He spanked a little harder and it started to sting, but in ever such a nice way. It made me feel good, and made me more full of mischief than ever, so before too long I'd said the words that were in my head.

'Do it properly . . . on my panties.'

I'd said it, and I meant it, but my heart was going crazy as he started to tug up my skirt. There was no going back. I had to have it, but I was biting my lip to stop myself from telling him not to, as my skirt came up my thighs and over the bulge of my cheeks and my hips, showing off the seat of my knickers to him, to the photographer, and to the world.

He chuckled. 'You are a bad girl, Angel.'

Once again he began to spank.

Now it stung, quite a lot, making me gasp and kick my legs, but I knew just how that would look and I wasn't stopping for anything. Besides, my bottom had begun to feel warm, and so had my pussy, a feeling so good I was wishing I'd had it before, and I knew I would have it again. I wanted more too, the full spanking experience, and that meant my knickers had to come down. I didn't even care about Evangelina de Sevilla any more, I just wanted my bottom bare and his hand against my naked flesh, spanking my bottom for being such a naughty girl. My voice was a sigh as I spoke.

'Get me bare. Pull down my panties and get me bare.'

And he did. Now that was naughty. He hesitated for just a second, but he couldn't resist my offer. I felt his fingers touch my knickers, pulling the waistband away from my skin, and down, baring me slowly, and, as my bum came on show to the world, I was whimpering with pleasure for what I was doing.

He did it well too, took them right down to my knees so I was showing it all from behind, my pussy and my bottom hole too. And he adjusted my blouse so my top was showing as well, nothing hidden, breasts and bottom and pussy all bare in a public park as once again he began to spank me. Now it was hard, a proper spanking, man to woman, telling me off for being such a bad girl as he slapped my burning cheeks. I couldn't stop kicking, and the ridiculous poses I was getting in as I thrashed about over his lap with my legs trapped in my knickers had nothing to do with the photographer, except that the more I knew he could see the more it turned me on. I wanted to show everything, to have every rude detail of my body on open display for my man and for the camera. Then I wanted to take his lovely cock in my hand and in my mouth to say thank you for the lovely spanking, and to get myself off at the same time.

Which was what I did. By the time he'd finished I felt as if my bottom was on fire, and I have never, ever been so aware of myself sexually, nor so wet. He put a hand between my thighs to feel me, and I just stuck my bum up for more. A finger went in and I was wriggling on it, and if he'd wanted to take me off like that I'd have let him, camera or no camera, but he spoke.

'No, you have to do it, Angel. You have to.'

I nodded, and down I went, on to my knees to him, kneeling on the hard path with my blouse open and my bra up, my bare breasts showing, with my skirt tucked up behind and my knickers around my knees, with my bare red bottom stuck out for all to see as my man freed his cock from his trousers and put it into my mouth. He was calling me all sorts of dirty names as I began to suck, but I didn't care. I just wanted him in my mouth and to have my body bare while I sucked, to think back on the way he'd exposed me and spanked me, in public, on camera, and to come.

He was already moaning and clutching at my hair, so

there wasn't much time. Back went my hand to my wet eager pussy, and I was masturbating in public as I sucked a man's cock, so rude, so naughty. I deserved spanking. I deserved spanking hard, hard and bare, hard and bare and in public, with my breasts pulled out of my bra and my knickers taken down in front of a hundred people, a thousand people, all with cameras to take pictures of me as I had my bottom warmed, and as I sucked on a cock to say thank you for my punishment.

I'd gone far, far further than I'd meant to, but I didn't care. Never had I felt so dirty, or so full of mischief. When my man grunted that he was about to come, I pulled him free and took what he had to give me in my face, and with that I hit my climax too. I was screaming as it tore through me, rubbing like crazy, my head so full of dirty thoughts and so full of ecstasy I really thought I'd faint. Only his voice brought me back down to earth.

'You always were a noisy one. We'd better tidy up.'

He was right, and then some. We were safe enough in the park with the dark hedges all around us, and just the single light above, but it could only be a matter of time before the racket I'd made attracted attention. I made myself decent just as fast as I possibly could, and told him to go the other way so it wasn't obvious we were a couple. He said to meet outside Champers and Oysters.

I didn't, for obvious reasons. Maybe he still thought I was Evangelina de Sevilla, maybe not, but any further conversation would have been extremely awkward. I went home instead, catching a lucky cab in Minories, and fifteen minutes later I was back in Butler's Wharf, drinking coffee and somewhat ruefully considering my pink bottom in the mirror, but smiling too.

The rest, as they say, is history. I'd never even realised the second photographer was there, nor the third, nor the fourth. He went to the papers anyway, earning a tidy sum for his kiss and tell, complete with pictures. Evangelina de Sevilla went wild. No, she went crazy, berserk, apeshit, throwing the diva tantrum to end all diva tantrums in the middle of Heathrow airport. She threatened to sue, naturally, but what was the use? There she was, bare bottom over his knee in glorious technicolour, titties out and legs kicking in her panties, enjoying her spanking with a big grin on her face. At the time she'd been asleep in her hotel room, not half a mile away, and, with her reputation and his testimony, even her lawyers didn't believe her. Me, I kept quiet and collected the cuttings.

Monica Belle is the author of the Black Lace novels *Noble Vices*, *Valentina's Rules*, *Wild in the Country*, *Wild by Nature*, *Office Perks*, *Pagan Heat*, *Bound in Blue* and *The Boss*.

Marianna Multiple
Kristina Lloyd

Marianna was a showgirl, a stripper, an artiste of bejewelled burlesque. She was originally from Margate but now she travelled the world, going to places she never got to see. She had a turquoise snake tattooed on one leg, climbing up from neat little ankle to bare pouting pussy. You should have seen what it cost her in waxes. Her boss was Irwin Lockhart, the man with the marquee, and a total bastard if ever there was one.

'More ass, Marianna! More tit! Work it, you bitch!'

He had no finesse. Marianna could make a man come by the way she took off a glove.

One day she decided to teach him a lesson.

'I have some very important friends in this town, Marianna,' he said. 'I want 'em to remember tonight for the rest of their lives.'

'Go fuck yourself, Irwin Lockhart.' She could talk to him like this. It didn't hurt at all. 'I do what I do, OK?'

Marianna shared a trailer with her new husband, Mental Micky. He was a sword-swallower and fire-eater, a shabby, sinewy fellow with a goatee beard and a sleeve of tats on his right arm. He smelt of cigarettes, whisky and paraffin. When he wasn't eating fire, he was eating pussy, usually Marianna's. He had a tongue you could stub cigarettes out on, and it was rough and tireless on her clit. She loved him and he loved her, but she would never let him kiss her, not with that mouth. Sometimes, for a taste of something sweet, Marianna would eat cherries as they fucked. She'd pop them into her mouth or dip her head into a little bowl, spitting out stones as they rode. 'Loves me, loves me not.'

'I hate that Irwin Lockhart,' she said.

Micky was lying naked on the fold-out bed, a hand around his upright cock. 'I love it when you're angry,' he murmured.

'Don't touch me,' Marianna warned. Standing, she bent towards the dressing-table mirror, arse out, twisting up a stick of scarlet lipstick. Marianna was a flaming demon of a woman, auburn haired with death-pale skin and a penchant for all things red. She was dressed in a scarlet-sequinned micro bikini, magnificent red feathers towering above her head. Her heels were red spikes and, when she moved, her buttocks wobbled around the strings of her tiny thong. In the harsh trailer light, you could see a trace of blue veins beneath her fair-maiden skin and the faintest of dimples puckering her arse. Micky was smart. He knew the intimacy of those imperfections, and it was a privilege to be this close. He got a real kick out of cellulite: God's own spangles.

Rising from the bed, he strolled over to stand behind Marianna, resting his erection in the split of her cheeks. His mauve-tinged glans gleamed wetly against her ruby sequins, and her skin shimmered with a hint of silver. Her shoulder blades were sprinkled with freckles, just a dusting of cinnamon. Marianna, elbows on the dressing table, pouted at her reflection in the bulb-lit mirror. Her eyelids were encrusted with midnight-blue glitter and her lashes were nearly two inches long. Sparkling on her cheek was a five-pointed star, in ruby red, of course. Micky held her hips. He had crude jailbird tattoos on his knuckles: LOVE on the right hand, LOVE on the left.

'So what do you want me to do about Irwin?' he asked. 'Shoot him?'

Marianna bared her pearly whites, running her tongue over them to remove stray flecks of Rimmel.

Micky slipped a hand between her thighs, sawing back and forth.

'Don't make me wet, Micky.'

Micky carried on.

'Anyway, there's no point shooting him,' said Marianna. 'We'd be out of a job.'

'So what do we do?' asked Micky.

'I want to make him come.'

Micky laughed, his gold front tooth glinting. He was permanently red eyed and he had a haggard, scarred face that made you care about his liver. 'You make him come every night, babe. He goes to his trailer, gets on his knees to pray and gets his tiny dick out. Uh-uh-uh. Takes around five seconds. Amen and goodnight. You already won.'

'That's different,' said Marianna. 'I want to make him come on *my* terms.'

Micky nudged aside Marianna's G-string and penetrated her with three slim, calloused fingers. With his free hand, he kneaded one fleshy buttock, gently so as not to mark her.

'A tough one,' said Micky, his arm shunting lazily back and forth. 'He won't let you near him. The guy's so repressed he's a walking stomach ulcer.'

Marianna looked at Micky in the mirror, her gaze thoughtful. 'You think he's got a tiny dick?' she asked, arching her perfectly plucked brows.

Micky grinned back, crooking his little finger at her.

Marianna smiled. 'A shame not many people get to see it.'

Micky laughed and landed a sharp slap on her arse. 'You are one sick bitch,' he said proudly.

'Don't mark me,' she said.

Mickey slapped her again, hard enough to bring heat to her cheek.

Now Marianna was hot for him. 'I said, don't mark me,' she repeated.

'You telling me what to do?' Micky twisted his fingers inside her, pumping them faster. The plumes of her red feathers shivered above her head.

Marianna fought hard not to groan.

'Hmmm?' Micky looked at her reflection, his face smug and threatening. 'You telling me what to do?'

'Christ, Micky, not now. I've a show to do.'

Micky withdrew his fingers and brought his hand down smartish on the other side of her rump. He clutched her buttocks with clawed hands and roughly rotated her flesh, making her cheeks open and close like a pair of sparkly bellows. Marianna moaned softly. Under his breath, Micky began singing: 'They called her Lola, she was a showgirl. Yellow feathers in her haa . . . ir.' He bent his knees to slot his erection between her thighs and rubbed his length along her near-naked folds. 'Hmmm?' he said again. 'You telling me what to do?'

There was a sharp rap at the door. 'Five minutes, Miss Multiple!'

Marianna pushed back, knocking Micky out of the way with her powerful arse. She dabbed a tissue between her thighs, made a small adjustment of her feathered headdress then slipped on a pair of red satin evening gloves. Draping a fluffy red boa over her shoulders, she stood tall, breasts thrust out, a brilliant fake ruby glinting in her navel. Amidst the chaos of the trailer, she was all fireflies and stardust, a delicious, devil-red creature haloed by a shimmer of silver, a sea-coloured snake entwined around one leg. Her coppery curls bounced, her lustrous skin gleamed and, when she turned to preen, shards of light glanced off the sparkly red scales of her itsy-bitsy costume. 'How do I look?' she purred.

'Like a goddess,' said Micky, wanking hard.

The tent was a touring dance hall from 1920s Berlin with booths of carved wood and velvet. An enormous chandelier hung over a circular stage and, in the smoky haze, countless bevelled mirrors made a kaleidoscope of mist and glitter, beaded with the eager eyes of the reflected audience.

Irwin claimed the tent had come to him via a great-great-uncle who'd once slept with Marlene Dietrich who'd then given him the tent as a token of her gratitude. Irwin was full of shit.

Nonetheless, Marianna loved that tent. On its stage, she was all woman, larger than life and breathlessly sexy. She gloried in being adored, and, boy, how they adored her! With a shimmy, a shake and a big kitsch wink, she had them eating out of her hand from the moment she walked on, to the final flutter of her feathers. She made them laugh, cheer and gasp, guys and gals alike, every single one from the sweet little albino glass-collector to the sequins and swells sat in the best seats in the house.

She performed solo, had done ever since her original partner, Miss Rhoda Retox, had hung up her nipple tassels to make babies with a plumber from Nebraska. Marianna's career had soared. Alone, she was in her element. Being up there gave her a buzz like no other and, for several twinkly years, she hadn't given a thought to sharing even an inch of those scratched teak floorboards with anything bigger than a flea. Which is why she was momentarily wrong footed by the sight of Micky approaching the stage to join her.

She saw him before the audience did, realising at once he was in full mental mode, his face bright with suppressed gleeful rage.

Uh-oh, thought Marianna, instantly moist.

Dressed like a Mafioso at rest, braces over a white vest and baggy trousers of a zoot suit, Micky swaggered down the aisle, dishevelled and hard, his tattooed biceps flexing. In one hand he held a flaming torch, in the other was Irwin Lockhart, tethered to a leash and silenced by a gag. Irwin, naked save for a pair of Union Jack boxer shorts, was as plump and pale as a large hairy baby.

Micky leapt up on to the stage, raised his torch and blew a huge cloud of fire several feet high. The crowd screamed as the flames evaporated with a whumph, singeing the air black. Male laughter, boorish and approving, roared above the applause as Irwin's very important friends spotted their old chum, cowering on all fours and as meek as can be. Micky stood there, bristling with arrogance, and surveyed his audience, flashing them his psychotic gold-toothed grin.

Marianna's groin went supernova. Did a more handsome specimen ever walk this earth? Cheeky as cheesecake, she wiggled seductively, cupped the curls of her hair and blew him a lipstick kiss. Micky winked back then lowered the wand of fire into his open mouth. He closed his lips over the flame – gone! Marianna made a show of being wowed, knocking her knees together, hanging out her tongue and clutching her glittery crotch. The audience laughed.

Hell, we ought to do a show together, thought Marianna. And then, Jeepers, looks like we are doing. Choreography zilch. With a flourish, Micky removed the wand from his mouth, flames emerging from his lips, before he sent another stream of fire rippling noisily into the air. Marianna felt the heat of it on her skin as it massed into a glorious orange ball then exploded into nothing. Irwin's eyes bulged above his gag.

Tilting a hip, Marianna stretched out a hand to Micky. 'Come to Mama!' she cooed, inaudible below the music. Micky grinned, stabbed his torch in a socket by the stage and wiped a grimy rag across his face. He strolled over, all nonchalance and menace, then turned to check on Irwin who trotted behind like a good little dog.

Oh, how she loved him when he was coiled and crazy. Right at that moment, Marianna had eyes for him, and him alone The audience faded into the twilight of the tent and, as Micky scooped her to him, she was aware only of diffuse puffs of light spinning away from her as they dropped into a tango-dancer pose. Against her sparkling flesh, Micky's body was dirty and dangerous, his pale semi-painted shoulders curving with fine strength, a fuzz of chest hair peeping above his vest. His skin was smudged with black, his face shone with paraffin and sweat, his eyes glinted with madness and he stank to high heaven.

He was filthy, physical, rough and mean. Marianna, plucked and perfumed, oiled and glittered, gleamed with decadent, showgirl purity. It was a heady combination. Even so, she rejected his kiss. Ew. For richer, for poorer, for better, for worse . . . but no tongues, dude, OK?

'Sit!' Micky ordered Irwin, letting go of the leash. Irwin did as he was told, dropping back on his heels, his piggy eyes about to pop out of his head. His paunch swelled, all solid fat and yellow-grey tufts of hair, and he cupped his hands over the jolly little tent erecting in his Union Jack boxers. His eyes got even piggier when Marianna planted a spike heel on his shoulder and Micky, whipping his hands behind his back, snapped a pair of cuffs on him, as white and fluffy as two goose-feather nests. Irwin glanced down at the red toenails on his shoulder, beads of sweat breaking out on his forehead.

'You like what you see, Irwin?' asked Marianna.

Irwin's eyes travelled up her tattooed leg until they were fixed on the point where the snake's forked tongue reached for her groin. He grunted from behind the gag, nodding enthusiastically.

Marianna rolled her hips, lowering her crotch closer and closer as the crowd whooped and cheered.

Micky stood behind her and began caressing her thighs, running a hand up and down her flesh. Poor old Irwin couldn't take his eyes off that hand. He stared at it when Micky massaged her tender inner thighs; followed it like a dumb cat when he stroked along that shimmering skin; and looked fit to burst when Micky dropped to his knees and slipped a finger within those dazzling red panties. Grinning at Irwin, Micky raised his brows enquiringly as he traced a leisurely line around the edge of his beloved's skimpies. Irwin, all eager eyes, nodded in response.

Marianna arched her back like a temptress. As Micky's finger travelled beneath the hip string of her briefs she swept a caress down her body then toyed deliberately with the fastening of her bikini top. Oh, what a thrill to be centre stage, charming them all with a big brash image, while down below some blissfully intricate fingerwork was making her pussy melt. Marianna tingled to feel Micky's finger slide over the mound of her bare pudenda and down, oh so slowly down, to tease her sweet, swollen love lips tucked, but only just, within that tiny glittery gusset. Hidden from all eyes, Micky's finger wiggled deeper. He parted her silky folds and stirred circles around her seeping entrance. He dabbled at her juices, smearing them along her groove, and rocked her perky little clit to near ecstasy.

Marianna began to feel weak in the knees and even weaker in the brain. She wanted to come. She could feel the moment gathering. She wanted Micky's lips sucking on her clit and his mighty schlong hammering deep in her pussy.

'Honey,' she said to Micky, 'we should get a room.'

Still on his knees next to Irwin, Micky grinned up at her, light darting off his gold tooth. He looked from her face to her crotch to Irwin and back again. Then he drew her gusset aside, giving Irwin an eyeful of luscious bald puss. Wolf whistles swooped around the tent, piercing the music. Irwin stared as if he'd never seen such delights, sweat drops amassing in his unruly grey eyebrows. Deliberately cruel, Micky teased him, his fingers playing gently with Marianna's plump vulval frills. Irwin craned his neck, grunting and straining to get closer.

'Ain't she a beaut, Irwin?' said Micky. 'That's top o' the range coochie, I tell you. She's hot, she's wet and she's hungry. You wanna see pink?'

Irwin groaned, a noise of pain that made Micky sneer with amusement. Murmuring words of soft filth, he splayed Marianna's lips, pressing them open to show Irwin her dark shiny crease. 'You wanna play with her clitty?' asked Micky, giving it a dainty wiggle. 'You wanna fuck that tight little slit? Mmm? Or do you want my Marianna to get on her knees and give you the best cock-sucking, ball-busting blow job you ever had?'

Irwin made a strangled moan, head nodding so hard it nearly fell off.

'Well, go swivel,' snarled Micky, giving Irwin the finger. 'You only get to watch.'

With that, Micky swooped between Marianna's legs, his wiry beard scouring her inner thighs as he squirmed and lapped with his asbestos tongue, a bunch of fingers pumping in her hole.

Micky's tongue was out of this world. Irwin's eyes were nearly out of his head. The audience were agog. And in next to no time, Marianna was coming like a steam train.

'Ohhhh,' she wailed as Micky sucked her clit, fingering her to a pitch.

'Ohhhh,' cried the crowd, spurring Marianna on.

'Ohhhh,' she echoed, and 'Ohhhh,' again as her climax opened and clenched, and her thighs trembled with wave after wave of pleasure and she thought her knees would surely buckle. She drew long deep breaths, her heartbeat calming. 'Oh, boy.'

At this point in the music, it was usual for the cute Cuban stagehand to come on with a black café table and chair. Marianna could see him hovering in the wings with his fold-up furniture. Once, after he'd missed his cue, she'd threatened to force him into a threesome with her and Micky. He looked nervous now, understandably so. They'd eat him alive, spit his bones out in a heap. Bones and cherry stones. Jizz, sweat and lube. Oh, a woman's work was never done.

Marianna beckoned the cute Cuban onstage. Quick as a flash, he sprang up, positioned the table, weighted it and scuttled off. On a normal night, Marianna would invite some unsuspecting Joe Schmo to sit there and be entertained with a spot of bump and grind. Man or woman, Marianna didn't mind but woe betide anyone who tried to touch even so much as her aura. Tonight, Micky was in the hot seat. And, hot dang, he was hot, hot, hot! That handsome hunk of muscle could touch whatever he damn well liked.

'Heel!' he called to Irwin. On his knees, Irwin shuffled after Micky, leash trailing from his neck. 'Sit,' said Micky, and Irwin knelt by his master's chair.

Marianna sashayed around them, hips a-wiggle as she trailed her boa over their shoulders.

'You want more pussy?' Micky asked Irwin. Irwin nodded hungrily, eyes popping. 'More of my Marianna?' Again, Irwin nodded. Micky bounced invisible bosoms to his chest. 'You want to see my Marianna's big, beautiful puppies?' Irwin certainly did. 'You want to see my Marianna slamming her juicy little snatch on my mean ol' cock?' Irwin nearly came in his boxers.

From his chair, Micky reached down, slipped a hand into the vent of Irwin's shorts and gave a few gentle tugs on his erection. Irwin began to overheat, his face puffing up in bright-red fury. 'You want me to stop?' asked Micky. Irwin nodded, his protestations muffled by the gag. Micky released him, leaving his prick poking out. 'You wanna go back to your trailer?' asked Micky. 'Say g'night to all these nice ladies and gents?'

Irwin was apoplectic. If looks could kill, Micky

would've been nuked ten times over. Then Marianna shimmied by, draping the boa over Irwin's shoulders. She let the red feathers trickle into his lap then coiled the boa around his erection, surrounding it in fluffiness.

'You want to leave, Mr Lockhart?' she cooed.

Irwin's rage subsided. He gazed up at Marianna, shaking his head.

'Then how about you stay right there,' she said. 'And imagine I'm doing this to your very own tiddler.'

With that, she dropped to the floor between Micky's open thighs, put her hands on his knees, and swallowed the boner that sprang mightily from his fly. Irwin's prick twitched in its feathered nest and he looked on enviously as Marianna's ruby-gloss lips slid up and down, up and down.

'Ohhh, baby,' growled Micky as Marianna did that special tongue thing he liked. Micky delved into her bikini top and fingered her big crinkly nipples. The audience began a slow celebratory hand clap, their hands sounding in time to the bobbing of her head. By drawing a few quicker lengths, Marianna found she could ruffle the applause. Slow, slow, quick, quick, slow. The audience chuckled when they lost their rhythm, then their beat resumed, as steady as the pulse drumming in her panties.

Heck, I've still got them on, thought Marianna. All I've taken off are the gloves.

Micky, as if mind-reading, lifted her head from his lap. He tipped up her chin with one finger and looked her in the eye. Coolly, he said, 'Get those hot little panties off that hot little ass and spread yourself for Daddy.' He hooked the braces off his shoulders. 'Bend over that table. Show Daddy your pussy. Show everyone your greedy wet puss.'

Marianna didn't move.

'Now!' barked Micky. He stood up, jerking his fist around his hard-on. 'Daddy wants to fuck you. Daddy wants to stuff his big cock in that tight little cunt. Ain't that so, Irwin?'

For one terrible moment, Marianna thought he planned on handing her over to the boss. 'I want to make him come,' she remembered saying. Oh, holy Moses. But, no. Micky would never do that. He loved her. And besides, Micky needed seeing to. He wouldn't step aside if Jesus H. Christ wanted to poke her, though Marianna didn't think she was quite His type.

She stood, uncertain now how to strip. Her usual routine seemed kind of inappropriate. What would be the point of teasing at this point? She stretched her arms high, wiggling sinuously, giving herself time to think. Micky, however, had never been much of a thinker. He clasped her bikini top, snapped the strings twice, then began tugging at her G-string.

'Hey, you'll ruin them,' cried Marianna, tottering in her heels.

But Micky took no notice, pulling and pulling until the string gave way. The scrap of red dropped to the floor and the audience went wild, whistling and hooting at Marianna's brave, beautiful nudity. In a flash, Micky joined her, whipping off his clothes so he too was butt naked and ready for action. He grasped her, twisting her with an armlock and pushing her down over the table. Marianna, tits squashed flat against the plastic, braced herself for the plunge of Micky's cock. But Micky had other ideas. He kicked her ankles wider, opening her up to the crowd, and left her on display. With his cock in his hand, he began slowly circling her.

Marianna lay there, feeling very gynaecological. Never in her life had she felt so naked and exposed. She could feel the air cooling on her wetness, and a thousand pairs of eyes boring into her pussy. She ached to be stuffed with flesh, to have Micky slam his meat in deep. Oh, please, dearest husband, don't make me wait too long.

As Micky sauntered by, hand still wrapped around his boner, she peered up at him. He grinned down, eyes ablaze, looking very mental. Marianna got even juicier, her cunt all lonesome. Then she felt Micky's hand on her arse, rubbing gently. He stood by the side of her. He trailed a finger down the crack of her cheeks, teasing her ring and the ridge of her perineum before he poked her entrance, widening it with slow rotations. Marianna heard the audience murmur. Voiced approval hovered uncertainly. Micky held her buttocks apart. Laughter bubbled.

Marianna craned but couldn't see Micky's face. She imagined him playing up to the crowd, grinning and appealing to them as she lay there, passive and powerless. All she could do was stay still, held open for public inspection, her body being manipulated like she was some worthless piece of trash. God, it felt good.

It felt even better when warm breath touched her buttocks and her cleft grew humid with Micky's closeness, his whiskers prickling. A tongue tip danced on her pretty little rosebud, then squirmed deeper, probing where the sun don't shine.

Marianna groaned loudly. 'Oh, fuck me,' she cried. 'Just fuck me, you no-good fucking bastard.'

Micky stood. 'Ask nicely,' he said, wiggling a couple of fingers in her pussy.

'Please,' she wailed. 'Please, fuck me.'

'Please Daddy,' dictated Micky. 'Please fuck me with your big fat daddy dick.'

Marianna moaned, 'Oh, please, please fuck me with your big fat daddy dick. Please!'

'See Irwin?' said Micky. 'She loves daddy dick, don't you?' Micky landed a hard slap on her arse. 'Mmmm?' He spanked her again, making her cheek shiver like jelly. 'Have you been a good girl?'

'Yes, yes, yes,' said Marianna through gritted teeth.

'But see, Irwin?' continued Micky. '*I'm* the daddy now!

You got your tent, you got your gold, your limos, your fancy cigars but they don't mean jack-shit because I've got my Marianna. You see? I got my Marianna right here and till the end of time so I'm richer than you'll ever be.'

Irwin and Marianna groaned in unison but for very different reasons. Micky moved into position behind her, his swollen end shoving at her slit, his hands clutching her hips, LOVE on the right knuckles, LOVE on the left. He penetrated her with a hard deep thrust. Whistles, catcalls and applause nearly blew the canvas off the tent. For a while, Micky held steady, his solid girth filling her to capacity. Then he fucked her, hips pumping fast and hard, dick slipping along her wetness. Marianna gasped and panted, whimpering when he teased her with a few smooth slow glides. Then again, he pounded away, whipping the audience to a frenzy as he slammed her on to his driving cock, fingers digging into her soft white flesh.

Marianna was on another planet. The noise of the audience lifted her right out of herself and she was half delirious, coming hard as her clit chafed the plastic. No sooner had she climaxed than Micky clutched her to him, lifting her off the table. She was a rag doll in his arms as he edged them back to the chair. Micky sat and Marianna sat astride him, reverse cowgirl. Micky's hand flew over her clit as she ground herself on his cock, her feathered headdress shaking, her big breasts jiggling. The audience liked this even more. Irwin was in torment. Marianna smiled at him and grasped her tits, massaging them especially for him, although it has to be said, she got something out of it too.

She came again.

'Once, twice, three times a lady!' hollered Micky. He withdrew from her and scooped her up on to the table again, this time laying her flat on her back. He grinned down at her, hair all rumpled, face flushed and raw, and raised her tattooed leg high and straight so that blue-green snake of ink spiralled towards her snatch. He held her by the calf, the light glinting on her red spike heels as he drove his cock in once more, eyes locked on hers. They could never do just the one position. They weren't the type.

'Hey, Irwin,' called Micky, 'what say you give us a pay rise?'

Irwin nodded enthusiastically.

'Hear that, doll?' Micky said. 'We just got a rise.'

'Hell, we earned it,' she replied. 'How about more time off, Irwin? And a bigger trailer?'

Irwin nodded again.

'Yeehah! Going up in the world!' cried Micky.

'Manners,' gasped Marianna. 'We have to thank the man, don't forget. Show him our appreciation.'

'Sweetheart, you're right,' said Micky. 'Hey, boss! You wanna shoot your load? Your cojones must be turning blue.'

Irwin looked at him with eyes half appealing, half terrified.

'How'd you like to feel a pair of hot lips slipping up and down your wiener? You like that, huh? Like I said before, my Marianna, she gives the best head in the world.'

Micky pulled out of Marianna, helping her to her feet. Marianna fluffed at her auburn curls and straightened her headdress as Micky unwound the boa from Irwin's prick.

'Oh, baby, that needs attention,' said Micky, eyeing Irwin's bright ruddy erection. 'What are we gonna do, hon?'

Marianna stood in front of Irwin, posing vampishly with her arms outstretched, the fat furry boa draped over her shoulders. 'You could give him his hands back,' she suggested, twirling the end of her feathers.

'Could do,' said Micky. 'But I kind of like him cuffed.'

'I love him cuffed,' said Marianna.

Micky's face lit up in a crazy grin.

In a flash, he was full length on the floor in front of Irwin, his mouth around Irwin's prick, doing press-ups by his knees. The audience cheered, howled and stamped. Irwin stared wild eyed at Marianna as if by sheer force of will he could make her swap places with Micky.

No, sireee, not for the biggest pay rise in the world, thought Marianna, admiring her husband's rippling, multicoloured back and his tight little butt cheeks, muscles all working as he fellated the boss.

It didn't take Micky many press-ups. He pulled away, spitting on the floor and jumping to his feet as Irwin obliged with the pop-shot.

The audience whooped and howled, applause crackling as Micky clasped Marianna's hand and raised it in triumph. The two of them stood there as naked as Adam and Eve, although Adam had a hard-on and Eve, in heels, had got the better of the snake. Someone in the crowd rose to their feet, then another and another, and within seconds they had a standing ovation.

Micky drew Marianna close. She inhaled the heat, sweat and paraffin of him, feeling his cock nudge between her thighs. Then suddenly his lips were on hers, that rough scorched tongue seeking out her own, and he tasted of fire and swords with back notes of nicotine and whisky. The tuft of his whiskery beard scoured, tickling not just her chin but her heart too. To her shock, Marianna couldn't help responding and her mouth began kissing him back.

He wasn't as sweet as cherries, not by a long chalk, but he was Micky, her husband, and it was nothing a little Listerine couldn't fix. All around them, the audience cheered and roared, filling their ears with thunder. They hardly heard a thing. They were lost in a world of magic, Mental Micky and Marianna Multiple, kissing like there was no one watching.

Kristina Lloyd is the author of the Black Lace novels *Darker than Love* and *Asking for Trouble*, and her short fiction appears in other themed Wicked Words collections.

Make Me Come at the Ball Game Sophie Mouette

I was somewhat overdressed for a major-league ball game.

I didn't even *like* baseball, and Dirk was only mildly interested – he'd watch the World Series with the guys at the sports bar, toss a ball around at picnics. But a client he was wooing invited us to share his private box for the day, and Dirk couldn't turn that down. So I'd dressed up a little to play the part of the supportive corporate wife.

The appreciation in Dirk's green eyes didn't hurt a bit.

It was another sweltering summer day, so I'd chosen a fire-engine-red halter dress with a swirling skirt. No bra – something I couldn't imagine – and just a scrap of a thong in matching scarlet. Even though we'd be inside most of the time, I thought the straw boater with red-and-black-dotted ribbon added a nice touch. Throw on a pair of Marc Jacobs stack-heeled espadrilles that laced up my calves and voila.

I'd thought I looked casual but elegant, but I felt overdressed as we were carried along by the crush of fans wearing shorts and T-shirts, carrying mitts and ice-cream cones, and all of them apparently shouting at the tops of their lungs. I couldn't wait to get into the relative seclusion of the box.

We were nearing the escalator to that section of the stadium when Dirk's cell buzzed.

'It's Preston,' he said when he saw the caller ID. The client we were meeting. 'I should take it.'

I nodded and we stepped out of the flow of foot traffic beside a buttery-smelling popcorn stand. I'm not sure how Dirk could hear – I certainly couldn't make out his side of the conversation, and I was right next to him. The look on his face as he snapped the phone shut spoke volumes, though.

'He's got a migraine and won't be making it,' he said. 'He said to go on up and enjoy the amenities. There'll be champagne and hors d'oeuvres.'

My initial instinct to flee back to the quietness of our home and fall naked into the pool vanished at the magic 'champagne' word. Free champagne? Take me out to the ball game, baby!

Blissful air-conditioned coolness enveloped us as we entered the box, properly escorted when our tickets were flashed. The full-length glass wall gave us a wide, clear view of the diamond. Comfortable chairs awaited us, along with binoculars, scorecards, pens and souvenir programmes.

A waiter in neatly pressed pants and a crisp shirt, which echoed the colours of the home team's uniforms, opened the full magnum of champagne and poured glasses for us before settling the bottle into an ice bucket, saying he'd check on us later, and retreating. On the buffet in the back were shrimp cocktail, a sushi platter, Brie and little toast rounds with grapes, Swedish meatballs simmering in a chafing dish, spicy hummus and fresh pitta, and a chocolate fountain with ripe red strawberries.

I bit into a mouth-wateringly plump shrimp, tasting the firm flesh and perfectly spiced cocktail sauce. Washed the delectable morsel down with tart champagne. God, it was good. I think I might have moaned aloud.

OK, maybe I could get to like baseball. Just a little bit.

When I opened my eyes, Dirk was staring at me, in a way that touched me. As if his gaze were an extension of his hands, sliding slowly along my body.

The air conditioning had nothing to do with how hard my nipples peaked, thrusting against the fabric of my dress. Huh. Check it out.

'What?' I said, feigning innocence even as I posed provocatively, tossing my hair back.

'Enjoying yourself?' he asked.

'As much as one can at a baseball game,' I said. 'You?'

His answer was physical, not verbal. There was a definite bulge in his crotch, one that had me stirring down to my core.

'You want to go home?' I asked, blatantly licking my lips.

'No,' he said. 'Let's see at least some of the game.'

But before I could load up my plate with food and refill my wineglass, he kissed me. His tongue toyed and teased mine, searing my mouth. Carrying promises of things to come.

I had no idea just how soon they would come. Or how soon I would.

We stood for the national anthem. I even took off my hat. Separated from the rest of the stadium crowd as we were, we could have ignored it, pretended we were watching on TV, but it was half manners and half, I don't know, part of the experience.

When the song had ended, but my hands were busy fumbling with the hat, Dirk slipped behind me and started kissing my bare back.

The first kiss, on my shoulder, was light and romantic, the kind of kiss that would make you think 'how sweet' if you saw another couple enjoying it. But it still made me shiver.

The next kiss, on my spine between the shoulder

blades, was more intimate. He sucked and licked at the skin, a gentle but firm pressure that called to mind the way he would kiss my mound and inner thighs before turning his attention to even more sensitive areas.

I dropped my hat and closed my eyes to savour the pleasure of the caress and the thoughts it provoked.

The crowd roared, and I jumped.

Despite a split second of amused panic or panicked amusement on my part, they weren't cheering on Dirk, although some people might have cheered if they'd known about my fantasies. It was just the game starting.

I glanced out. The visiting team was up to bat.

'Just on principle,' Dirk said and leant away from me long enough to hit a switch, sending the announcer's voice booming through the box. He fiddled with something and the volume corrected itself.

The announcer was saying something about Goldenarm Gonzalez.

Ah, *him*. Even *I* had heard of our team's hotshot pitcher. His preening presence on the pitcher's mound must be inspiring the cheers.

I picked up the binoculars, took a peek.

Kind of homely. Kind of chunky, too, except for nice muscular arms. Disillusioning. I know you don't have to be gorgeous to be a pro athlete, but I'd have thought you'd at least end up with a good body.

I set the binoculars back down and between the various distractions – topping off our glasses, trying a meatball (not bad, but I'd stick to the other treats), selecting the most interesting-looking bits of sushi, kissing Dirk, Dirk grabbing my ass – it took a few minutes to get settled down in our seats.

Very comfy leather chairs.

Sweet. This was definitely the way to watch a baseball game, not in the baking sun, butt falling asleep in a hard plastic seat, snacking on hotdogs, pretzels and cheap beer.

At first I tried to follow the game, and actually made it through most of an inning without too many breaks to refill my glass or get more nibblies. But between champagne and my almost complete baseball ignorance, I got bored eventually. It's easy to tell a home run from a strikeout, but I certainly don't understand the finer points that must make it interesting for fans. Why *was* bunting sometimes the best course of action? Can anyone explain that to me?

And let's face it, it's not exactly the fastest-moving game on earth, and the players don't even look that great in their uniforms. (I don't understand soccer any more than I do baseball, but I speak sweaty hunks in shorts fluently, so I enjoy watching the World Cup.)

Dirk, on the other hand, looked pretty damn great. Of course I'm biased, and after the teasing and the kisses and the still more kisses, I was also turned on and a little giddy. The champagne was carrying that feeling through my bloodstream in its bubbly wake.

Towards the middle of the second inning, I started leaning over and feeding him tidbits. Semi-innocently at first, then not so innocently, with nibbling and teasing, and a bit of imposing my cleavage between him and his view of the game.

Then I got the bright idea of putting a piece of sushi into my own mouth and sharing it with him that way.

Hmm, it seems you *can* improve on a spicy yellowtail roll, and I'd always thought they were pretty much perfect as they were.

Before long I was straddling his lap, licking wasabi from his lips, and we'd abandoned any pretence of either watching the game or enjoying the hors d'oeuvres in favour of making out like a couple of teenagers in the back row of the movie theatre.

OK, a little more than any but the boldest teenagers might do in the theatre. Dirk's hands were all over my breasts, moulding, caressing, tweaking my nipples, biting and sucking through the fabric and then blowing on the wet spots he'd made, making my peaks even harder. I could feel his touch all the way to my crotch.

My skirt was hiked up, flashing my thighs and a bit of my butt, and Dirk and I were grinding together. His pants and my tiny thong stood between his hardening cock and my pussy, but the less sensible parts of my brain were helpfully suggesting ways to overcome that challenge. The way both my clit and his cock were straining to meet through the fabric, it was only a matter of time before we listened.

The door to the box clicked open.

I flew to my feet at roughly the speed of light, probably giving whoever was there an eyeful of leg and ass in the process, and ending up looking rather ruffled, but not lewd.

Not Preston miraculously recovered from the migraine, thank goodness, just the waiter, who smiled a bit as he asked if we needed anything.

Dirk blew a kiss, then stood up and drew the waiter aside. There was a quick whispered exchange, some masculine laughter. I picked up the binoculars, elbows covering my chest, and looked out, watching the tiny figures moving about the field below, doing my best imitation of a cat who'd fallen off the sofa and was hoping to erase your memory of it by being extra dignified.

So far, so good for our guys. The other team hadn't scored yet – maybe Golden-arm Gonzalez was as good as they said – and we had. Once.

I still couldn't muster any real interest, though, not in the face of the more interesting game Dirk and I had begun. Sure, it was a little embarrassing to be caught in a clinch like that, but my nipples felt like they were on fire.

My thong, on the other hand, was too damp to catch fire easily.

The waiter retreated, having clearly been told we were fine, didn't need a thing, and Dirk came back to me, grinning rakishly.

'Take off your thong,' Dirk said.

Giggling a little, I complied. I reached underneath my skirt and shimmied out of the scrap of slightly damp material, not revealing a thing. At the last minute, I flashed him. Just to show who was in control.

Dirk held out his hand. 'Give it to me.' I dropped it into his palm. I didn't feel like giggling any more. My eyes widened – and my insides fluttered – as he brought it to his nose and smelt my private scent. With a wicked smile, he pocketed the wad of satin.

I wondered if he'd give them back to me before we left, or if I'd have to walk all the way down out of the stadium and to the car completely naked beneath my dress.

My thighs weak, I sat down. A good thing, too, because Dirk's next words might have just caused my knees to buckle.

'Prop your feet up on the window ledge.'

We were too high up for anyone to see anything and, besides, my skirt flowed around my knees, leaving my private parts in shadow. Nobody could see my bare shaven lips, darker than the surrounding skin of my belly and thighs, growing shiny and slick with desire.

Didn't matter. The cool brush of air conditioning on my hot core had me shivering not from cold but from arousal. I was well aware of how naked I was, how exposed, how vulnerable beneath my dress.

And I liked it.

I almost wished someone besides Dirk could see. Almost wished the waiter would pop back in, or that some other couple could catch a glimpse and decide the game in the ballpark was less interesting than games they could get up to somewhere else.

My brain didn't want to cause anything that would get back to Preston, let alone get us arrested for indecent exposure. The less thoughtful and more sensual parts of me, on the other hand, were throbbing and pulsating and all but dripping from the sense of naughty daring, the hint of risk. And between champagne and kisses and this sexy quasi-exhibitionist game, those parts of me were definitely winning.

He left me that way – legs spread, exposed but not quite revealed – as he fed me chocolate-dipped strawberries.

Better for the purpose than sushi.

I licked the rich dark chocolate from each one as sensuously as I could, revealing each bright, swollen-looking ruby fruit before I ate it. I sucked the chocolate from his fingers, sucked them clean and then sucked the fingers themselves, because I could, and because it made Dirk make wonderful noises. Because it made me imagine sucking his cock.

Between strawberries, we sipped more champagne and shared bubbly, chocolate-tinged kisses.

With each strawberry, with each kiss, I could feel my almost-visible sex swelling and getting more and more slick.

By the time he stopped feeding me and started caressing my nipples again through the soft thin fabric of my dress, I felt as though I had a beacon between my legs, pulsing, red as the strawberries, visible from orbit, let alone from the cheap seats. And my nipples might as well have been exposed too, the way they were pressing against the fabric as if they'd tear it away, hard and erect and sending waves of sensation through my body.

Every once in a while, cheers or jeers from the field

made it in through the lust fog clouding my brain. They served to remind me that we weren't alone – which I could almost have forgotten, focused on Dirk and on the heat gathering inside me. And every time they did, I could feel my sex twitch and clench, feel a stronger surge of pleasure pass through me knowing that we were playing with fire in front of thirty-odd thousand fans, plus the TV audience, and none of them had any idea what we were doing. Who'd be looking up at a private-box window while the game was going on, anyway?

But when Dirk knelt down between my legs, reason reasserted itself for a second.

He couldn't be seen from outside the booth – maybe someone who happened to look up would catch a glimpse of movement, if that – but still I glanced nervously at the door.

'Don't worry,' he said, apparently sensing my motion, or maybe my attack of nerves. 'They won't bother us. I gave that guy an extra twenty just to make sure.'

Then he settled himself into place.

Mostly hidden by my skirt, but if twenty dollars was an insufficient bribe these days, or, God help us, Preston recovered from his migraine and decided to show up anyway, his position would be low on the plausible-deniability scale.

Then Dirk put his hands on my thighs, pushed to splay them even wider, and I ceased to care very much.

He pressed his lips against the naked curve of my mound.

Began the delicate, yet insistent nibbling and sucking he'd demonstrated earlier on my back.

Worked his way around until all the skin around my vulva was sensitised, tingling, feeling like the blood there had changed to champagne, and I was pressing against him, fingers laced in his thick hair, torn between wanting to direct his mouth to my aching clit and wanting to enjoy the prolonged teasing he could be so good at giving me.

Slow licks down my labia, closer to where I needed it most, but not quite. Pressure building, making my head swirl with need.

Nibbling my lips, tantalisingly and gently. The announcer was saying something, but I couldn't hear above the blood pounding in my ears, the frantic beating of my heart.

Finally, he closed in on my clit.

My own cries drowned out the announcer, drowned out the roar of the blood, almost drowned out the roar of the crowd as something that must have been exciting – relatively speaking – happened.

Dirk made some very bad joke about how we weren't the only ones scoring. When my eyes focused a little, I saw that 'our team' had apparently gotten a run while we were busy.

I was happy, giddy, but far from sated. Something about the setting, about the bubbles in my bloodstream and our place high over the ball field and the near-but-not-real exposure was crying for more, more.

And of course there was Dirk, and Dirk's lovely hard purpling cock, requiring attention.

I stood, leant forwards on to the window sill, raised my skirt and thrust my naked bum up and back in clear invitation.

'Looks like things are finally happening out there,' I purred. 'Might as well watch their game while we play ours.'

Sexy, but not obvious. If anyone saw, we'd look like eager and affectionate fans, too excited to stay in our seats.

Well, the last part was true, anyway.

Trust Dirk to raise the stakes a little. Raising my hair out of the way, he nibbled at the nape of my neck, distracting me while he untied the bow that held my halter top in place. The red fabric draped forwards at my waist. My bared breasts were almost pressing against the glass.

And when he leant over me, started rubbing his cock slowly and tauntingly against my dripping sex, his weight moved me forwards a little, so I really was pressed against the glass.

Cool on my heated nipples, a strange caress. My mounds were mashed against the glass, but I still felt as though my nipples were hard enough to score it. I could only imagine what it looked like from the other side, if anyone chanced to look up.

Would they chance to look up? Distracted somehow while the teams changed places, maybe curious to see if someone famous was inhabiting the private box?

Would they be turned on to see a half-naked woman pushed against the glass, being thoroughly fucked?

If only that were the case. Dirk continued to tease me, rubbing the head of his turgid cock against my wet lips. I knew he was teasing himself as well, delaying the inevitable for both of us. If anything, it made him grow harder, sliding the sensitive head of his penis against my opening.

Of course, the more it bumped up against my clit, ground across it, the more aroused and needy I became, too.

'Fuck me,' I begged him.

'Here? Now?' he taunted me, his voice hoarse with desire. 'In front of everybody?'

'Yes!' I wailed. 'God, yes!'

'God, yes,' he echoed as he drove into me.

I was so wet that it was like the proverbial hot knife through butter, at least until he was buried up to the hilt in me, the head of his cock nudging up against my cervix and sending shivers of arousal through me. I fluttered on the edge of orgasm.

Dirk could feel those vaginal ripples; I heard his sharp

intake of breath before he started moving again, slowly at first but ramping up to hard sharp thrusts. The thrusting, the sensation of the hot hard length of him inside me, set me off. I screamed, fogging the window in a halo around my head as my whole body cracked and shattered into orgasm.

I shoved back against him, prolonging my pleasure and urging his on. We'd been teasing each other long enough that he wasn't far behind me.

His thrusts changed to short staccato ones, signalling his release. I cried out his name.

Below us, the star hitter slammed a home run.

Screams that weren't our own filled the box. I opened my eyes, registered the situation.

The ball was coming right for us.

And the Jumbotron camera was tracking it.

Oh shit.

As the ball hit the Plexiglas we were already collapsing backwards into one of the cushy leather seats. I caught a glimpse of myself on the giant screen, wild hair and eyes, blurred breasts.

Below, everyone was on their feet.

I was reasonably sure it hadn't been entirely clear I was naked to the waist. Just an excited fan . . .

'Home run, baby,' Dirk gasped in my ear, and all I could do was convulse in laughter.

It was, we realised a moment later, the winning hit that had sealed the game for our team.

Go team!

I was cleaning myself up (feeling vaguely guilty about what I was doing to a formerly pristine linen napkin) when Dirk's cell rang.

He didn't have the phone tight against his ear, so I could hear Preston's voice as he asked, 'So how are you enjoying the game?'

There was laughter in Dirk's voice as he answered, 'Oh, very much, sir. I'm sorry you couldn't be here.'

'That's OK,' Preston said. 'I've been watching on TV. Quite a home run . . .'

Sophie Mouette is the author of the Black Lace novel *Cat Scratch Fever*, and her short fiction has been published in numerous Wicked Words collections. Part of the writing team that is Sophie Mouette also writes as Sarah Dale, whose first Cheek novel, *A Little Night Music*, will be published in June 2007.

Fee, Fi, Fo, Fum Madelynne Ellis

'Fee, fi, fo, fum, I'm going to bite your sexy bum.'

That's how it started, with a stupid rhyme as he chased me through the park. It was October and the leaves were swirling around the menagerie like demented butterflies, gold, orange and red. The smell of winter was in the air, its crisp, frosty tang filtered through the leaf mould and the mulch of rain-sodden grass to tweak our nostrils. The evening was hovering on the verge of twilight, and every now and then a whistle or a bang would signify the incineration of yet another firework in a waste bin.

There was laughter on the wind too, not just Jake's and mine. Children's voices imitating witches' cackles, and the gruff hollers of the teenage boys hanging by the loos.

'Fee, fi ...'

'Stop it,' I squealed, as Jake backed me up against the wire front of the birdhouse. 'Jake, please! You're killing me.' I bent double trying to prevent my sides from aching, while I frantically tried to ward off his hands. Despite the lateness of the season, I felt the same exuberance for life that day as a spring lamb. Everything seemed vibrant and beautiful, as if bursting with energy.

'Got you.' He clapped both palms over my rear, then forced me upright against the wire mesh. Giggling, I let him pin me, and watched his lips expectantly as they hovered inches over mine, slightly parted. Jake had a sadistic streak that wove through his psyche, but I was a tease, so I guess that made us even.

'Thought you were going to bite me.' I drew my teeth over my fleshy lower lip.

His eyelashes dusted his cheek as he smiled. 'I'm just working up to it. Course, if you want me to. I might have to reconsider.'

Reconsider, no way. I didn't want to be bitten, just like I didn't want to be tickled, but there was something alluring about the proposition all the same.

Jake snuggled closer, pushing our hips into contact, and forcing me on to my toes. Apparently, his sap was rising too, considering the size of the bulge now spearing me through several layers of clothing. I'd always known he'd had a thing about my bum. Six months earlier, he'd caught me trying to wriggle into a pair of skintight jeans, and had me stand there a full ten minutes with them halfway up, just so that he could stare at my cheeks.

'Ever thought about doing it here?' His voice was a husky sigh into my ear. The warmth of his breath was far more arousing than his proposition. It left tingles all through my throat, while the idea of exposing even an inch of skin to the elements made me long for a blanket.

His eye tooth grazed my ear lobe.

'Ow!'

I jerked forwards into his hard body. Knocked off balance, he sat with a thump on the broken pathway. 'Jeez, Luce!'

'Sorry,' I whimpered, hastily rubbing the top of my thigh. 'Shitbag!' I glared at the silver pheasant who'd just pecked me. He returned my gaze unblinkingly, which, combined with the arrogant tilt of his head, told me exactly what he was thinking – my territory, fat arse. Shift your bum.

'Grrr!'

'Hey, buster, that was my move.' Jake pushed himself on to his feet, grinning hard while trying to look concerned. 'You all right?'

I twisted to show him but there was nothing to see besides a new scuff mark on my jeans.

'Hmm, this calls for a closer inspection.'

'Not here.' I batted away his hand. 'There are children about.'

'Aw, come on, live a little.' His easy grin broadened and made the twinkle in his pale-blue eyes that bit more intense.

'No. And you can bugger off too,' I added to the pheasant, who was still eyeing my rear in a particularly vindictive manner.

'I ought to check it out, Luce. I mean, it could be nasty.'

Jake was all hands again, his large soft palms roving over my hips and thighs in persuasive circles. It was a motion that was all about desire and instant gratification, but, as I said, I was never one to give in easily.

'Stop it. I'm not unzipping in broad daylight in the middle of a park just so you can stare at my arse.'

'The light's nearly gone...' He drew the knuckle of his thumb along the back seam of my jeans, down into the shadowy hollow between my thighs. His breath whispered across my lips as he leant closer, teasing me with the promise of his kiss.

I wasn't being drawn. 'The answer's still no.'

'Fi, fo...' he muttered into the fabric covering my chest. He dipped below my elbow, and emerged at my back, where he nuzzled along the path his thumb had just taken. 'So – here, at the back of the birdhouse, or shall we get artistic on the swings?'

'I said, no.'

The trouble was I could picture it so clearly, me face down over the old tyre base of the swing, and him standing, driving into me from behind. All done with only a few slivers of skin on show as our bodies rocked back and forth.

I looked at him, he looked at me, and I'm afraid to say, I ran.

I ran so hard that my legs were jelly by the time I staggered, panting, up to our front door. You see, I know how my flights of fancy go. A few choice words and a subtle caress or two from Jake is all it would have taken. And it's just not dignified for a teacher to get caught out like that. Not to mention that it would likely cost me my job.

Jake unlocked the door, while I was busy catching my breath. Bastard had followed me home at a leisurely jog. I guess regular five-a-side matches gave him the edge in the fitness stakes.

In we went, me collapsing straight on to the stairs, while he just shrugged off his jacket. 'Better check that bite.' He curled over my prone form to nibble my shoulder.

The stair carpet rubbed my cheek as I turned towards him. 'You could have offered me a drink.'

'Oh, no.' He shook his head. 'Not when there's another injury to check first.' His hands slid around my waistband to my fly, and popped the button. 'Now, don't worry, Ms Lucy.' He planted a kiss just above the level of my panties, then tugged down the denim. 'Dr Jake's gonna make it fine.'

Half-heartedly, I swatted at his arm. OK, he was being kind of cute, particularly the way his hot breath was buffeting the sensitive, rarely touched skin of my bum. And now that I wasn't desperately fleeing from becoming the next local newspaper headline – SWINGING EXHIBITIONIST IN SEXY SOUTH PARK SHOCKER – I was coming around to the idea of a little attention.

'Oh, dear! Naughty bird.' Jake traced the back of my thigh with his thumb and forefinger. 'Evil, evil pheasant.' His lips pressed up against the bruise, adding heat to the already tender skin.

'Is the skin broken?'

He prodded a little. 'No, just coming up a lovely shade of blue. Needs some butter.

'It needs some arnica.'

'Nope.' He drew his tongue across the tender lump. 'My nan always used best butter. And it always worked.'

I raised my head and peered back at him. Jake's legendary nan was also the world's finest pastry chef, an expert car mechanic, knitter, trivia expert and had probably swum the Channel. 'But it's an old wives' tale. I have done a first-aid course.'

It was no use. He was already off to the kitchen to rummage through the fridge. He reappeared a moment later with a block of butter.

'How big is this bruise?'

'Oh, not that big.' He scooped off a piece with two fingers, then lovingly rubbed it into my skin in ever-widening circles.

'I thought you said it wasn't that big.' His fingertips brushed along the crease of my bottom, sending twitters of excitement across my thighs. 'Jake.' A single digit twanged the elastic of my thong. I could feel myself getting wet.

'I'm just making sure. I thought it might need a kiss better too.'

Not that his kiss landed anywhere near the bruise. It grazed the fleshy cheek above.

'Get off.' I jerked my hips, but he clung on tight.

'Damn, Luce. I love the way your bottom jiggles.' He patted the cheek, just to make it wobble again. 'I could just . . .' His teeth grazed the surface of the skin, nipping a little, exciting me a whole lot more. 'I could just . . .'

I remembered how hard he'd been when he'd pressed me up against the birdhouse. His breath tickled. Each tender brush of his lips was making hairs rise all across my body and, as I instinctively moved with the rock of simulated sex, my nipples brushed the coarse threads of the carpet. OK, I was gagging for this as much as he was – fast, unpredictable sex. The sort that tossed me about like a battered ship in a storm, that got hot, sticky and squelchy, and left you exhausted and gasping for air.

His tongue dabbed into the valley between my cheeks and an erotic shiver rolled up my spine: instant intense arousal. I gulped a breath to replace the one he'd just stolen.

'S-s-sensitive!' His tongue danced around the puckered ring of my anus. We'd talked about doing this, but he'd never actually done it before. More shivers trembled down my thighs. The dabbing, flighty touch was incredible, excruciatingly sweet and borderline ticklish. I didn't want him to stop, though. I wanted him to be braver. I wanted him to push just a little way inside and take the taboo that little bit further.

'Fee, fi,' he began again. There was a rustle of cloth, and then his T-shirt landed on the stairs just above my head. 'I'm going to fuck your sexy bum.'

'Oh, no!' I tried to push myself upright, but Jake was right behind me.

'Oh, yes,' he said. His bare chest rubbed up across the backs of my thighs.

We'd talked about this too, but . . . 'Jake, it'll hurt.'

'Relax, Ms Lucy. No, it won't. You're in safe hands.' Jake's code for 'I've done this before, sugar plum.' He scooped up another knob of butter, and this time smeared it down the shadowy valley between my cheeks. Another good-sized knob he circled around the puckered rosebud until I couldn't help but sigh. There were reasons why this area was taboo, and I guessed I was appreciating one of the reasons people did it regardless. It felt good, incredibly, mind-bendingly good. So good, it left me trembling against the stair carpet and relaxed me enough for Jake to slip me the tip of a finger.

The wicked intrusion instantly awakened all the over-eager nerve endings I'd been expecting him to tease with his tongue. I swallowed slowly. Deep sparks were kindling where his fingers pressed. They ran like threads of fire towards my cunt, which eagerly plumped.

OK, if we were actually going to do this, I wanted to watch him slide in. I turned my head, and sought the long mirror hung across the hall. There he was, in perfect view. Naked on top, with his jeans coiled below his knees, and his erection, thick and hard, pointed dartlike towards my up-thrust bum. My apprehension didn't die, but my protests did. He was beautiful. There was no other way to describe him. Jake was neither tall, nor traditionally handsome. His features were softer, more feminine than that. Apart, of course, from his cock, the precise icon of my lust. I wanted it. I wanted him inside me, rocking me towards bliss. My cunt was gaping, waiting, but of course, that wasn't his target.

'Relax, we'll take it slow.' His fingers spread out to girdle my hips. His cock-tip bumped my arse.

He curled a hand over my cunt from the front and rubbed back against my pubic bone: instant, liquid heaven.

'Gawd, Luce,' he drawled again. 'You are so fucking hot.' And a saint for letting him do this, I mentally added. Everything felt so tight, so weird. My muscles fought the intrusion, while my nerve endings sang in welcome. The buttery tip was in, stretching me, branding me with its heat. Jake's gasp said it all. It was intense; a feeling magnified tenfold when he slid in deeper. 'That's it, baby.' His low voice was a gentle caress against my shoulder. 'I'm right inside you.'

My nails raked against the stair carpet. I wanted a sheet to cling to, to bite, to shove into my mouth. My nipples were aching, my cunt felt empty, but he was filling me so well, jerking my hips to meet his shallow thrusts.

I'd always thought it would hurt, that there'd be no joy in having a cock thrust where it was never intended to go, but it had lifted me into a world of pure sensation, a world where a second heartbeat had taken up residence in my bottom and where every shiver of motion exploded pinprick stars across my skin.

'So, tight. I can't hold it much longer.' Jake's words seemed to drift down to me through the sex haze. I braced myself on one arm, and mashed my hand over the one he was using to knead my clit. In the mirror, I could see he was sweating. Gritting his teeth and holding on to his libido so tight the slightest thing might upset the balance.

'Harder.' I jerked his fingers over my clit in short rhythmic strokes, but the buzz seemed to be wholly centred in my rear.

'I'm going to come up your arse.' He gasped, and held himself still for just a moment at full penetration.

And that's when it came to me, the perfect Halloween present sex.

We had a sort of competition going, you see; on those special days of the year, Christmas, New Year, Valentine's and so on, we'd do our best to create the other's special fantasy. Jake, naturally, was a complete whiz at it. On Easter Monday, he'd borrowed a fedora and raincoat and even arranged for us to meet at some half-forgotten airstrip full of vintage planes. His Bogart a perfect match for my Bergman, as we enacted a farewell scene that never made the final cut of *Casablanca*.

Anyway, I didn't have Jake's connections, but I had read this article once, 'How to tell what your man really wants in bed', and it recommended paying particular attention to where he concentrates his caresses. The gist being that, if he's into slowly circling your navel with his tongue, he's probably got a really sensitive tummy, and, if he's all over your breasts, he probably loves having his own nipples sucked. Now, I'm not sure if there was any real science behind the study but, when it came to Jake, this is pretty much the way I'd found things to be. That meant that all this bottom loving he was doing might be a cry for a little anal experimentation of a different kind. So, armed with this insight and his hefty hints about doing it alfresco, I had the seedlings of a plan. A risqué, dangerous, stupid and oh so irresistible in its naughtiness plan.

'Luce ... Oh, God, Luce.' Jake was so close, his movements had become jerky and indecisive. A shiver of pleasure ran up my spine, causing me to arch my back and raise my hips to meet him. Streamers of joy rippled through my bottom and abdomen. 'You've gotta come now ... Please!'

The needy, plaintive little cry was so cute it made my heart turn over. I mashed his fingers harder against my clit and, as the swell of my orgasm reached its pinnacle, vague ideas solidified into an image of Jake bent over a swing and me buttering him up with a huge black strap-on. Brilliant! Sordid, and sexy too. Yum!

Eventually, after we'd cuddled and cleaned up, we hurried up to bed. Jake in typical post-orgasmic fashion immediately flaked out, but I was up, up, up. My mind was racing. There was so much to prepare. For starters, I needed to shop for the right kind of toys, and find time to practise with them while he was out of the house. There was also a location to scout out. The idea of the swings was delightfully wicked, but completely impractical, being both too open and acrobatic for a first attempt.

Hark at me – I snuggled up against Jake's back – the girl who ran home from the park because she was scared of showing a sliver of butt in public was planning a session of bend-over boyfriend in a nature spot. On which subject, I needed to check my facts about Jake's obsession before I launched myself into this full throttle, and that meant I needed to initiate a few little warm-up exercises in that area.

I was too excited to sleep well that night; consequently, I was up with the dawn chorus, feeling hopelessly randy. It seemed like a good time to make a start. So, after a few minutes brushing up on my technique with some online sex guides, I armed myself with a latex glove and a bottle of lube, and slipped back into bed.

Jake was still snuggled up beneath the duvet, all toasty warm. Heavenly. I ran my fingers over his quarter-inch of golden-brown stubble, then transferred the caress to the diamond-shaped thatch on his chest and sucked one of his nipples into my mouth.

'What are you after?' he drawled, and half opened one eye.

'Nothing.' I looked up at his face wearing my best innocent-as-a-daisy smile, all the while imagining him impaled and jerking to my rhythm. I even added a corn field as a backdrop.

Jake cocked an eyebrow in response. 'Guess I'll go back to sleep, then.'

Bastard. I was supposed to be the tease, not him. Still, there was no way I was letting him doze. I released his nipple and licked a shiny line down his torso to just above his cock, which, if Jake wasn't awake, certainly was. It perked up, happy to see me. Too bad, because for once it wasn't my primary target.

I skipped the hot treat and instead planted a smooch on his upper thigh, a move that brought a brief murmur of complaint, but soon had him parting his thighs for more.

'Jake,' I crooned as I pushed my head down further between his thighs.

'Mmm.' The tip of my tongue traced his balls. 'Yes.'

'Do you ever think about rimming?'

'Yeah – duh! Don't you remember last night?'

'Course.' I traced the line of his perineum. 'But I didn't mean like that.' My tongue reached his puckered ring.

Suddenly, his shoulders were up off the bed and he was staring down at me like I'd just electrocuted him.

'I ... um ... What are you doing?' He squirmed against my tongue.

'Rimming.' I drew the word out to heighten the impact. 'Don't you like it?' The musky taste of him was thick upon my tongue. A dewy blush swept across his cheeks and neck. Jake sucked his bottom lip into his mouth. It was an apprehensive look, but one I liked. It was a rare treat to see him look so vulnerable, so shy.

'I think you'd like me to take it a bit further.' The snap of the lube-bottle lid made him jump. I dangled the latex glove between us like an omen.

'But ... uh ...' he blurted, and his eyes never left my hands as I slowly drew on the glove.

'Exactly,' I replied.

Jake's tongue worked nervously across his lips. He looked so ripe for a kiss, but my attention was already firmly focused on a different puckered pout.

'Are you still a virgin?' I whispered.

His gaze flicked nervously about the room as if there were spy cams mounted in the corners.

'How many fingers shall we try? One ... two?' I held them up, and dribbled lube down them. It pooled in the V. Jake gave his cute nervous lick again, but I wasn't really waiting for permission. I didn't need him to tell me how turned on he was, it was plainly visible. His eyes were bright, his cock was stiff and his throat was so choked up with nervous excitement he was starting to pant.

I dribbled more lube down his cock, then curled my palm around the shaft and drew my thumb tip up over the sensitive eye. 'Aah!' The exclamation rippled through the tensed muscles of his abdomen.

Jake flopped back against the pillows. 'Oh, God!'

His slit was oozing pre-come and his knees had risen to give me better access. It seemed my prediction had been spot on. He was gagging for a little rear-entry action, and I was going to give him some. I slipped him the tip of my index finger, but his body sucked up the intrusion so hungrily, I suspected mine weren't the first digits to explore down there. 'Do you do this while you wank?' I was pretty certain he hadn't done it with a partner before.

Jake just groaned and lifted his hips in time with the

movement of my hand. Apparently, the demands of his body were too urgent to ignore, or else he was avoiding a confession out of embarrassment. Still, seeing how he was really into this, I pushed a second finger in alongside the first and scissored them apart, preparing him for the real treat yet to come.

Last night's experiment had taught me what this felt like, and it seemed Jake was experiencing the same fountain of sparks. Just watching him, the desperate motion of his body, feeling the heat of him, called down a gush of cream from my own body. But it wasn't about coming for me this time. It was about exactly what all this was doing for my beautiful boy. Make that my beautiful, blushing, double-scoop-chocolate-and-rum-truffle-ice-cream delicious boy, because he looked scrumptious enough to lick up one loving slurp at a time. I couldn't resist. My mouth closed over his glans, while I continued to finger his hole. Orgasm hit him like a thunderclap. It shuddered through his body, while I milked his cock and clasped my fingers tight.

'Luce,' he whimpered. 'Oh, Luce.' Shaky with arousal, he smeared kisses over my face, and then supped my clit until I came.

Well, after that, I thought it would be impossible to contain my excitement until the weekend, but a week of marking dire essays is a pretty effective passion killer. There was also the small matter of shopping for the specialised accoutrements, and a location to find, which was a bit of a mare. You see, while I knew I could always fall back on the bedroom, this was supposed to be about fulfilling Jake's fantasies, not mine, which meant my fear of going at it outdoors was going to have to go. Still, I quickly vetoed the park, for all the same reasons I'd given Jake when he'd had me pinned up against the birdhouse. It was too open and too risky, and anal sex with a dildo isn't exactly the stuff of discreet quickies.

Other options included the local abandoned theatre, the cinema and the public toilets. All were quickly dismissed. The latter because the council-run amenities were just gross, and there'd be too much through traffic in the rest room of a pub, club or restaurant. This left me rather stuck until a chance errand on Friday afternoon took me to the art department at school. And there it was, the choicest location this side of Fiji, conveniently displayed in a poster.

Jake muttered more than a few protests on Saturday morning when I rolled him out of bed and into a taxi. So many, he didn't even question the full-length leather coat I was wearing, despite being used to seeing me in just a tee and jeans.

'The Tate,' he said sulkily. Staring at art just wasn't Jake's thing. Guess it was just as well that wasn't where I was taking him, although, we were heading for one particular installation.

Confused, Jake followed me across the road and past the conservative iron railings to a shiny mirrored box that rose out of the pavement like a space-age obelisk. I guessed he was thinking we'd be doing the Halloween treat once it had gone dark, not in broad daylight.

'You first.' I clasped the utilitarian door handle and tugged, revealing a brushed steel washbasin–WC combo and a waft of floral air freshener.

Jake's eyebrows disappeared into his hairline as he moved inside. I shuffled in behind him.

Shiny box on the outside, yeah, but on the inside . . .

'Whoa, goldfish bowl!' Jake stared through the transparent walls at the procession of tourists heading into the gallery. 'Brilliant, you get to piss in front of everyone, and they don't even know it.'

I really hoped that was the case, not that I intended to watch him piss. Although, we hadn't been able to see in from outside, my own paranoia was working away at my confidence. What if there was a switch that activated when you stepped inside and exposed you to the world? What if people started queuing and pressed their faces to the glass? I trembled at the thought of film crews and newspaper headlines – DIRTY DILDO DIVA, DON'T MISS A SEC and TATE-FUL SODOMY SHACK EXPOSÉ.

Jake was harbouring no such qualms. 'I love it, Lucy.' He bent over the shiny washbasin and stuck his tongue out at a group of suits outside 'Wee hee! Wankers!' I think the real potential of the place hit him then, because his voice dropped to a husky drawl. 'Say, let's get dirty.'

That was my cue to bury my butterfly nerves. Attitude, I goaded myself. Stand tall, be strong, be brave and, most of all, commanding. I looked the part with my scarlet nails, kinky coat and waspish heels. Now all I needed to do was act.

'Drop your trousers, bunny boy.'

Jake turned on the spot, his eyes alight with wonder, and now focused on the leather raincoat. 'Ooh! Role play. I love it when you talk dirty to me. Let's see the succubus outfit.'

I gave him my best Dietrich pout. 'I said drop 'em.'

Jake licked his lips, as his gaze followed the path of my fingertips along the edge of the coat lapels down to the belt. 'OK.' He fumbled with his belt, and frantically pulled down his trousers and pants. 'Show me.'

I coyly teased open the belt.

'Lucy. Oh my . . . fucking hell!'

Hand on heart, he stepped backwards into the sink.

Despite the beauty of the black satin corset, with its tight lacings and the steel bones that cinched my waist to nothing and showed off the womanly flare of my hips, despite the stockings, the garter belt, the heels, and the flimsy wisp of silk covering my modesty, all he appeared to see was the silver-buckled leather harness fastened around my hips and thighs and the beautiful black dildo supported there.

His mouth dropped open. There were no words to accompany the emotion, nothing to express his incredulous surprise, but there was a glint of something besides shock in his eyes. The same sparkle I'd seen when I'd shown him the glove in bed.

One hand stroked frantically through his spiky hair.

'Do you like?' I sucked my little fingertip into my mouth.

He looked around frantically at the people walking straight past us, reached for my leather coat to cover me, then changed his mind and pressed his palms to the walls as if to confirm they were real.

'They can't see us, Jake.'

'Are you sure?'

A nod was all I managed. I had too many doubts about the glass box to risk voicing an actual opinion. It was taking a supreme effort just to stop myself checking over my shoulder every four seconds. Why did I think Saturday afternoon, outside a famous art gallery would be less risqué than midnight in a deserted park? Blind stupidity, I guess. There were people walking past us eating their sandwiches, and I was wearing an enormous rubber schlong.

Sweat bathed my skin, but despite my reservations I wasn't about to chicken out. After all, there was a special kind of thrill associated with being this rude in the open. And wearing little more than lingerie and a fake cock was pretty damn rude. It pumped the adrenaline in the same way that sneaking boyfriends upstairs had when I was a teenager.

'Shit! I must be dreaming.' Jake slapped himself, hard.

I gave my hips a playful wiggle. The dildo bounced in response, lewd and full of promise.

Jake's grin stretched from ear to ear. 'How do we do this?' he asked, his voice breathy with longing.

How, indeed?

While the idea of holding him face down in the sink,

my scarlet claws clamped around the back of his neck and his luscious arse sticking out all peachy fuzz and ripe for me, this was Jake's treat, so I gave him the choice. 'Either bend over, or find a perch.'

He frantically searched the cubicle for comfortable spots, but there wasn't much choice or space. Comfort for sex had not been the designer's primary concern. Or mine, when I'd picked this location, and I dare say a park bench might have been more accommodating.

Jake settled on the edge of the toilet seat, having wriggled free of his trousers.

'I want to see you do it.' The confession coloured his cheeks with a pretty ruby blush. Wow, he looked fantastic, stripped naked from the waist down, his legs and cheeks splayed and a look of complete overexcited adoration in his eyes. Suddenly, I wished I'd brought a camera, but hell, if this went well, maybe I'd get to see it again regardless.

The floor was scrupulously clean, but I shed the coat and knelt down, mostly to flash the exquisite beauty of the corset's lacings. The move wasn't lost on Jake, who made an immediate grab for my breasts. 'Ah-ah.' I batted away his hands. 'Touch yourself, not me.'

'Aw!' He risked my wrath by raising a fingertip in order to jiggle my cleavage.

'Hands off.' I clasped his wrists and moved his hands to his swelling erection.

Shyly at first, he grasped his shaft and worked it with long steady pulls. I grinned at the persistence of his rhythm. He was so up for this, any reservations seemed to have imploded, although his gaze constantly followed the movements of the passers-by. I wondered if he was watching their expressions in fear of being caught or in the hope of being seen.

For my part, I was ignoring everything outside the tiny box. If I was being watched, I didn't want to know.

'Easy. Steady now.' I slowed Jake's pumping fist, and

lifted the lubed dildo to his arse. The pert flesh was hot as I parted his cheeks and worked lube into the puckered crease.

'Sure you're man enough to take it?'

Jake swallowed so his Adam's apple bobbed. 'Sure.' His inflection sounded syrupy.

The tip of the black cock, *my* cock, butted his bum. Jake pushed against the tantalisingly persistent pressure, too eager to let me take charge. 'Don't tease, Luce.' He captured the smooth head between two fingers and guided it to its target.

'Oh, yes,' he crooned as the head of the glossy dildo slipped past his anal ring. 'Do me good.' He braced himself against the panoramic view of the street. 'That's right. Lady, you are hot. So. Fucking. Hot.'

He was getting a little too vocal, and I doubted that the box was soundproof. A quick jerk of my hips set him back in line, and quietened his voice to a soft kitten-like mewl. I guessed I'd just found his prostate. But I wanted to fuck, not just wiggle. I echoed his croon as I pulled back so that only the very tip of the rubber cock remained inside him. Lube dribbled down the shaft between us, like treacle raindrops, they trickled down his thighs, an image so lovely it nearly had me bending down to lick it off.

Jake began to whimper. Hot sweat bathed my skin beneath the leather. The musky sweet scent of arousal permeated the air between us. Like a narcotic, the smell was intoxicating. It demanded action – sweaty, sticky, hard-core action.

'What about you?' Jake was suddenly serious, his gaze focused upon the liquid evidence of arousal on my pants. There were goosebumps across his bare skin. He was desperate for more, but he needed to know this was good for me too. What a sweetie.

'Don't worry about me.' With one hand, I drew aside the scrap of silk covering my sex to reveal a tiny butterfly vibe held in place with elastic loops – time for power on.

The buzz rippled straight through my clit, causing me to draw a hissed intake of breath. 'Fee, fi,' I growled on the release. Jake's mouth went slack in response. 'Fo, fum. I'm going to fuck your sexy bum.' And the black shaft slid inside his body, until our loins almost kissed.

It seemed unreal, my jiggling and his adulatory expression of dizzy bliss. I stroked in and out of his body with leisurely ease, while Jake took care of his cock and the vibe took care of me. With all that stimulation, and the audience, the hum of the traffic faded into insignificance. The passers-by became no more than ghosts. The glittering space-age box was no more than our personal paradise. A whole host of faces pressed to the glass wouldn't have stopped us.

I watched Jake's eyes close and his head fall back against the sink as his cock bucked. My own orgasm shook me just moments later, leaving me tingling and shaky on my heels.

Jake's mournful exhalation said it all as the black cock came reluctantly free of his arse. He looked at me, at the harness and the dildo. We both knew it wasn't farewell. Then he crushed me with an embrace. His kiss, the first kiss of the day, was hungry and hard. The second and third, he smeared across my face. 'How did you know?' he asked, as he turned the handle to let us out.

I laughed. 'A bitchy pheasant told me.'

'Fee, fi,' he replied. 'Let's go to the park and thank it.'

Madelynne Ellis is the author of the Black lace novels *A Gentleman's Wager*, *The Passion of Isis* and *Dark Designs*.

Innana's Temple Olivia Knight

Mina climbed the steps of the temple with slow grace, a slight smudge of white against the steep staircase, flanked by her two dull-robed escorts. Beneath her, on the plain around the ziggurat, the people watched her ascent. All of them were staring in silent awe, in raptures at the sight of such cleanliness – such whiteness! – and the distant priestly chant, which echoed among the crowds. Was I ever so dirty, she wondered, before they took me? She could feel the soft brush of her hair against her bare back – was it ever as dull and matted as that of the people below her? Her dress hung by a gold thread at her left shoulder, falling sharply to expose the rounded side of her right breast, the undulating curve of her waist and hip. The hollow of her back disappeared beneath its folds just above her bottom, and the ornate hem trailed on the stone behind her. She reached the top, where the broad stone of the uppermost tier stretched around all four sides of the square squat temple. The dying midsummer sun scorched the red brick, turning it florid. The shadows' edges were just beginning to blur.

For the first time, she stepped through the temple doors. Within the hall stood a ring of naked priests, their hands clasped in front of them, their eyes wide and reverential. She flinched, and stopped. The sharp fingers of the priestesses escorting her grasped her bare arms. The priests' lips were parted, but the sound didn't seem to come from them. It reverberated around the columns and played down her spine. The hands were digging harder into her flesh, but she could not bring herself to take a single step forwards. Then she saw Corin. Shaking, she stepped forwards again. She would not let him see her weak.

Long before the temple, before the baths and fine clothes, before she was a precious guarded jewel, it had been her and Corin. Corin had taught her to fish in the Indigna, waiting as still as a tree without casting a shadow on to the water, until the silver flickered and the spear flew. Corin had taught her to swim in the canals and shown her where to find the best figs. When she had run crying from one of her father's beating, Corin had known where to find her.

He climbed over the rocks, athletic and powerful already at fifteen, and crawled on his belly down the narrow tunnel. Soon his shoulders would be too broad, but then he could just slither his body along. In the cavern at the centre, in the shaft of light from far above, he found her crying and rubbing her arms. He said nothing, at first – just put his arms and legs around her and pulled her to his chest. When her shaking stopped, he nudged her matted hair aside with his chin and whispered into her ear. 'If you were my wife, I would never beat you.'

'Let me be your wife now, Corin!'

'Mina . . . Mina . . . It's not possible.'

'I'm fifteen,' she said angrily. 'Essuru's fifteen, and she's married *and* pregnant!'

'Shh . . .' he whispered, rocking her. 'It's not that. I'm going to Uruk. I'm going to be a priest.'

She wiggled around to stare at him. His face was lit with a distant dream, staring beyond her, through the rocks of their secret place, into a luminous world.

'No,' she whimpered, her eyes filling with tears again. 'Please don't.'

'The gods have spoken to me,' he murmured.

'Well, they didn't ask *me*,' she snapped waspishly. She was going to marry him, leave her horrible father's hut and spend all day in his company. She was just starting to realise how sweet it might be to spend all night with him, too.

He chuckled, and fluffed her hair as if she were a toddler. 'And you wonder why your father complains of your sharp tongue.'

She pulled out of his grasp. 'So what am I to the gods? Nothing? Must I just stay and be beaten and ... and ... never see you again?' Anger and tears fought for her voice.

'Don't question the will of the gods,' he said warningly.

'I will if they steal you!' she yelled back. 'I will if they steal everything I want in my life, and they have the whole world to choose from, and I only have you – if that's how they are, I hate them!'

She didn't hate them, however. She knew nothing about them – their names only crossed her father's lips when he swore. Why hate what you don't know? Corin, on the other hand, was right in front of her.

For the rest of the summer, she refused to speak to him. On his last day before the priests came, he tracked her down in the stubbled barley field, his face stained with tears.

'Mina, my darling, my heart's sister ...'

She turned her face away. It had hardened and thinned in the past few months. Her breasts had abruptly begun to swell, and pressed out against her blouse. 'Your sister is not what I wanted to be,' she said coldly.

'I will petition the gods for you – I will make sacrifices – everything you want will be yours, wealth, peace, pleasure.' His hands were on her knees as he crouched before her. She twisted further, hiding her misery. His palms pulsed with heat; his fingers lay lightly on her thighs.

'You won't sacrifice for the one thing I want, so why should your gods be any different?' Her words emerged clipped and scornful.

'Is this my Mina, so hard hearted?'

At that she whirled around and leapt up. 'No!' she screamed. Her face shone with Kalimâth's fury. 'I'm *not* your Mina, and *I'm* not hard hearted!' She pelted across the ground before he could see her break, and up the hillside, as fleet-footed as a goat. He could no longer fit his shoulders into the tunnel and her heart ached, wishing he could. She sat at the centre, rocking and crying silently, listening to him call her name.

The next time he saw her was three years later, lining the road with the group of girls watching the priests' procession. She stood a head taller than those around her, her face was thinner still and hard as flint. Even the swollen purple bruise under her eye couldn't spoil her beauty. That evening the chief priest approached her father.

'Vouch for her?' sneered her father. 'That bloody cat wouldn't even look at a man, no one's good enough for *her*. Stares them down and spits words like arrows. She's chaste, all right. Who'd bed a cold thorn like that? Can't even *give* her away.'

'Then perhaps,' said the priest delicately, 'this will be sufficient?' He lifted a few coins from the bag on his belt.

'Cut-price goods for the gods?' broke in Mina. She appeared from the shadows like a graceful column, towering over her squat father. 'They must have fallen on hard times.'

'If you come with us,' the priest answered, dumping

the rest of the bag on to the table, 'you will be subject to a vow of silence for some months.'

'Fine.' She shrugged disdainfully. 'Get me out of this hellhole and I'll go one better – I'll hold my tongue till the gods themselves speak to me.'

'The gods will accept your vow.'

With that, she closed her lips.

Not speaking was better, she learnt. The priests didn't seem to beat people, but even so, it was safer. Her silence wrapped a secret world around her, to which she could retreat. Her bruises were healing, the clothes were soft and the food was regular. She tasted dates for the first time, their rich, pulpy flesh filling her mouth. She drank creamy milk as often as she wanted. She ate millet buns, dripping in sesame seed oil which ran over her lips and down her chin, and gulped grape wine. The two old priestesses who guarded her laughed at her greed. Her face and figure softened a little. From gaunt and lovely, she became slender and breathtaking. She rarely saw Corin – she was kept mostly in her quarters with her guardians, and in their private courtyard. She was the priceless gem, reserved for the gods. She was protected.

Best of all was the baths. The warm spring bubbled out of the cave into daylight and shallow froth, but far within the winding tunnel it lay deep, dark and hot. The first time they took her there, she shook with memories of her and Corin's secret place. This was no sandy crevice, though. Brackets on the walls held brilliant orange torches, which shimmered across the water's surface and reflected off the intricate mosaics around the edge. She eased into the voluptuous warmth, lay back against a submerged ledge and surrendered herself to it. They gave her handfuls of lye to scrub her skin and years of dirt melted away. She was addicted to the spring. In the half-dark, she could watch her golden flesh float, ripe and glowing. The heat held her and penetrated her as she had once longed for Corin to do. Almost every day, she walked up the path towards the cave and the priestesses, sighing, followed her. After all, the plaything of the gods was allowed to indulge. When they objected, she turned her peaceful, silent face to them and smiled remotely. Let them think the gods were leading her. The truth was, her health was returning, her body was coursing like any young woman's, and in that luscious water her dreams could run riot in her head. The truth was, she wanted to be naked.

While the two old women sat with their backs to the pool, talking softly, her mind drifted to the priests. She saw them from the windows, sometimes, walking slowly, looking as sober and peaceful as eunuchs, but after the lunar eclipse she changed her mind.

The priestesses veiled her and took her by moonlight to the temple steps, where all the priests had gathered. They stood with their heads flung back, their faces wild and eager. As she swayed behind her escorts, she felt their eyes sliding over her hips and round the curve of her breasts, and her spine straightened. The tips of her breasts tingled strangely. Despite herself, her eyes flickered behind the gauze, looking for Corin. He was staring straight at her, his mouth parted and his eyes soft. Her blood rising in her face, she was glad of the veil. She stood in the centre of the stone flags and turned to watch the full moon. The priests were chanting their haunting notes, their deep voices shuddering through her bones. From behind her, within the temple, came a stream of pure high sound. A river of women parted around her, their skirts hanging low on their hips, their waists curving deeply in, their breasts exposed. The music floated from their lips as they swayed past and ranged themselves across the front of the temple.

Silence fell. Darkness began to eat away at the moon.

So quietly that she could not say when it began, the song started again. One voice slid over the other, one note overlaid another. As the shadows on their faces deepened, their song grew wilder and more demanding. Spread across the wide tier, the robes of the priests were falling to their feet. She gaped at their muscular backs and exposed buttocks. They were whirling around, they were beginning to dance, and she swayed against the old women. The men slammed their feet into the ground and flailed their arms, as if begging the singing women. They caught each other's arms by the crook of their elbows and slung each other across their backs, then on to the ground again. They stormed forwards and retreated.

As the dance's ferocity grew, so did their fleshy staffs – but they were hardly visible now, the moon was almost stripped from the sky. When its blackness was complete, only a thin ring of silver to show where it had ever been, the priests fell as one to their knees before the temple. The priestesses took her arms, and led her through them, down the stepped ramp. Her nostrils flared with the smell of their fresh sweat and the lips between her legs slithered and clenched. She glanced behind her, where the naked priests were storming through the doors – but the old women took her away, back to her rooms, where she lay sleepless and watched the moon grow back.

Now, when she glimpsed one of the priests, she imagined the powerful bare skin beneath his skirts. In the hot springs, she relived those naked bodies. Her imaginings varied with the moon. Around the new moon, before and while she bled, her body longed for violence. She imagined bulky muscles pinning her down and stubble scratching her breasts or lean strength gripping her and sharp teeth nipping at her neck. In the happy calm of the waxing moon, she daydreamed that one of them, someone gentle and only a little older than her, crept into her room at night and woke her with kisses. She painted the details patiently – her surprise, his soft lips, the slow travel of his mouth down her neck towards her waiting breasts . . . her shift, lifted over her shoulders, and his breathstruck wonder . . . She knew, theoretically, what the outcome should be. She'd heard the grunting at night, when her mother was still alive. She'd seen the shadows of the men's tools in the fading moonlight. She knew, from animals, that, when they looked like that, they were ready. But her body knew nothing, and her fantasies fizzled into confusing thoughts of skin and bodies and something that would make the ache between her legs better.

At full moon, her nipples stood like pebbles and she wanted them all. In her mind, the naked dancing men advanced towards her and ripped her veil and silky gown away. They rubbed their thigh muscles against her, and passed her between their strong arms. She was queen of them all, stroking their jutting flesh and yielding to their hands. She granted their wishes with her lips and let them suck benediction from her breasts. And then – and then . . .? She knew enough to think of them pushing that part into her, but didn't know enough to imagine how that might be. All this beauty, she thought forlornly, admiring her nakedness in the water, wasted. She wondered constantly what they wanted her for. She'd assumed they wanted her to be a priestess, but the chief priest called her Bride of An, they pampered her, and she was given no duties. She was also given little instruction. They seemed to assume she knew much more than she did about religion, but she'd learnt nothing. Pride stilled her tongue and her face. She'd made her vow and she'd keep it.

When the cold winter winds came, the old priestesses muttered more loudly about her trips to the spring. They hated leaving the shelter of their rooms. She ignored it, kept her face impassive and walked anyway. Somehow she knew they wouldn't physically drag her back and had to follow. One evening in early spring, the rain was lashing down and her body raged back and forth with the storm. She stalked from room to room until she couldn't bear it any more and lifted her woollen cloak with an imperious glance at the priestesses.

'Gods, isn't this enough water for her?' grumbled one. Half a year into her silence, they seemed to have forgotten she could still hear. 'I'm not dragging my bones out into that; she can just sit back down again.'

'Oh, let her go,' said the other. 'They're all up at Innana's Temple anyway. She'll be safe enough.'

The other hesitated, and shrugged. 'Go,' she said loudly to Mina, miming with her hands. 'We stay here. You go. If you want.'

Mina nodded, and left.

Alone in the cavern, she hung her single torch on its bracket and undressed slowly. Her hands ran lightly over her breasts, relishing their new weight. As her fingers brushed her nipples, she shuddered. The water lapped at her skin as she slipped in, sending new shivers through her. Already, the fantasy was unspooling in her head and it was men's admiring hands, not water, caressing her. She played gently with the slopes of her breasts, feeling how the tremors rushed and receded with each stroke. Each time, her hand drifted a little further and the newly awakened skin came alive. Then the skin just beyond that would tingle agonisingly, begging to be touched, and she would return her fingertips to her collarbone and stroke slowly down again, just a bit further. Without those two old witches here, she could do what she liked. Her head fell back, and lifted again to watch her little buds clench. One elbow supported her against the ledge while her body floated to the surface. Her fingers reached her nipples and she lurched with excitement. Her eyes closed as her hand began to trail down her belly. Her body was telling her what to do, where to touch next, how to tantalise the fleshy inside of her thighs and the little valleys where her mons met her thighs. Her palm skimmed her floating downy hair. She could feel how her lips pulsed and yearned to be parted, and let a finger nestle closer in. The shock of pleasure made her whimper. She heard it echoed, and her eyes sprang open. There, by the side of the pool, stood Corin. Swiftly, she curled into a ball, hiding herself. Her eyes shone with anger.

'I'm sorry,' he said, 'I didn't mean to spy.'

She raised one eyebrow, sardonically.

'I know.' He hung his head for a moment. 'But I couldn't bear it any more. I slipped away from the temple to find you. I had to know if you forgave me now – now that the gods have answered my prayers.'

All her old fury, lulled by comfort and lust, returned. She turned her back.

'Mina, *please*. Look at where you are – what you have. How could I have condemned you to life in a clay hut, scrabbling in the earth for crops? *That* would have been our life together. The gods *told* me this was better. I trusted them, they gave you everything I asked for . . . Isn't this better? My love?' His voice was breaking. She turned around and looked into his tear-filled eyes. She spat in the water, and swung back.

You may think food and hot water is all there is to life, she thought angrily as his footsteps receded, but I'm kept from the one thing I wanted. To know you sliding into me. To learn what my body's howling for, with you. I'd rather have lived in a cowshed with you than the finest palace alone.

The thought was grand and elegant. She repeated it to herself several times, trying to shake the feeling that it might not be entirely true. She slept on down, not hard-packed dirt. She wore flowing silk, not rough cotton stained with dirt. She wallowed every day in the hot water of the spring. Her hands were soft and her skin glowed with good health. The walls around her at night were clay, not reeds, keeping out the howling winds of winter and the baking sun of summer. And yet, for all the comfort her body was kept in, its most vital purpose was denied. She wanted to scream into the echoing chamber, *What do you want from me?* Silent till the gods speak to me, she reflected bitterly. Silent and unused to the grave.

The spring tormented her. Fresh breeze and new sun played with her hair, tickling it softly across her shoulders and back. The trees in the courtyard budded, their sap flowing and erupting in blossoms. The birds leapt on to each other among the branches, and insects spiralled through the air conjoined. Will I stay here, she wondered, feeling my veins thrum, until old age withers them like these two? Is that what the so-called gods they all worship want? She longed to speak again, to demand answers from the old women. Anger and stubbornness wrestled in constant argument in her head. She could surely escape – they'd be no match for her – but then, where would she go and what would she eat? Late summer would be a better time to leave, when the fruit was ripe and the barley was gold. Forgetting for a moment that she hated him, she wondered if Corin would help her. An unbidden fantasy wove itself swiftly, of running through the land together, stealing food, sleeping in fields and opening herself to him under the stars. Covered with old sweat, she reminded herself curtly, and rocks digging into my back.

Summer was beginning, and the old women seemed to remember her presence. For hours, they combed her hair and oiled her skin. They no longer left her alone to drift in the water, but rubbed stones over her and scrubbed her hair. More lengths of cloth arrived, shimmering and transparent, which they measured against her and sewed with tiny stitches. Around the hem, they embroidered hundreds of silver stars. On the evening they finally draped it over her, her body shone through like gold in the setting sun. They laid a veil against her face, looping it over her ears, clasped copper bracelets around her wrists and ankles, and fastened a necklace of gold and lapis-lazuli triangles around her neck. Outside, a chariot was waiting, festooned with ribbons and harnessed to a donkey.

She turned her head sharply to them.

Where am I going? What's happening? No words came out – it was a year since she had spoken, and the habit was lost. She was suddenly terrified. I vowed to non-existent gods, she told herself, I *will* speak.

Where am I going? Her mouth opened, but her lips couldn't even form the words. Her eyes were wide with horror.

One of the old women smiled gently, and stroked her cheek through the veil. 'Have no fear, my dear,' she said. 'Innana will protect you as surely as she has honoured your vow of silence.'

As the horses trotted slowly through the late slanting sunlight to the temple, Mina's mind danced desperately. I can't speak, I can't speak. Innana, have you taken my voice? If you have, if you're real, keep me safe!

At the bottom of the temple's soaring sides, they gestured for her to dismount. The slopes were covered in crowds, all of them staring. The priestesses began to escort her up the steps. The swollen red sun was setting.

She stepped into the temple, and heard its doors swing shut behind her. On the far side, beyond the ring of naked priests, she could see a vast statue of a naked woman, her hands upraised, bird wings emerging behind her. At the centre was a low stone dais, draped with heavy fabric. The air was cloudy with sandalwood and cloves, stirring her blood. The chanting grew louder, and the silvery song of the women crept over it. They emerged in two graceful lines from behind the statue, their breasts bare and their skirts tied beneath their bellies. Sinuously, they wove between the priests, hips shifting easily from side to side, until they reached Mina's side. The men's eyes never strayed from her. The first woman to reach her lifted the necklace, laid it on the floor and edged her forwards a step. The next removed her veil, and put it behind her. Her four copper bracelets followed, one at a time. The six items stood in a row behind her. She was almost at the dais now. The men's song ceased. The piercing sweetness of the women's voices lingered in the air, and fell away. She felt the soft hands of the women untie the gold thread at her shoulder and the silky fabric cascaded down her body. Low, hushed gasps echoed around the circle. She stood completely naked, feeling their eyes devour her. They began to sing again, words emerging, repeating – 'Welcome, bride of An, welcome, emissary of Innana,' over and over again. The women took her hands, and led her to the dais. One held a cup to her lips. The liquid was bitter, twisting her lips, but it was kept in front of her until she drained it down. They laid her back against the fabric. Around her, the two circles of men and women began to move in opposite directions, dizzying her, as they sang faster and faster, their feet twirling. The drink fogged her thoughts and exaggerated the ribbons of song.

'Stop!' cried a woman, and both voices and feet halted abruptly. 'Let Innana's chosen one step forward.'

One of the priests stepped forward from directly beneath the statue. It was Corin.

Low humming filled the hall as he paced towards the dais. The circle of women slipped through the ring of men, standing outside. Her throat contracted. His muscles gleamed. All his body was packed and hard, and his shaft stood upright. So now I find out, she thought, weak with fear. He knelt by the platform, pressed his forehead to it and looked into her wide eyes. She saw the same tender compassion on his face that she'd seen each time since that awful day in the cavern four years ago, but this time a smirk of triumph played on his lips.

'What have they told you?' he whispered beneath the hum.

She shook her head, wordless.

'Don't be afraid,' he murmured. 'Innana is with you – and so am I.' He leant over and brushed her lips. Her body spasmed with the brief contact and he smiled. 'You will have what you want, my love, everything you want, but not till dawn. Until then, I will show you just what wanting can be.'

He ran one finger over her collarbone lightly. She groaned, sinking back. The light flickering sensations she had given herself were intensified tenfold under his hands. His hands trickled over the same paths she had discovered, but even slower than she had forced herself to be. Each hair's breadth of skin he conquered sent fluttering wings of feeling across her. Back and forth he went, making her untouched nipples stand like tents. The deep humming seemed to keep pace with his movements, guiding him or him guiding them. She opened her eyes again, imploring. He was smiling lazily down at her. All around her, the priests were watching his hand tantalise her and how her breath came faster through her parted lips. When his knuckles brushed her nipple, she gave a tiny scream.

'Oh yes,' he sighed hoarsely. 'Forgive me, Innana.'

He bent and flicked his tongue across it. She screamed louder. He closed his eyes, fighting for control. Her breath wavered. She felt his tongue on her ankles, his hands sliding up her calves as his mouth followed. Her head tilted further back, succumbing to the surges of lust. The wildest of her fantasies had never made her feel like this. She looked straight into the eyes of the priests behind her, in the circle, and saw how they glowed with ardour. Corin was on his knees by the dais, licking up her side and around the curve of her breast. She lifted her arms above her head, stretching her sides luxuriously. A sly smile crept on to her face as she watched their reaction, their eyes darting from her swollen breasts to her face. Then Corin's tongue slid into her armpit and her body bucked. He pressed his face against her sweet-smelling skin, sucking fervently while she shook. For hours, it seemed, he kissed and lapped at her, turning parts of her she'd never imagined could be sensitive into trembling fires. Beyond that one brief brush and lick, he didn't touch her nipples. Nor did he lay hand or mouth on her cleft, where her longing was turning to agonising pain. She writhed in a dream of sensation, her body dancing a highwire of desire. She floated on the humming voices, feeling the ring of lust around her growing. She could smell the delicious glow on their skin and it melted the core of her. She was rocking her hips rhythmically, in time to their song. It seemed she was both feeling their gaze and at the same time she was the hungry eyes seeing her pleasure, wanting to be the one giving it, the one to fulfil it.

Innana, she cried out in her head, let him touch me *there*.

Through the roar of passion in her ears, she heard a rushing wind, saying, *Yes*, as if all the men were sighing their assent in unison. Corin's hands were tracing her thighs, parting them slowly. She let them spread, pushed ever wider until her calves hung on either side of the dais. The air teased her wet lips and she pushed her hips upwards, opening up even more. Look at me, she thought, think of that, imagine it's you I'll yield to. Somehow, she was giving herself up to all of them through the beautiful man touching her – they were all An, sharing His pleasure. He'd found the taut skin inside her thighs, the backs of his fingers stroking the swell of her mons. She looked at him through blurred eyes, and saw his head dip slowly towards her. His tongue touched her small swollen, twingeing bead, and she wailed. Her body seized up with bliss as he began to suck and nibble at her, his fingertips prying at her entrance.

'Yes,' she howled, 'please, Innana, yes!' She heaved against his mouth, crying incoherently, as his fingers began to push into that sweet slippery tunnel. She was clasped tightly around him, slick as oil and barely yielding. His hand dug harder in, wrestling for space, sliding back and forth faster and fiercer. Her head rolled from side to side, only half-seeing the avid witnesses in the dim grey light. She was riding the crests of the sea, skirting the edge of an abyss, falling down a tunnel towards a golden light ... But every time she thought the light must surely burst over her, turning all her body white hot, his hand edged out and stilled. She sobbed, begged, railed at him, but he only looked at her with hunger, his chest heaving, and shook his head. When he pulled his hand right out of her, tears ran down the sides of her face from the corner of her eyes.

'Too cruel, too cruel,' she whimpered.

'I hope not,' he answered, his voice strained.

She stared up at him. He was hovering above her, supported on one hand, his knees between her open thighs, guiding his tool. Its blunt head nudged her opening, parting her outer lips. On the far wall, behind him, the pale gold of sunrise painted Innana's face. His staff was sliding against her, struggling to gain entrance. It felt smooth and huge, impossible to accommodate, and every prod made her cry out. At last, a fierce shove lodged him inside, and her legs shot into the air.

'At last,' she was wailing.

He was struggling to control himself, longing to force the rest of him inside her. Just the tip was held, constricted in her welcome, and he pushed harder. Her words were incoherent, babbling yes and no – but there was no more choice. She had to have him now. She yelped in shock, as still more of his rod fought its way in. She was being torn in two, split as an axe splits wood. She realised dimly that the singing had stopped, replaced by ragged gasps as eager for ecstasy as she was. Corin's arm cradled her head, the other seized her waist.

'I must, now,' he ground out.

Holding her tightly, he heaved his full length into her too-narrow space. She screamed long and loud, glorying in the pain and the feeling of being stuffed full of him, beyond bearing. He thrust repeatedly, feeling the warmth of her wrap round him again and again, each time forcing her tight walls to part for him. She could see nothing, drowned in the ecstatic agony. It seemed they were all impaling her as Corin's spear dived in and out, she could hear their moans alongside her shrieks and his rising roar. The brilliant light crashed over her, running through her veins, turning her into a burning sun, and still he kept stabbing into her. Each time his body crashed into hers, her ecstasy came again. He hurled himself ever faster on to her, yelling his yes to her joy, and, with a final lion's roar, flung her through the light into the absolute darkness of sheer feeling.

When she came to, the priests were on their knees around them, patches of the flagstones glistening with their spurted pleasure. Corin's eyes were dilated with love, his shaft still fat inside her, their bodies glued together with sweat. He parted her lips with his tongue and kissed her deeply.

'Corin,' she whispered.

'Now you've also heard the voice of the gods. Welcome to Innana's Temple, my sweet.'

Olivia Knight is the author of the paranormal erotic romance novel *The Ten Visions*, published by Black Lace in July 2007.

Public Domain Portia Da Costa

Breathing deeply, I pause before the door to the Entertainment Chamber. Efficient as ever Cicero steps forwards to open it for me. Not for the first time, I admire the sight of his deliciously taut buttocks, and the way they roll and tense enticingly beneath the skintight leather of his trousers as he moves. My fingers itch to reach out and give his firm flesh a squeeze, or even a pinch, but I distract myself by flicking out my fan.

Propelled by his strong arm, the door swings smoothly open, and as he steps back to let me pass, I swear he winks at me. A second later, his face is a picture of innocence.

Oh, but my Cicero is a prime specimen!

My tall dark companion is the perfect body servant. He has the face of an angel, he keeps himself in supreme condition and he knows what I want before I know it myself. Hiding a smile, I congratulate myself for having selected him. It helps, of course, when one's mother is the Matriarch of all the Islands, and one always gets first pick of the annual crop up from the farms.

My heavy figured satin skirts swish around my thighs and bottom as I sweep into the room, and I imagine Cicero, behind me, dreaming of what's beneath them. He's as familiar with my nether regions as he is with his own, even if it's not really his place to lust after them without my permission. His daily duties include washing every part of me, anointing my body with oils and perfumes and then dressing me from the skin outwards. And as he's a man, my sex must be ever in his thoughts even if tradition decrees it's not supposed to be . . .

The Entertainment Room appears small and intimate, the walls hung with rich tapestries, the lighting warm, the air perfumed with aphrodisiac spices. On the ceiling there's a painted fresco of muscular males toiling naked in a field, their sweating flesh so realistic that one can almost feel the heat of it. Several of my fellow mistresses are already here, lounging on their couches, their body servants just inches away and, as ever, I wonder just who it was who originally decreed that entertainments like this are to be part of public domain. I've asked my mother more than once, and she says she doesn't know either. But it's tradition, and the Matriarchy is big on tradition.

Cicero helps me on to my velvet-upholstered couch, and then decorously arranges my many-layered skirts across my knees and ankles. I say decorously, but in the process he manages to touch me several times, his fingers hot but gentle on my bare skin. With each contact a surge of delicious power arrows upwards and sets a light between my thighs.

Carefully schooling my rising excitement, I affect the same mask of boredom and ennui as the other mistresses. And that's another thing. When did it become the fashion, then the custom, to find coupling with a strong and well-set-up male tedious? I know it's a tradition, but to me it seems a delightful one. Is there something wrong with me that I still look forward to a tumble?

But just look at them . . .

Mistress Layla and her Liam.

Mistress Tanya and her Timon.

Mistress Rosa and her Ryan.

They all look weary and as if they were being seriously inconvenienced. Anyone would think this was a council meeting about the trading figures for meat or metals or wheat, and yet for me the sexual tension makes my loins tingle. As I attempt to settle myself more comfortably, Cicero readjusts my skirts. Other mistresses continue to file in and take their places, and all the while he's caressing my skin with slow light touches.

The last of our number to arrive is Mistress Jenna and her body servant James and, leaning towards him, I sigh for Cicero's ears only. He makes a show of fussing with my hem and gives my calf a delicate squeeze of reassurance.

Hopefully their performance today will be better than usual. I don't hold out much hope, but perhaps we'll all be pleasantly surprised by some original thinking.

Jenna is beautiful, tall and blonde and willowy, imperiously dramatic in a royal-blue gown – but of all of us she has the least enthusiasm for these proceedings. Her James has an excellent body and very fine genitalia, but I always feel that his mistress never really shows him off to his best advantage. Their performances lack 'spark' and originality somehow, even though the sight of any kind of sexual congress always stirs me.

'Good evening, Cerise, how are you?' Jenna's voice is brittle as she catches my eye. Have I revealed my low opinion of her in my expression? Or perhaps she detects my wish that either she, or someone else, would show some daring?

'I'm very well, thank you, my friend,' I reply, giving her a bright smile, 'and looking forward to your pleasure. James is looking in particularly fine fettle today.'

'Which he is, as ever.' Her tone is curt and defensive and she gives me a narrow look, her eyes flicking enviously to Cicero at my side. My man is the acknowledged prize amongst the body servants in our assembly. 'Your Cicero is looking well too. Has he put on a little weight?'

Aha, trying to belittle my beloved stallion!

'Why, yes indeed he has. He's been following a new exercise routine, a most rigorous one. Designed to increase muscle mass and stamina.'

She makes a harrumphing noise. Score a point to me.

'Attend me,' she snaps to James, who hurries forwards.

He removes his clothes, which naturally aren't many. First he kicks off his boots, and then he unbuckles his trousers. A second later, he's stepping out of them, nude, but for his collar of servitude.

His penis rears up eagerly, ready to perform, and I eye it critically, ever the connoisseur.

He's big, but not as big as my Cicero. Not one of the body servants around this circle possesses either his length or his girth. But that doesn't prevent me appreciating the charms of other males. Especially when that male takes his meat in his fist and begins to work it to a sturdier, stiffer erection with considerable enthusiasm. Perhaps we're going to see something special after all?

'Hurry up! Don't take all day!' instructs Jenna, leaning back on her couch, making no effort to hide the fact that she wants this to be over quickly. What a spoilsport! Me, I'd much rather see an extended performance. Something that's wild and energetic and sweaty. Something that's intricate, luscious and unusual. For a moment, I take my eyes from the couple before me and glance at the real man who's standing so close to me that his leather-clad thigh is actually pressed tight against my bare ankle where my gown has slid aside. He's dutifully staring at his polished boot toes as decorum decrees, but as if he's sensed my scrutiny, he turns, ever so slightly, and catches my eye.

There's the faintest superior smile upon his sculpted lips.

You devil! I think.

The rules of our society say that it's not his place to judge a mistress or even her servant, but Cicero is ever the uncommon one, and not just in the physical perfection of his body. Only he and I know how much he breaks the mould.

His erection brought to full stand, James reaches reverently for his lady's gown and folds it neatly out of the way. Beneath it, her loins are clad in an elaborate undergarment of ruched lace and silk and Jenna tuts and sighs, rolling her eyes in exasperation as her man removes it. His movements are deft enough, but she finds fault all the same. When her underwear is removed and set aside, she appears, to my eyes, completely unaroused – despite the presence of a fully erect male member barely inches away from her niche.

Indolently, Jenna nods, and James moves obediently to help her into position – adjusting her hips, parting her thighs and then slipping his hand between them.

He rubs. He fondles. He fiddles. And yet still she seems disinterested.

'Use the lotion,' she instructs, sighing again and taking a long swig from the glass of wine at her side.

I glance again at Cicero, and there's still that little smirk playing around his generous red lips. He never has to use the lotion on me.

'May I pour you some wine, mistress?' he asks softly, as a distractionary tactic. It wouldn't do for my fellow mistresses to get wind of his secret insubordination.

Or would it?

A tantalising idea forms in my mind. Something so outrageous that it whips through my imagination like a forest fire, so vivid that I fancy Cicero himself might be able to see it. As he pours a measure of ruby wine into my goblet and hands it to me, his great head cocks on one side a little, and his brown eyes twinkle. Out of sight of the other mistresses, an expression of pure devilment and wonder flashes across his handsome features.

Do we dare, he seems to say, and in answer I nod.

The wine suddenly tastes twice as sweet as I sip and scheme.

Meanwhile back at Jenna and James, the blond man is coating his fingers with the rich scented herb-laden lotion, preparing to anoint her diffident flesh with it. Huffing and puffing, she hitches her bottom along the couch, every action exhibiting impatience and boredom.

Oh, poor Jenna, I think suddenly, feeling pity.

To give James credit, he applies himself with unstinting diligence. Gently massaging, circling, flicking. Jenna's lips tighten as if she's actually resisting the sensations he's seeking to induce, but I can barely keep my pelvis still, imagining I'm being fondled in her place.

I lounge back further on my couch, tweaking and fluffing at my skirts as a cover for the fact that I'm pressing my calf against Cicero's magnificent leather-clad haunches. Through narrowed eyes, I study his hands, clasped loosely behind his back, and imagine those fabulous fingers playing my sex.

He's a virtuoso with those divine digits of his, instinctively seeking out the most responsive and fugitive of sensitivity zones. Pressure. Speed. Angle. He employs subtle variations of all, divinely orchestrated. Even while James perseveres with his unresponsive mistress, my own sex quickens and trembles, just at the thought of the same caress at Cicero's hand.

I glance around at the other mistresses. A little interest is beginning to stir in some of them, I can tell. Which makes me wonder whether I'm quite so different after all? Who knows what goes in the secret privacy of all their residences?

Perhaps Jenna is the only one of us who finds coupling a bore?

And even she is beginning to stir now, thanks to the industrious James. Her narrow hips are shifting now, hitching to and fro on her couch.

'Mount me, you fool!' she cries suddenly. 'I'm ready now!'

So am I, I murmur in silence, aiming my words at the back of Cicero's strong, dark head.

James obeys. And we all gasp when he takes her firmly by the hips and pulls her into position. Precious little deference now, and only the most cursory mumbled words to ask permission. He almost shoves her on to his penis, and thrusts in hard.

Well done, lad! I want to shout. Well done!

Jenna's eyes fly wide open, staring, but for once she doesn't protest.

As James thrusts, and his pale buttocks clench and tense, all eyes around the circle are on those flexing muscles. I bite my lips as Cicero secretly takes advantage. His warm hand is higher on my leg now, under cover of my many layers of flounced and silken skirts. The tips of his fingers are fire against my skin.

As James labours on, and Jenna slowly and almost painfully rises to meet him, my own sex gathers and moistens, excitement fizzing. I press myself against the slow, hot pressure of Cicero's fingertips, surreptitiously adjusting my position to coax him further.

If only it was our turn. If only we could flee the Chamber, be alone . . . and be ourselves.

Eventually a high, clear and strangely abandoned cry signals Jenna's crisis and, despite my excitement, I feel a sense of relief for James. He has despatched his duties, and is now free to relax and take his own pleasure. Jenna kicks him away from her, and he retreats, his moist and reddened member swinging before him. He snatches a cloth from the adjoining console, retreats behind the couch and ejaculates into it.

Cicero catches my eye. His broad handsome face is troubled, and I understand how he feels for his fellow servant's lack of dignity.

That will never happen to you, I tell him without

speaking. I will never demean you that way, no matter what the others think or whatever rules and tradition decree. Anything that happens to you will be your choice. I don't know how, but I know he hears my silent pledge.

If Jenna were not so arrogant, I would say she looked shamefaced now, and she snaps and fusses as James attends to her, cleaning her crotch and straightening her clothing. She glances around, looking for someone else to begin a coupling and take the limelight.

I smile at Cicero, and he smiles back.

Let's play, he seems to say. Let's really show them.

With great deliberation, he nudges my elbow and what's left of my wine spills on my dress.

'Oh, Cicero, what have you done?' I cry. 'It's not like you to be so careless or so clumsy.'

'Forgive me, mistress,' he murmurs, falling to his knees, his dark head bent as he takes one of the cloths on our console to blot my clothing.

In a show of fussing worthy of Jenna herself, I primp and prink at my gown, tutting over the damp fabric. 'This is one of my favourite gowns, Cicero,' I say, mock stern. Well, at least he and I know the sternness is feigned. The others around the circle don't seem to see anything amiss, other than a mistress who has been let down by her man.

'I'm sorry, mistress,' he intones solemnly, head still bent. I wonder if the rest of the mistresses can detect the minute shaking of his shoulders which indicates that he's fighting to suppress his laughter. 'Please let me atone for my clumsiness. Please punish me, if it pleases you. I am at your disposal.'

A gasp goes up around the circle. Nobody admits to corporal punishment, but there are always whispers. Whispers of spankings and beatings – and the dark pleasure that overtakes the mistresses who inflict them.

'I think I may have to take you in hand, Cicero. You've

been lax in your attentions, and you've displeased me,' I lie. This man has never ever disappointed or displeased me. I doubt if he could let me down if he tried.

'If it is your will, mistress,' he murmurs, bowing lower, pressing his noble brow against the carpet.

'It is my will,' I reply. 'Get up. Strip off your clothes. And give me your belt.'

Light and elegant, despite his great height and his massive muscles, Cicero rises. Within moments, he's naked ... and so magnificent it makes my heart ache. His body looks as if it's cast from bronze and polished with silk; the plains of his chest and belly are ridged with sculpted muscle. His penis, though not erect yet, is a heavy swelling promise. Lowering his head reverently again, he hands me his thick leather belt.

My hands shake, though I try not to show it. I suspect I'm not the only mistress in this circle who gets pleasure from games like these, but I know I'm probably the only one who'll ever reveal it.

Without a word from me, Cicero bends over, presenting his perfect buttocks for my perusal, and his punishment.

'Do you presume to anticipate me, Cicero?' I ask imperiously, letting the leather swing and swish, flicking it against the back of his thighs.

'Forgive me, mistress,' he answers gravely, and begins to straighten.

I flick him again, and command him, 'Stay where you are.'

He resumes his pose, maintains it immaculately and with dignity.

I strike him. Hard. And accurately. This is far from the first time I've done this.

My beautiful servant makes not a sound, and across his backside appears a crimson stripe. I step back, stare around, and discover eyes, hot and avid, locked upon the mark.

I strike again, struggling with my control, but not showing it. Between my legs my sex glows – just like Cicero's arse. I feel an almost overwhelming compulsion to throw up my skirts, crush my sex against his pain and massage it.

What would my fellow mistresses think to that? I wonder. In fact what indeed do they think of this performance in itself? I know it's impossible, but I can almost seem to taste their fascinated revulsion in the air. The same sense of horror, but also hot, erotic wonder that I experienced the first time I accidentally happened upon this game.

Cicero remains motionless, twin stripes of crimson shimmering across his perfect flesh. Those broad red lines seem to twist and tighten around the very core of my pleasure and embrace it in a fierce and dark caress.

I swing the belt again and it cracks in the air before crashing down on Cicero. He barely flinches but he lets his breath out harshly. He will never cry out, but he's not immune to the glowing agony.

And I'm not immune to the power of his stoicism. Beneath my gown, my sex swims with silken honey.

I continue. We continue. The mistresses continue to gasp, following every stroke.

At last, though, my beloved servant's bottom is one mass of simmering line-blotched red, and I can see tension and emotion quivering in every line of his bowed yet majestic body.

'You may stand,' I instruct him coolly, even though my heart is as wild and flaming as his flesh.

He straightens, still regal despite his ordeal. His broad back is taut, strong and resilient. His noble head is still bowed as he stands tall, facing the couch, and his arms hang at his sides, the light clench of his hands the only sign of his internal struggles.

'Turn now,' I command, unable to prevent myself

from licking my lips in anticipation. Slowly, oh so slowly, he obeys my command.

Oh, my Cicero! I'm not your mistress ... *I* worship *you*!

He is erect, as I knew he would be, his penis jutting from his dark-furred loins like the unyielding branch of a mighty oak.

I want it in me.

I want it now.

I cannot wait.

His eyes meet mine, arrogant and sultry, and there's no time now to play games of remonstration and imperious disapproval. I throw myself backwards on to the couch's edge, fling up my skirts and open my legs.

Without instruction of any kind, my lover moves between them, sinks naked to his knees again and presses his face between my thighs. Somewhere in the background I hear a faint ripple of outraged disapproval – probably as much for the fact that I'm wearing no undergarments as for Cicero's presumption – but there's nothing they can do about this and they've never been more distant.

To me now, and to him, they no longer exist, even though we all still operate in the public domain.

His tongue seeks out my pleasure, furling to a point, examining my intimate topography with its sensitive touch. He licks, he laves, he teases, cruising this way and that, and up and down, side to side, visiting every part of my sex from top to bottom and back again.

At first he avoids the most critical nexus, delicately skirting around it, except for tantalising flicks. My hips begin to lift of their own accord, seeking him, almost pleading with him mutely to grant release. He's on his knees before me, and I'm the one begging with my body for his beneficence.

I groan, 'Please,' and for a moment I'm dragged out of

our zone of inclusion by the ricocheting gasp of outrage and amazement. Even though they all envy me, they can't break the rigid conditioning they're barely aware of.

But still I plead. I mutter. I groan. I whimper. I implore, inarticulately, to be granted ecstasy.

And because he loves me, Cicero smiles against my flesh ... and grants my wish. He closes his warm lips around my centre and delicately sucks.

I rear up from the couch. I howl and buck. I grab at Cicero's crisp dark hair and jam his face closer to my crotch. My feet and ankles pummel his broad bare back, thumping and pounding against his bare skin.

It's too much to bear. I black out. Crying his name ...

Just moments later, I return to myself again. But not to the ghostly babble of feigned indignation and disapproval that I'd dimly perceived as a soundtrack to my pleasure.

No, as I open my eyes, and reach for Cicero, I see a blank white ceiling, not the fresco of labouring slaves. I turn and see the 'off' light glowing red upon the console.

We're alone now, just the two of us, no longer a part of the public domain of the holo-sphere.

'I don't think you're going to be very popular after that performance, my love,' murmurs Cicero wryly, settling his long, glorious and still rampant body on the couch beside me. 'I feel there will be reports of your recidivist behaviour winging their way, even now, to your mother.'

'I'm sure there will, but do you know? I really don't care,' I proclaim, reaching for the gleaming red-hot bar of his rigid penis. I'm not sure I really want to talk about my mother the Matriarch whilst handling my lover's genitalia in a way that's far from mistresslike. But even so, I decide to clarify my bravado. 'Who do you think I get my wicked ways from, Cicero? Who do you think recommended a rogue like you to me as my body servant?'

Cicero laughs softly, reaching, with a large strong hand, for the back of my head.

Compelled to bow before him, I smile happily and become servant to his master. Taking him into my mouth, I bestow a very private pleasure . . .

Portia Da Costa is the author of the Black Lace novels *Gemini Heat*, *The Tutor*, *The Devil Inside*, *Gothic Blue*, *Continuum*, *The Stranger*, *Hotbed*, *Shadowplay*, *Entertaining Mr Stone* and *Suite Seventeen* (published in June 2007). Her short fiction has also appeared in numerous Wicked Words themed anthologies.

Day Fifty-One Maya Hess

Annabel and Mick are in the kitchen. Mick is opening a bottle of wine and Annabel is washing glasses. The rest of the housemates are lounging in the garden except Glen, who is in the Confession Box.

'Hello, Glen. How can we help you today?'

'Forgive me, but I have sinned. I have been having unclean thoughts about another *Public-Eye* housemate and if I don't get it off my chest then . . .'

'Who have you been having unclean thoughts about, Glen?'

Glen buries his face in his hands and begins to laugh.

'Who, Glen?'

'Annabel. It's Annabel, OK? She's asking for it.' Glen looks up and musses his hair.

'In what way is she asking for it?'

'Short skirts, running round in her bra and panties all the time, flashing her tits at the camera. Everything. She wants it bad.'

'The other female housemates wear short skirts, Glen. Why do you think Annabel is asking for it any more than the others?'

Glen shakes his head and leaves the Confession Box.

It's 82 degrees in the *Public-Eye* garden and Annabel and Mick have given everyone chilled white wine. Annabel steps out of her sarong and jumps into the pool.

'Look at her, will you?' Selena says.

'Sshh, she'll hear you.' Gilly leans over and whispers in Selena's ear, spilling wine on her neck.

'Hey –' Selena jumps up.

'Lick it off, Gill, why don't you? Go on, give us a show.' Pedro, grinning, pours more wine.

'Can Gilly and Selena please come to the Confession Box immediately?'

'Oh dear, girls. You've done it now.' Pedro sips his wine and then dives into the pool with Annabel.

'Hello, Gilly. Hello, Selena. You have been chosen to perform this week's challenge. If you complete it successfully, you will be rewarded with a special dinner party on Friday.'

'And if we fail?'

'Then there will be no dinner party and only a budget box of groceries will be delivered to the *Public-Eye* house. Do you understand?'

'Yes, we understand. What do we have to do?' Selena wraps her arm around Gilly's bare shoulders.

'*Public-Eye* wants you to do a little matchmaking. In order to come to the dinner party on Friday, everyone must have a date. It is your responsibility to ensure that this happens but you must not let the other housemates know you are scheming. Do you understand?'

'What, so you mean we've got to secretly make everyone fancy each other and then we can have a party?' Gilly and Selena look puzzled.

'Yes, Gilly. Everyone has to be paired off to be allowed to the dinner party, including both of you. Plus, there must be one special host couple.'

'What do you mean, special host couple?' Gilly and Selena look worried and then giggle.

'*Public-Eye* wants you to make sure that every housemate is attracted to someone of the opposite sex. But in addition to this, one couple must show their attraction as a sexual action. *Public-Eye* will inform you if and when we deem this has happened.'

'But there are only three guys left and four girls.'

'*Public-Eye* knows this, Selena. Whichever housemate

is not paired off by the end of the week will not be going to the dinner party and will be removed from the house.'

Gilly and Selena remain silent and leave the Confession Box.

The housemates have come in from the garden. It's raining and a thunderstorm is overhead. Rosa is painting her toenails in the lounge and Annabel and Mick are in the kitchen preparing dinner. Pedro and Glen are playing cards, while Gilly and Selena are talking in the bedroom.

'Everyone knows that Glen likes Annabel. All we have to do is tell him she fancies him like mad and we've got our host couple.' Selena takes off her shorts and kicks them under the bed. She pulls a skirt from the drawer and holds it against her chest.

'Yeah, but they have to snog or grope or something and we all know that Annabel's truly madly deeply about Mick.' Gilly sighs.

'Oh, Micky, take me, Micky,' Selena says in a silly voice. She hugs her skirt and begins to kiss it theatrically.

'Shh, someone's coming.' Gilly pretends to read a magazine.

'Dinner's ready.' Annabel pauses and stares at Gilly and Selena but she is reanimated by the sound of her own name.

'Would Annabel please come to the Confession Box?'

'Oh, great timing.' And she bursts into the cubicle angrily. 'Can't this wait until after I've eaten?'

'Annabel, *Public-Eye* has chosen you to perform this week's challenge. If you complete it successfully then you will be protected from eviction for two weeks and all the housemates will receive a celebratory dinner at the end of the week.'

Annabel sits down, pleased to have been chosen. 'So, what do I have to do?'

'Firstly, Annabel, you must agree to keep this a secret. If you tell anyone, then you will immediately fail. Do you understand?'

Annabel nods, leans forwards and listens to her instructions.

All the housemates are chatting in the lounge. Gilly is giving Selena a neck massage while Glen fetches Annabel's dinner from the kitchen.

'What did *Public-Eye* want, Annabel?'

'Nothing much.' Annabel shrugs. 'They just asked about our shopping requests and stuff.'

'Why don't I believe you?' Glen sits next to Annabel and tries to feed her. When she pulls away, he puts his hand on her shoulder.

'You look good today, Annie. Shall we go in the pool later? Just you and me?'

Annabel's cheeks flush and she looks around to see who has heard. 'No,' she says, while continuing with her dinner, 'we can't.'

'Why not? We could have a cuddle and stuff.'

Annabel sighs. 'It's the "and stuff" that worries me.' She looks to Mick, who quickly turns away when he sees Glen touching her. Annabel sighs again.

Glen leaves but Selena quickly takes his place. 'Oh, go on, Annabel. Go for a swim with Glen. Anyone can see he really likes you.'

'You an expert, are you?' Annabel puts her empty plate on the table. 'Nope. Glen's nice but not for me.'

'Then who is?' Selena slips her long hair out of its band.

Annabel thinks, staring at the ceiling, careful not to look at the camera, before whispering in Selena's ear. 'No one. I'm a virgin and I think I prefer women.'

'Women?' Selena says loudly, while pulling a face at Gilly. 'You can't!'

At Selena's remark, Annabel runs out of the lounge. None of the remaining housemates sees the smile spreading across her face.

It's 9.42 p.m. Annabel is in the Confession Box.

'Hello, Annabel. How are you this evening?'

'Fine, thanks.' Annabel pulls her legs up into the large chair. Her skirt has ridden up and she idly strokes the pale skin on the inside of her thigh. 'Not fine, actually.'

'Go on.'

'It's just this week's challenge. I don't know if I can do it.'

'You do understand, Annabel, that, if you don't complete the task we have set you, there will be no party and you will automatically be nominated to leave the house.'

'I know. It's just that there's this, well, *feeling* in the house at the moment. Like everyone's about to crack or do something crazy. I don't know if it's the weather. It's been so hot. Made everyone so hot.'

'You have been set a task, Annabel, and *Public-Eye* wants you to carry it out to the best of your ability. If you fail, you will be up for eviction this weekend.'

'I think you chose the wrong person. Set the wrong task.' Annabel leans back. Her finger walks further up her leg and her face is a mirror of her conflicting thoughts.

'Why do you think that, Annabel?'

She pauses before answering. Allows the tingle in her leg to trip a path to her brain, telling her that they are wrong, oh so wrong, to have chosen her for this task. 'None of us has had sex for nearly two months and Mick's driving me crazy because he won't even look at me and, when I look at him, I can hardly stand it. The way he fans his shoulders out, makes it so his muscles show even through his clothes. *Everything* shows through his clothes.'

'Annabel, the other housemates, even though they don't know it, are relying on you for the dinner party. Morale will be low if you don't succeed.'

'I know, I know.' Annabel buries her face in her hands, moans and then stands up quickly. She pulls her skirt down. 'OK. Leave it to me. I can do this.'

Annabel leaves the Confession Box.

Rosa is in the bathroom taking off her make-up. Pedro is lying in the bath.

'Go on, get in with me, honey.' Pedro pats his hand on the bubbles.

'Really, you're mad. Me get in there with you?'

'You may as well. You've seen all of me now anyway. Seen what that ass of yours has done to my cock.' Pedro raises his hips out of the water.

'That doesn't mean I'm going to get near it or touch it.' Rosa laughs and turns from the mirror. The raised circles of her dark nipples bleed through her sheer nightdress. 'I'll scrub your back though.'

Pedro grins and sits up. 'I'll take whatever I can get.'

Rosa is washing Pedro's back with a sponge. She is leaning over the bath and her breasts are pressing against the side near Pedro's face. Mick comes into the bathroom.

'Oh, sorry,' he says and turns to leave.

'No, Mick. Stay!' Rosa beckons him back, grinning. 'You have to protect me from this beast.'

'Bit higher, hon. Mmm, just there.' Pedro closes his eyes and drops his hand between his legs as Rosa grinds the sponge across his shoulders.

'Pedro, a beast?' Mick laughs and tries not to look at the hem of Rosa's nightdress, which has lifted above the crescent of her ass as she leans over the bath.

'He wants me to get in there with him. Don't you?

Naughty boy.' Rosa plunges her arm into the water and Pedro yelps.

Pedro grabs her by the shoulders and pulls her close. 'You know you want it really, Rosa. Stop being so stuck up with your posh accent and expensive clothes and haul your sexy little ass next to –'

'No . . . stop!' Annabel runs into the bathroom screaming. She is panting and her face is flushed. 'What's going on, guys? What's up?' She is trying to sound cool, despite her frantic entrance. She casts a glance over Mick, who has just removed his shirt. He smiles at her before cleaning his teeth. Annabel screws up her eyes and looks away. 'Rosa, come into the bedroom with me. I want to tell you something.'

'Sorry, Pedro. Bath time's over.' Rosa winks and splashes Pedro. She follows Annabel into the bedroom. The two women sit alone.

'So, what's up?'

Annabel sighs. She looks at Rosa's perfect body and wonders how she will sound convincing. Rosa has a porcelain face, hair the colour of the hottest embers and legs long and slim enough to wrap around Mick, Glen and Pedro's backs all at once.

Keep her guessing, Annabel thinks. 'Do you think I'm attractive?' She twists a strand of hair around her finger.

Rosa laughs and her long neck stretches back. Annabel sees the line of muscle running down her throat, across her breastbone and beneath her short nightdress. She looks away when Rosa straightens. 'I could have had my hand around Pedro's cock and you called me away to ask me that?' Rosa stands. 'Babe, you're beautiful. That's why they put you in here. Glen's so hot for you he –'

'Photos!' Annabel jumps to her feet. 'I was going to show you photos.' She scrambles around in the mess beneath her bed and eventually retrieves a battered album. 'Look, this is when I was a kid and –'

Pedro and Mick come into the bedroom. 'Rosa, there you are. I thought I was going to get a good scrubbing but you disappeared.'

Rosa smiles sweetly and turns back to the photographs. She hears a television camera wheeze overhead. 'Keep on thinking, babe.'

It's 10.30 a.m. and Gilly and Selena are in the garden eating breakfast. Already it's 73 degrees.

'We have to think of ourselves, too,' Gilly whispers to Selena. She begins to plait Selena's long hair in order to whisper in her ear. Selena smells of suntan lotion. 'Glen's going to get it on with Annabel, I can feel it. Pedro's hot for Rosa, which only leaves Mick for one of us.' Gilly doesn't know why, but her lips take a taste of Selena's skin, right beside her ear.

'We could do him together,' Selena says with a giggle just at the same time she realises what Gilly has done. 'Then neither of us would be up for eviction because we'd have both got off with Mick.'

'I'm not sure *Public-Eye* wants everyone having sex,' Gilly whispers again. 'We're on TV, don't forget. They'll pull the plug and nip off to some washing powder commercial if we do that.' Both girls splutter into laughter at the thought just as Mick joins them.

'Tired, Micky?' Selena asks.

'Yep.' Mick's dark hair is a mess. His eyes will hardly stay open.

'Go back to bed then, stupid.'

'Not in that room. With all that going on.' Mick takes Gilly's coffee. 'It's Pedro and Rosa,' he confirms, when the two girls frown.

'Quick!' Selena squeals and they run inside leaving Mick blinking in the morning sun.

Pedro and Rosa are in the bedroom. Mick is in the garden talking to Glen, while Annabel is frantically preparing a breakfast tray. Gilly and Selena are listening outside the bedroom door.

'Open it quietly,' Gilly instructs. 'There's not long left so someone's got to do something if we're going to get a party.'

The bedroom is dark. Gilly and Selena slip inside unnoticed. They see that both Pedro and Rosa are in the same bed, hidden by the duvet.

'What if someone comes in?' Rosa asks. 'What if the cameras see us?'

'Stop asking questions and take this off.' Pedro's voice is urgent, impatient.

An arm and several legs appear from beneath the duvet and then Rosa's lace nightdress is dropped on the floor. Rosa moans loudly.

'God, you've got beautiful breasts.'

'Do you think he's sucking her tits?' Gilly whispers to Selena. The two women knot fingers in the dark corner, desperate for Pedro and Rosa to be exposed, desperate to win the challenge. Desperate for something.

12.32 p.m. Gilly and Selena are in the Confession Box.

'Well, well, do we pass? Can we have the party now? Glen's so hot for Annabel, and Rosa and Pedro have just done it in the bedroom and both of us are going to be Mick's dates. Have you seen the way he looks at us, as if he wouldn't take us any other way except as a pair?' Gilly and Selena sit on the edge of the Confession Box chair. They hug each other in anticipation of *Public-Eye*'s reaction. They desperately want the dinner party.

'I'm sorry, Gilly, sorry, Selena. *Public-Eye* doesn't believe that the task set has been completed. In our eyes, Rosa and Pedro haven't displayed any public physical attraction towards each other. Five minutes of romping beneath the duvet does not count. *Public-Eye* must be able to witness the act on at least two cameras. And Glen may like Annabel but the feeling doesn't appear to be mutual. Finally, double dates aren't allowed in this task. Good luck, girls. Remember, there are only a few hours remaining.'

'But ... but it was Annabel's fault. If she hadn't brought breakfast in for Rosa and Pedro and disturbed the whole thing, they'd have –'

'Thank you both. You can leave the Confession Box now.'

Gilly and Selena do as they are told, eyeing the camera positions even though they are familiar with the locations. Behind each mirror, sweeping from every corner, an addition to every smoke alarm, is the invasive arc of television broadcasting their every move to the nation.

'It's that Annabel,' says Selena thoughtfully. 'She's sabotaging everything we do.'

'Then,' says Gilly, leading her friend out to the swimming pool, 'we have to do something to stop her.' Smiling, they both strip naked and allow their tanned bodies to cut perfect dives into the still water. The thought occurs to them simultaneously as the cold water rushes through their hair, across their breasts and between their legs.

4.19 p.m. Rosa and Pedro are asleep in their own beds, while Gilly and Selena are pretending to be. Glen is dozing in the lounge. Mick is weight training by the pool and Annabel is in the garden sunbathing and reading.

Annabel's eyes can't help but flick above the pages every few seconds to admire Mick as he works out. Even though the book she found lying around – Selena's book, she recalls – is turning her on no end. She's lying on the sunbed apparently unaffected by the words that flow from the pages, but really this book is as hot as Mick's metal weights glinting in the sunlight as he pumps them from his waist to his chest. Really, she shouldn't be reading this given the task she has to perform. *Public-Eye* has said it is her job to ensure that none of the housemates display any public sexual acts or gestures, otherwise the task will be failed and there will be no dinner party.

'What are you reading?' Mick asks, breathless from effort.

Annabel wishes he was breathless from pumping her instead. She wants all of his strength inside her, on top of her, behind her, all over her. Perhaps, she thinks, he'd like her in the pool. 'It's Selena's book.' She wants to say how erotic it is and how she's imagining that it's them within the pages but she can't. She mustn't turn Mick on in any way if she is to secure the dinner party for tonight. Despite the charged atmosphere in the house, Annabel doesn't believe that anyone's done anything they shouldn't.

'Hey, give us a look then. It's a bit horny that, isn't it?' Mick grins and clanks his weights down before approaching Annabel. She pulls her sarong down over her legs and wishes she'd put on a shirt now that Mick is right beside her, reading a sexy novel over her shoulder.

'Bit boring, actually,' Annabel lies. She can smell the sun, the skim of fresh sweat and the chlorine from his earlier swim on him. 'Going back in?' she asks.

'What?' Mick has read a couple of paragraphs and stands up and walks away. He wants to read that book later. After he's unravelled Annabel and her aloof ways.

'The pool. Are you going back in the pool?' She doesn't mean to say that and certainly doesn't want to cause the shedding of jeans that follows. The pool isn't very big and by the time Mick dives in, takes a couple of strokes, he is at the other end. He shakes water from his hair.

'Coming in?' He front-crawls to the edge nearest Annabel. 'You've got your bikini on. Go on. What's the harm?' Water beads on the sheen of his toffee-coloured skin. Strands of dark hair wrap around his face and Annabel is struck by how like the character in the book he is.

She smiles. 'Maybe I do need to cool off,' she says, trying to lose her sarong as demurely as possible. She sits on the edge of the pool but, when she sees how Mick is lapping up everything about her from the tiny diamond stud in her navel to the white triangle of fabric barely covering each breast to her bunched blonde hair at her neck, she plunges into the water for modesty. The chill takes her breath away.

'They're on to us today.' Mick swims alongside Annabel. '*Public-Eye*,' he says in answer to her silent question, while staring in turn at the six cameras positioned around the garden. Over the weeks, it has become easy to ignore the robotic whirring of the machines as they watch and monitor the housemates' every move. 'Something's up, for sure.'

Annabel chokes on pool water and starts splashing about. Mick grabs her by the shoulders and hauls her against him. Annabel is fine but Mick doesn't know this. Annabel finds herself coughing more even though she doesn't need to. Instead of the kiss of life, she gets shaken vigorously.

'Hey!'

'I thought you were drowning.' Mick is still holding on to Annabel and their legs are tangling beneath the surface – foot brushing foot and thigh sliding over thigh. They don't need to say they both like it. The crystal sparkles bouncing from eyes to pool to eyes are words enough. They laugh and Annabel wants to drape her arms around Mick's neck but she can't. Not until the challenge is complete.

'What are you doing?' she asks, trying to flipper away from the sudden tighter grip around her waist. Mick's arms encircle her completely.

Mick doesn't reply. He pulls Annabel's weightless body closer until she is just about sitting on his knee as he bobs in the water. He draws a line up and down the ridge of her spine, feeling for her bikini-top strings although he doesn't pull them undone. There's something comforting about knowing that, with a gentle tug, Annabel's soft warm breasts will spill into the water.

4.45 p.m. Selena and Gilly are in the bedroom, trying not to wake Pedro and Rosa. Glen is still dozing in the lounge. Gilly slips into Selena's bed so they can whisper under the covers.

'Look at your nipples,' Gilly says with a giggle, surprising herself. She wants to reach out and touch them, maybe with her mouth or finger but resists the urge. If it comes to it, to save themselves, they are going to have to get it together anyway. 'How would you feel if, you know, we had to do it to win the challenge?' Gilly, unexpectedly, is salivating like she is being told to keep her hands off Belgian chocolates, not Selena's nipples.

'It's the camera bit that worries me,' Selena confesses, 'not kissing you.'

'I don't mind the cameras. Guess that's why I'm in here in the first place. Imagine my first girl experience being on the telly.' Gilly and Selena snort back giggles and, in the aftermath, Gilly finds herself eating those chocolates anyway.

Annabel and Mick are still in the pool. It's 83 degrees in the *Public-Eye* garden and Annabel is telling Mick about a school nativity play she was once in. She is perched on his knee in the water.

'And then I fell over and dropped the lamb and by mistake I tripped on the manger and the doll fell out and –'

'Annabel?'

'Yes?'

'Shut up about nativity plays.'

'OK.'

No one speaks for a couple of minutes but, when Mick pulls the ripcord of Annabel's bikini, she screams.

'Sorry!'

'OK!'

Annabel likes the cool water rushing about her breasts. She likes it that the white stringy fabric floats up and away and she can see Mick's eyes straining through the ripples to get a clear glimpse of what he has released. She likes it, too, that she has to grab on to his shoulder as she starts to slide off his knee. She doesn't want to lose contact even though she is getting close to breaking the rules of the challenge.

'Mick,' she says thoughtfully, a smile widening her face. 'Do you think the cameras can see much down there?'

'Nah,' Mick says immediately. 'No way. Plus, the deeper we go, the less chance there is. Why?'

'No reason,' says Annabel before front-crawling to the deep end. She can't stand up so has to tread water until Mick catches up and takes her by the waist again. This time he pulls her close so that her naked breasts press against his own toned chest. They huddle in the corner of the pool, out of sight of the cameras.

'Camera shy?' Mick asks.

'Don't ask,' Annabel replies, wishing how she could tell Mick it's her fantasy to have sex with him while being watched by millions. She doesn't tell him about the challenge.

'I *am* asking,' he says and takes a tug on the side strings of her bikini knickers. Like the top, the garment floats away leaving Annabel with a delicious rush of cool water between her legs.

'Truth is,' she says, reluctantly breaking away from Mick, her voice wavering like the surface of the water, 'that I love to be watched. You know, having sex with the possibility of being caught.' Annabel floats on her back and sculls with her hands to keep everything that Mick has just revealed in full view of the cameras. No one can accuse her of sexual relations doing this. All the girls show off their bodies. The challenge will not be lost. Annabel prays that the others are behaving themselves inside the house. Last time she looked, they were all asleep.

'Come here then, if you want your dream to come true.' Mick's voice causes Annabel to splash and splutter again and then she swims swiftly to him.

'You like me?' Annabel notices an aching deep within the folds of her sex. She wants someone, something, to touch her and bring her to orgasm quickly, just to get rid of the feelings that will lose her the challenge.

'You're gorgeous,' Mick confesses. 'Although I backed off because I know how much Glen likes you.'

Annabel finds herself on Mick's knee again. This time, his fingers are waiting to explore what he uncovered and now Annabel doesn't know what to do. If she screams and kicks up a fuss or even mentions that he's doing it, then the game will be lost and *Public-Eye* will know that a sexual act has been committed. She decides to keep quiet because there's no way the cameras can pick up what's going on three feet underwater in the corner of the pool. She can't even let go the little moan knotted in her throat. But because she's not responding to his touch, Mick is delving further between her legs and winding his way inside her.

'Say stop if you like.'

'Sshh,' Annabel says as normally as possible. 'Talk about the weather or something.'

Mick shrugs and comments on the temperature while letting another finger drift towards Annabel's butt. That bit of her has intrigued him since the day she arrived in the house. It was wrapped in shorts so small and tight he thought it might burst out when she leant forwards, which was often.

'It's so hot, isn't it?' Annabel says shakily, as both her butt and sex are invaded by a cluster of large fingers. She wants to ride his hand, get so close that when she slips on to his floating cock she can come over and over before he's even had a chance to feel what it's like to be inside her. In her mind, Annabel pretends that all the cameras can see them, that the entire nation is getting off watching them.

'Very,' says Mick. Annabel has lowered his swimming shorts and has her hand round his cock but instead of beating him hard, which he's desperate for, she lightly massages the head until he can barely keep his eyes open.

'Are you sure no one can see us?' Annabel whispers.

'I thought you wanted to be watched?' Mick smiles and ducks his head beneath the surface to gorge on her beautiful breasts before his breath runs out.

'More than anything,' she replies when he comes up desperate for air.

'I'm game then. Let's finish this on a sunbed. Just us and the cameras.'

They are whispering but Annabel is concerned that *Public-Eye* can hear. If only she could warn Mick about the challenge. If only she could wait a few hours before pulling him inside her.

'Impossible,' she whispers, replying to both Mick's request and her own thoughts. Annabel washes her hands over the submerged parts of Mick's body as she considers a duck dive. They smile at each other and the sun on their faces, the flush in their cheeks, is signal enough that they want each other.

Mick tips back his head in the wake of Annabel's splashing feet. The cold water around his cock has been replaced by her warm soft mouth and, to keep herself from floating back up, Annabel has latched her legs around his and is rubbing herself against him. When he looks down, he can see the gold of her hair billowing in the disturbance. He can't quite reach her breasts but the feel of them against his skin makes him want to come in her mouth.

Seconds later, Annabel surges up gasping, smiling, laughing, and if she can't kiss Mick's open lips, taste the water and salt on his neck, then she thinks she might die.

'I want you in me,' she mouths silently and slides her legs around Mick's hips so that her sex – a little pink clam – can take him all in.

It's 5.12 p.m. and Gilly is kissing Selena. They are under the duvet while Rosa and Pedro sleep.

'Just practising, in case, yeah?' Selena whispers, unsure they should be doing this. She is sure, however, that she likes the feel of Gilly's womanly lips against her own and would never ask but hopes that Gilly might kiss away the unbearable ache in her sex.

Later, as Gilly prises Selena's legs apart, neither of them notices the cameras whirring frantically above as the duvet shifts and twists and exposes Gilly's tongue drawing a gentle exploratory line between the moist folds of her friend's pussy.

In the pool, Mick's cock slips easily into Annabel, aided by their weightlessness and the skim of natural juices that he discovers inside her. Glen has woken up and comes into the garden, where he sits on a sunbed.

'Good book, is it?' he asks, grinning and waving the novel at Annabel, who he sees panting, splashing and playing a silly game with Mick in the pool.

'Uhuh,' she manages, now incapable of keeping her movements undetectable. 'Take me harder,' she whispers to Mick, grinding herself against his groin.

Glen hears what she says, sees the willpower dripping from Mick's face, and so dives into the pool, remaining underwater with his eyes open. In the deep end, behind the tiny bubbles, through the waves and legs and discarded swimwear, Glen watches the hard line of his friend's cock entering and leaving the most inviting pussy he has ever seen. He stays underwater far longer than he should and is rewarded with a silent explosion, which he feels in his own erection as their orgasm ripples through the pool.

He resurfaces, spluttering, ecstatic, thinking he'll choose Annabel. Without a word, Glen climbs out of the pool and returns to the bedroom to dry. He finds Gilly and Selena in bed together where he left them, still exposed, still devouring each other and for a moment considers it could be one of them. The sight of purely feminine flesh tied together so intricately does something to him but his mind is set on the pretty place between Annabel's legs.

Finally in the corner, he's pleased to see that Rosa and Pedro have fallen asleep in each other's arms, spent, exhausted, their actions captured by the camera above the bed.

'Would Glen please come to the Confession Box?'

Glen smiles, towels his hair, and enters the cubicle. 'Hello *Public-Eye*.'

'Hello, Glen and congratulations. You have successfully completed the task we set you earlier in the week. By abstaining from any public sexual activities, we are able to offer you a night in a luxury bedroom with four-poster bed, spa bath and waiter service. And of course the person of your choice can accompany you.'

'Thank you, *Public-Eye*,' Glen says, thinking how easy it has been. 'I'll be taking Annabel to the room.' He feels himself stiffen within his jeans.

* * *

All the housemates are in the dining room eating beans on toast except Glen and Annabel who have gone to the luxury bedroom for the night.

'I just don't get it,' Mick says. 'We were right in the corner, as deep as we could go and always submerged.' He can't help but think of what Glen might be doing to Annabel, how he gets to taste her without holding his breath. Until she comes back, he saves the thought of her tight little sex gripping him, working him up. 'The cameras couldn't possibly have seen what was going on. As far as *Public-Eye* is concerned, we were just talking in the pool.'

Gilly and Selena begin to giggle, wishing their water was wine, their beans caviar. 'Didn't you know about the underwater cameras?' Gilly says. 'Your naked butt's been on national television!'

Maya Hess has written numerous short stories for Wicked Words and is the author of the Black Lace novels *The Angels' Share* and the paranormal erotic romance *Bright Fire* (published in May 2007).

Cowboy Up Kate Pearce

For the twentieth time, Cauy Warner looked at his watch and then back at the gate. Behind him, the crowd jeered as yet another bull rider crashed to the ground. The scent of cotton candy, hot dogs and kettle popcorn mixed uneasily with the raw smells of the rodeo. He scarcely noticed the noise and the dust, his attention fixed on the entrance where he hoped to see a miracle.

Suddenly, there she was. He studied her under the deep brim of his Stetson from the feet up. Red cowboy boots, an embroidered denim skirt and a silky halter top. With that amount of bare skin on show he hoped she'd slapped on plenty of sunscreen. In his eyes, she still looked like a teenager. He remained near the gate, one elbow propped behind him, one booted foot crossed over the other.

He waited until she turned around and slowly raised his head until he could meet her eyes. Her smile held a hint of uncertainty. No surprise really, considering the last time they'd met she'd told him to go to hell. He touched the brim of his hat.

'Hey, Jen. Long time no see.'

Her smile didn't quite reach her blue eyes. She tucked a wayward strand of black hair behind her ear. She'd always done that when she was nervous. Hell, over the years, he'd done it for her a thousand times.

'Hi, Cauy.'

He waited for her to say more but she didn't. What did you say to a man who had walked away ten years ago and never looked back? He checked her fingers. No rings but that didn't mean much these days. He gestured to the nearest concession stand.

'Shall we grab a cold one?'

She nodded and began to walk away from him. He caught her up in two easy strides and cupped her elbow. He sensed her stiffen but she didn't pull away from his casual touch. Damn, she felt fine. He inhaled her familiar butterscotch scent and was instantly dragged back into the past. Her eager body moving under his, his cock buried deep inside her until he knew he had to come long and hard into her welcoming warmth.

He was hard now. She was the only woman who had that instant effect on him. Since the first time they'd made out as teenagers, he'd always craved her. Ten years obviously wasn't enough for his body to forget her. Did she feel it too? The immediate connection and the tug of desire?

After dealing with some fans, he scribbled a few autographs, got two beers and carried them carefully back to the secluded table where he'd left her.

'Here you go.'

'Thanks.' She took a small sip before putting the beer back down.

'Why did you leave the ticket for me, Cauy?'

He fought a smile. That was his Jen, always quick and to the point. 'Because I wanted to see you again.'

She frowned. 'It's been ten years. Why now? Is it because you've finally made National Rodeo world champ? Did you come back to gloat?'

He took a moment to swallow some beer. He didn't quite understand why he'd come back himself unless it was to touch base with someone who once believed in him. Who knew he was not the salacious sex fiend being portrayed in the media.

'Perhaps that was part of it.'

'At least you're honest.' She pulled a crumpled

five-dollar bill out of her pocket and slammed it on the table. 'Congratulations. I'll pay for the beer and wish you good luck and goodbye.'

He laid his hand over hers. 'I said that was *part* of it.' He hesitated. 'Shit, I'm still no good at this emotional crap. We were best friends, Jen, long before we became lovers. Doesn't that count for anything?'

She snatched her hand out from under his and got to her feet. 'Friends don't walk away from each other. Friends don't cheat on each other either.'

She was already halfway to the exit before the full impact of her words hit him. Too angry to care what the crowds around him thought, he caught up with her and swung her around to face him.

'What the fuck is that supposed to mean?'

Even with her boots on she was almost a foot shorter than him yet she still managed to get in his face. 'You cheated. Don't lie to me.' She took a deep breath and tried to smile. 'But, hey, I shouldn't have said anything. It all happened a long time ago and I don't really care any more.'

He slid his fingers under her chin so that she couldn't look away from him. 'Like hell you don't.'

He bent his head and captured her mouth. His tongue probed and demanded entrance. With a moan, she opened her lips and allowed him inside. He kissed her with a slow thoroughness until she kissed him back, until her body was pressed against him, until her arms were wrapped around his waist. He slid his hand down until he cupped her butt and pressed her even more firmly to him.

Someone slapped him on the shoulder and yelled, 'Hey, buddy, get a room.'

He opened his eyes to find a crowd gathered around them. He had to move before someone recognised him, next thing their picture would be plastered all over the papers. He had no desire to have his intimate life picked over by the gutter press for a second time in one year. Jen buried her face in his shoulder.

He whispered in her ear. 'You're not going to like this, but could you just turn around and head for the arena railings over there? I'll be right behind you.'

She swallowed hard. 'I don't want to go anywhere with you. How dare you kiss me like that in front of all those people?'

'I didn't notice you stopping me.' Before she could retaliate, he placed a finger over her lips. 'Help me out here. I'm so hard I'm going to burst out of my jeans. Walk in front of me to the railings and we'll sort it out over there.'

She glanced down at his groin and blushed. 'OK, I'll do it. But . . .'

He turned her around and steered her in front of him, lowering the brim of his hat so his face was half-hidden. When they reached the sanctuary of the railings, he remained behind her, one arm wrapped firmly around her hips, his cock unwilling to relinquish the soft temptation of her butt.

'Give me a minute.' He kissed the soft skin behind her ear and she shivered. 'If we ignore him, maybe he'll go away.'

She surprised him with a reluctant chuckle. 'He never did in the past. Although you are ten years older.'

He deliberately undulated his hips and rocked into her, resting the palm of his hand over her mound. 'I'm just as capable, darlin'. Way better than I used to be. Ten years ago I could barely last ten minutes with you. Now I have more finesse, I can last for hours.'

Her breathing hitched and he smiled. She was as caught up in this tangle of lust as he was. 'Now what were you saying about me being unfaithful?' He braced his other arm along the top of the railing just about the height of her breasts. Her nipples contracted like two hard little bullets and bored into his flesh. 'I thought you dumped me because I'd decided not to go to college.'

She stared resolutely into the arena where the team roping was still going on. Dust flew up as a young calf stumbled and fell on the ground in front of them. 'That was one of the reasons.'

He nipped her ear, spread his fingers wider to investigate the curve of her mound. She didn't pull away. Encouraged, he pressed his long middle finger down the centre seam of her skirt, right where he guessed her clit would be, and started a slow rhythmic rubbing. She arched her back increasing the pressure on his swollen shaft.

'Do you really think we would have made it if we'd got married that young?' He took a second to study the people around them. No one was paying them any attention. 'Perhaps it was better that we went our separate ways and grew up a little.'

Jen sniffed. 'I've grown up but what about you? Nothing's changed. You're still trying to get in my pants.'

He blew softly on her exposed neck and then bit down hard. 'And you're still letting me.' After another quick glance at his oblivious neighbours, he grabbed Jen's ankle and placed her foot on the second rung of the metal fence. He slid his hand under her skirt and up her leg until he met the lacy edge of her panties.

'You're soaking.' He stroked the damp sliver of silk until he could feel her swollen clit through the fabric. 'I'm going to make you come right here in front of all these people, and you're going to let me.'

Beneath that calm exterior she'd always been wild with him. They'd had sex in any number of public places. The element of discovery had turned them both on. He wondered if any other man dared challenge her like this any more. He'd been the bad boy at school. The one the girls were told to keep away from. But he and

Jen had been best friends from their first day when she'd punched him for trying to look under her skirt.

Thinking of skirts ... he slid one callused finger beneath her panties and plunged it deep into her core. Her lush scent surrounded him as he worked her. The slick wet sounds were masked by the roars of the crowd.

'Cauy ...'

The breathy way she always said his name when they were together haunted his dreams. He'd fucked his way through the last ten years but no one ever made him hard by just saying his name the way Jen could. God, he wanted to lift up her skirt and take her rough and fast in a primitive display of possession that would leave no one in any doubt that she belonged to him and always would.

He added two more fingers, scissoring them wide to give her maximum pleasure. 'I never cheated on you. Why the fuck would I? You were everything I ever wanted.'

She moaned and rested her cheek on his forearm. Blood pounded through his cock in time to the fast beat of his heart. Her sheath tightened around his fingers and the first quiver of her release spasmed through her. He gritted his teeth as she squeezed his fingers tight while she came. He continued to caress her, bringing her gently back down again.

Rock music started up, echoing the strident thump of his heart. The bass notes made the ground shake beneath his boots as the arena was cleared for the next event. Cauy slowly withdrew his hand and turned Jen to face him. Still holding her gaze, he brought his fingers to his mouth and licked them.

'I didn't cheat, Jen. I left because I wanted this life more than I wanted to be tied down.'

Her cheeks were flushed, her pupils wide with desire. 'I saw you.'

He took a slow breath, wondered if his cock would

ever stop hurting. Wondered if he'd ever be able to forget the hurt look in her eyes. 'Christ, Jen. I don't know what you're talking about.'

She pushed at his chest and he stepped back a reluctant inch. 'That last night, I came out to your house to try and make things right before you left. I saw you and Linda Wilkes coming out of the barn. You were picking hay out of her hair just like you used to do with me.'

He took her hand and marched her towards the stables behind the area. There were still a lot of people milling around but most of them were rodeo competitors rather than gawkers. He hoped they would have their minds on their jobs rather than on him and Jen. A horse neighed and tried a little buck as it passed them in the narrow passageway between the stalls.

Instinctively, Cauy pressed Jen to the wall, covering her body with his own in case the horse decided to kick out again. Unable to resist the lure of her mouth, he kissed her, his body straining against hers. His breathing was ragged when he finally raised his head.

'Look, how about we get the fucking out of the way first, and then we can talk.'

He winced as she bit down on his lip.

'That's so typical of you, Cauy. It was always about sex, wasn't it?'

After a quick look around, he drew her into the empty corner stall and shut the door behind him. If anyone came in, they'd find them for sure, but from under the half-opened door, once he had Jen's legs wrapped around his waist, only his boots and jeans would show.

He trapped her against the wall, using his superior weight to keep her just where he wanted her. Not that she was struggling. Her body was pressed to his from knee to shoulder.

'I'm a man. It's always about sex. Now let me inside you and we'll talk later.'

She squeezed his butt. 'I guess it's the only way I'm going to get any sense out of you.'

Desperate now to get inside her, he hooked a finger in the side seam of her lace panties and ripped them off. One handed, he undid his gold belt buckle and unzipped his jeans. No time for foreplay now, just the instinctive need to mate. He lifted her until the crown of his cock brushed her pussy. Voices and laughter echoed off the walls of the barn as people passed by the door, barely a foot away from where they stood.

'Please, Cauy.'

He studied Jen's face, held her there, his wet stiff cock gently rubbing over her swollen clit. 'When I fuck you, I'm not stopping. Not even if someone opens that door and comes in. Is that what you want?'

She angled her hips, tried to take him deeper inside her. He kept her suspended over him. 'I said, is that what you want?'

'Yes. Just do it.'

He lowered her an inch until just the head of his cock disappeared inside her. 'I'm thinking maybe I'll wait until someone opens that door. I'd love to see how turned on some of the cowboys would get watching you ride me.'

'Dammit, Cauy. Do it!'

Her nails dug into his shoulders and he felt her come. It was too much for him to resist. With a groan he thrust upwards just as he slid her down over his shaft. The smack of her flesh hitting his made him want to shout out loud. He gripped her hips, pounding himself into her with all the force of his longing and all his regrets for the past ten years.

She climaxed again and he came with her, pumping her so full of come he thought the top of his head would come off. He wrapped his arms around her hips, and held her close, aware for the first time that the heels of her cowboys boots were digging into his bare butt like spiked spurs.

Shit, someone else was coming and not in a good way. Cauy hastily pulled out and zipped up his jeans. He pulled down Jen's skirt and stood in front of her. The door swung open.

''Scuse me, folks.'

Cauy only saw the shadowy outline of a cowboy before a black horse was shoved inside the stall. He held his breath as the door was shut. The horse ignored them and instantly made his way to his food bucket.

He turned back to Jen and tucked a curl of her hair behind her ear. 'Let's go and get cleaned up and then we'll talk.'

He waited for her outside the restrooms as the arena floodlights came on and the scent of warm beer joined the fug of overcooked barbecue and fried funnel cake.

'Hey, Cauy!'

He looked up to see his long-time room-mate and fellow world champion Jack Kenyon waving at him.

'You're on in five minutes. I've set up your ride in chute three, OK?'

Cauy nodded and turned to study the long line snaking out of the women's restroom. What did women do in there that took so long? He'd agreed to give an exhibition ride along with the rest of the newest rodeo stars. The invitation had given him the excuse he needed to come back to his hometown and show them he had done good despite their gloomy predictions. And, of course, an excuse to dazzle Jen.

His cock ached hard in his jeans. Damn, he wanted her again. That five-minute fuck had reminded him of their teenage years when that had been all they'd had time for. Now he wanted to lay her out on some nice silk sheets and take his time exploring her body and let her explore his.

'Cauy!' Jack shouted again.

This time, he raised a hand in acknowledgement. He couldn't let his sponsors down. He'd been paid well to perform his eight-second ride. With a muttered curse, he strode towards the chutes. Would Jen wait for him or had he lost his chance? Hell, she might think he'd had his fun and had no intention of talking to her after all.

The arena announcer called his name and the crowd applauded. He stood on the top railing and waved his Stetson. Jen would never understand the adrenaline rush competing against a wild horse gave him. It was the nearest thing to fantastic sex he had ever experienced.

He carefully slid on to the small saddle, wary of the twitching young bronc beneath him. No certainties in what he did for a living. One false move and he could be thrown off, stamped on or break every bone in his body. He didn't even want to think about what else might happen. Wild horses were never predictable. It was never a question of whether you were good enough to stay on, more a question of how soon the horse could get you off his back. His job was to react quickly enough to delay the inevitable for the longest eight seconds of his life.

He rammed his Stetson down on his head and nodded at the gateman. Poised like a dancer atop a pin, he anticipated the horse's first crazy leap to the left and quick spin on its back legs before it set off running. He always tried to make it look easy. Points were awarded for style as well as sheer grit. The sound of the buzzer was almost lost in the roar of the crowd.

He relaxed a little and vaulted off the horse with his trademark flip, landing safely on his feet in the centre of the trampled arena dirt. His grinning face loomed large on the screen at the end of the arena. He took off his Stetson and pushed a hand through his damp brown hair. On the screen, his hazel eyes looked green in the new checked shirt his sponsor had designed especially for him.

He signed more autographs and acquired a few unwanted phone numbers stuffed in the pockets of his jeans by the crowd of women who hung around the competitors' entrance. With one last smile, he turned back to the packed stands.

'That was some show you put on there.'

To his amazement, Jen stood in front of him. Her blue eyes serious, her lush mouth freshly painted with red lipstick. 'I can almost understand why you left.'

'You were going to leave too, remember? Your plan was that we would go to college, get married and move to a big city.'

She shrugged. 'What can I say? Somehow it didn't seem so appealing without you.'

He fought a smile. 'Jen, don't try the guilt thing on me. I'm the one who left, remember? I've already got enough guilt of my own, I don't need yours.'

She fiddled with the strap of the small purse she wore around her neck. 'I did go away to college, but somehow I ended up coming back here.'

He moved closer and took her hand. 'Was it because you wanted me to know where to find you in case I changed my mind?'

She laughed then. 'Jeez, Cauy, I haven't been sitting around pining for you. I came back because I was offered a great job.'

He couldn't decide whether he was disappointed by her last comment or relieved. 'I should've asked you earlier, what do you do?'

'I'm the chief editor of the *Lakeside News*.'

He let go of her hand and stuffed his own back in his pocket. His fingers crushed the slips of paper until they formed a solid mass. 'A reporter, huh?' A sour taste caught at the back of his throat and he swallowed hard. 'Is that why you turned up today? Were you hoping to get the dirty details of my so-called affair with Miss America?'

She produced a mini recorder and dangled it in front of him. 'Like you said, perhaps that was part of it.'

Turning on his heel, he pushed his way through the crowd. Christ, he was a naïve fool. He'd thought he'd be safe here, away from the city and the tangle of lies and innuendo that had surrounded him since Christmas. Obviously Jen had decided to pay him back big time.

A tug on his sleeve made him look down. Jen marched right alongside him, her expression as determined as his own. 'Cauy, you said you would talk to me.'

He slowed down and turned to face her, his professional smile firmly in place. 'Sure, darlin', what would you like to ask me? I'm sure your paper would love to run a story about a hometown boy who made good or were you planning on something spicy to sell to the *Enquirer*? You're a true reporter. Having sex with me first was a damned good way to get my attention.'

She stamped her foot. 'Will you just listen for a minute? I didn't mean for that to happen, OK? I was just going to ask you for an interview for old times' sake.' Her voice wobbled as she reached up to touch his cheek. 'Dammit, I didn't realise I'd still be so attracted to you. And then, before I could stop myself, all that other emotional crap poured out. Stuff I thought I'd forgotten about.'

He caught her fingers against his face, couldn't stop himself from rubbing them against the stubble on his chin. His anger died as swiftly as it had risen. She was only trying to do her job. And after all, he'd come back seeking his lost self-esteem. Perhaps there was a way to satisfy them both after all.

'It's OK. I'd rather give you an interview than anyone else.' He gestured to the press room. 'Let's go sit down and talk it through.'

To his surprise, she pushed on his chest until he was backed up against the wall beneath the overhead stands.

'I said that having an interview with you wasn't the only reason I picked up the ticket. I still want to know what you were doing in the barn with Linda Wilkes.'

Cauy tried not to smile as he stared down at her determined face. 'She came to pick up one of the kittens as a birthday gift for her little sister. We had to chase the critters around the barn before we caught the one she wanted. That's why I was picking straw out of her hair.' He held her gaze. 'You wanted to believe the worst of me. You were looking for a reason to send me on my way because you realised I'd never be happy following your plans and it scared you because you knew I was right.'

Jen looked away from him. 'I realise that now. I was glad to see you with her. It made it easier for me to tell you to go to hell.'

He stroked a finger over her full lower lip. 'But I came back.'

She looked up at him and smiled. 'Yeah, you did, didn't you?'

'I meant what I said about us being friends, Jen. I'd be happy to give you an interview. It's a chance to tell my side of the story to someone who might actually listen.'

'Friends, then?' He jumped as her hand cupped his groin and squeezed hard. 'When do you have to leave, Cauy?'

'Tomorrow morning.'

She eased his zipper down and closed her fingers around the rapidly expanding column of his shaft. 'Fuck first, interview later?'

She did understand. He closed his eyes as she stroked his cock and slid one of her hands around to his buttocks. 'Works fine for me.'

Kate Pearce is the author of the Cheek novel *Where Have All the Cowboys Gone?*

Talk of the Devil Primula Bond

Celia was hovering on the edge of a dance floor somewhere in Argyll when she first learnt what Scotsmen wear under their kilts. It made her hot under her lacy collar. It made her realise how far from home she was, how overdressed. She couldn't take her eyes off what she saw.

'Not too shocked with our ways, are you, hen?' Someone who looked and sounded just like Billy Connolly was pressing a third schooner of warm sherry into her hand. 'I mean, what's an innocent young Sassenach like you doing in the midst of these reprobates?'

'What makes you think I'm innocent?' she answered. The man just stroked his whiskers and looked her up and down knowingly. He'd already summed her up. They all had. 'Actually, I'm not even supposed to be here. I can see I'm out of place.' Her head was starting to ache. 'I think I'll call a taxi.'

But her words were drowned as the band struck up. The chap abandoned her, striding away over the worn carpet like all the others to grab a partner. Every single man in that stuffy room, young and old, looked spectacular once they were on the move. Any fat spotty English yob taking the piss out of Jocks wearing skirts should try it. Those kilts were the business. Distinguished tribal tartans, smartly knotted ties, fitted jackets studded with silver buttons – they reminded her of outfits of the world you could collect to dress your doll. But these were no mannequins. They were real men with great sinewy legs; flexing, determined knees. They had daggers shoved down their socks for God's sake.

They wore polished shoes laced up the ankle, which clicked smartly about on the flagstone floors of the church and managed to look not remotely girly. How was that possible?

And the sporran. Yet again she wished Bess was here. No-good Bess who had dragged Celia from the comfort of Hammersmith to the other end of the country, to this windswept hamlet to keep her company. Bess who at least belonged here. Bess who was Scottish, a cousin of the best man, had the same auburn hair as nearly everyone here.

And Bess who right now was doubled over the loo back at the bed and breakfast, covered with a ghastly livid rash and puking after eating crab which most definitely had *not* been freshly caught by some hunky fisherman from the grey waves crashing on the rocks below.

'Scottish women must spend their lives trying not to stare,' Celia said, giggling, as they were digging into their supper last night. 'I mean, great leather pouches dangling over the guys' crotches? Might as well stick a flag there saying "Here's my cock"!'

'Since when have you been obsessed with cocks?' Bess snorted, taking the first forkful of the treacherous crab. 'Airhead. The sporrans are there to keep their money safe, I think. No pockets in a kilt, see.'

'No,' Celia had tipsily argued for once in her life. 'They're there to keep their dicks under wraps if they get a hard-on!'

She recognised the opening bars of the Eightsome Reel. The men had grabbed their partners, and what a drab floral lot the women mostly were. Celia tugged at her drab floral dress. That included her. Bess had dragged her along with no time to buy something gorgeous. So it was the men who were the peacocks.

They started to set to the right, set to the left. She knew all the steps. And as they started to move, so did their kilts, swaying heavily from side to side. She caught glimpses of strong manly thighs. Her stomach tugged. She felt a smile, or more like a leer, pulling at her mouth. She crossed her legs, letting her skirt float up over her knees. She swigged some more sherry. So that's what kilts were for. Those thick pleats at the back were designed not for scaring the enemy shitless while roaring into battle but for skipping about on the dance floor.

She tried not to giggle. And then she saw it. Them. A pair, in fact, of tight buttocks. In front of her a man was circling his partner in a mad spin. The momentum meant the kilt started to swing with its own rhythm. Up and sideways, faster and higher, until there were his great manly buttocks, the dark cleft chiselled clearly between. Celia could see how taut they were – men have such gorgeous butts – as he danced and balanced and swung his drab female partner right off her feet, turning her into a bird.

Celia craned shamelessly forwards, blushing furiously. It didn't matter whether the flying Scotsman was young or old. She just stared at those buttocks, curiously youthful like a naked boy's but with thick muscles running through them. You never see muscles in a woman's plump arse, do you? This guy's bottom flashed under the giddy kilt. Celia wondered how his backside would look without the kilt, clenching tight, the strong legs braced, whirling the woman into a dark corner of the room, slamming her against the flock wallpaper so the breath was knocked out of her, one of those strong knees shoved between hers to trap her there, big hands pinning her wrists, hips drawing back to thrust, wait, first he'd have to get rid of that horrible plaid skirt the woman was wearing, he'd hook it up to her waist to reveal a pair of surprisingly good legs kicking feebly. She would be wearing one of those flesh-pink wartime girdles and suspenders. He would rip at her nylon stockings, rip away her silken knickers, her white thighs would try to close over her sudden nakedness but then they'd melt open, part for him, showing the black bushy shadow of her snatch. Her face would be rosy from the dancing and the excitement and her mouth would form an O as he was ready now, ready to get his cock out and start to fuck her . . .

'You look bored out of your skull. Will the Gay Gordons put a smile on your face?'

Celia couldn't help it. If only he knew what pictures were flickering through her skull. He'd drum her out of town. She burst out laughing. Forget the crab's revenge. This sherry was having a dreadful effect on her. Here was another inquisitive wedding guest come to suss out the gate-crashing wallflower. A wedding guest, admittedly, with the sexiest, deepest Glaswegian accent she'd ever heard.

'Look, I know I'm not welcome here, but you don't have to threaten me with a Highland fling!'

Still laughing, she shifted round in the stiff little chair. Her bottom squeaked on the hard seat and she felt the faintest prickle of wetness under her skirt. The laughter nearly choked her. Level with her nose was a massive sporran. Worn cracked leather, with a silver clasp, bulging with something – money or a couple of small pistols? – and trimmed with some kind of snowy hair or hide. Her face went hot. It looked like a bearded animal, biding its time, clamped over this guy's crotch. Maybe she was the only one with a filthy mind, but all she could think about was what lurked beneath.

'Och, believe me, that wasn't a threat.'

Celia moved her eyes up from the sporran. A flat stomach beneath the kilt's smooth front panel. The cropped evening jacket, a broad chest in pure white dress shirt, a strong neck and jaw then such a mouth, the full lower lip jutting with amusement as if one of them had just cracked a joke. His auburn hair stood up on end as if blown in a high wind.

'Oh my God,' Celia breathed, standing up slowly. She found herself running her fingers up the velvet jacket. 'You look just like the guy in the porridge advert.'

'The macho one eyeing up the girls and wearing nothing but a singlet?'

His smile was crooked, his lower lip bitten by the upper as if he was trying not to bellow. His nose was broken. Rugby broken, not boxer broken. Dented in the middle so it tipped up at the end, just like the guy in the advert, and he had the kind of brow that looked as if he might be permanently frowning, if his eyes weren't so bright.

'Yes. How come you all look so sexy in your kilts?'

'That's because all your men down South are a bunch of big girls.'

She flapped her hand at him in silly protest, but he caught at her and wrapped his arm round her waist. He pulled her against his hip. It was hard, and grated bony against hers. She thought of her fantasy Scot, kilt up to show his bare butt, knees bent, screwing his gasping woman hard up against the wall. Her stomach went tight.

'You know how a real Scot eats his porridge?' her Scotsman said, leading her into the middle of the room.

Celia shook her head as she stumbled along beside him. His body against hers was warm like a radiator.

'Standing up.'

He laughed, as if he knew exactly what had been going through her mind. Her fantasy Scotsman, doing it in the corner, standing up. He may as well have lifted up her skirt and run his finger over her crack the way the electricity crackled through her.

'So where's my little cousin?' he asked as the accordion went into its intro. Sure enough she recognised the Gay Gordons. All round the room couples were lining up two by two. Animals going into the Ark. Why did Noah need two of each? For mating, of course – God, this sherry...

'Your little cousin?'

'Bessie. You're her mate Celia, aren't you? How is the little nympho?' He took hold of her fingers, held them loosely, formally. 'I was looking forward to seeing how she's grown.'

'She's sick as a dog. Left me to come on my own,' Celia told him. For the first time that day she was glad Bess wasn't here. 'What do you mean, "little nympho"?'

But the music drowned his reply. Celia placed her arm diagonally across his front. She knew what to do. Those childhood years of thumping round draughty village halls with a harridan shrieking instructions had not been wasted after all.

As they started up she felt her dress swish and float round her legs, against his legs. Her heart beat faster as the music introduced the step. This was her favourite dance, though she wouldn't admit it. The harridan always made her be 'the man' because she was tall, but the harridan should see her now. Four steps forwards, four steps back, twirl nonchalantly under her dashing partner's arm. Try to look as if being dragged against a dangerously sexy chest was all in a day's work.

Then leave him as you turn and position yourself for the next man. How swinging is this, she thought, as another brawny arm wrapped round her waist, I never thought of Scottish dancing as sexy before, but it's an organised version of wife swapping. Women being spun about, getting passed around the room. All the guys having a go, handling us, passing us on – how kinky is that?

'Dancing with the best man, eh?' It was the whiskery guy who'd been plying her with sherry. 'You're honoured. The girls are all after him, but Stuart rarely dances with anyone.'

Celia twirled until she was dizzy. Everyone was watching her now. The blood was rushing to her head, and so was the sherry.

'You dance very well for a Sassenach. Better than this rabble,' said the next guy. It was the one with the buttocks. 'I think we'll have to kidnap you for the Dashing White Sergeant.'

'Oh really?' Celia said, batting her eyelashes and catching an evil look from a nearby woman, presumably his wife. She realised this was the bride's father. Once again the image of him hitching his kilt up to fuck the woman in the corner, now identified as his wife, burnt across Celia's brain. She leant closer to tease him. 'And what does he want with me?'

Like all the others he had a deep filthy laugh. Like all the others he was eating out of her hand. She caught the admiring nods of the men as the dance finished, the wary looks of the women. Each time she moved, they absently copied her gestures, so that everyone seemed to be nervously licking their lips to a shine, running their hands over their necks, smoothing their flimsy dresses over their thighs.

'I don't know about the Dashing White Sergeant,' the bride's father whispered into her ear as the dance ended, 'but I've a shrewd idea what our Stuart would like to do to you.'

Celia looked about, but Stuart had vanished. The fire escape had been yanked open to let a breeze into the sweaty room, and she walked outside, leaving the music and the sherry and the compliments behind. Past the hotel kitchens and the bins and through a scrubby garden. She reached a wooden gate leading to the cliff path, still catching her breath, and the cooler air clutched at her, making her skin come up in goose-bumps under her dress.

'Shame to leave when you're just getting warmed up?'

A drift of cigarette smoke pricked her nostrils. Celia

crossed the path, and there was Stuart sitting on a bump of grass right near the edge.

'I can't get a signal. I need to phone Bess. She'll be wondering –'

Stuart shook his head, looking out to sea. 'Bollocks. She'll be calling you a wuss.'

A gaggle of walkers was stamping along the sandy path, all boots and maps and rucksacks. Celia was blearily surprised to see that it was still broad daylight.

'She can call me what she likes. This was a mistake. She should be at this bloody wedding instead of me.'

'Yeah.' He handed her a silver flask. 'Then she could explain how come you two are mates.'

Celia's dress flapped in the wind, whipping it up over her legs. Stuart was looking at her. She let the dress flutter, wondered if he'd had a flash of her knickers. The whisky burnt into her chest. She kicked her shoes off and flopped on to the grass.

'Oh, we met at work.'

They were partly hidden by a small clump of heather bushes now. The walkers were passing behind them, their faces shaded by drooping canvas sunhats. In front, the grey sea crawled.

'No, I mean, how come you're mates when you're so different. Bessie's hot. Everyone fancies her. God, you should have seen her when we were kids. She was all tanned and blonde. Like a honeypot. We all used to come up here. She had us all – come on, you know what she's like.'

Celia's stomach twisted sharply. Was it envy? Or curiosity? She leant back on her elbows, tipping her face casually to the sun. 'Sure. I've seen her in action.'

Stuart's feet were tapping restlessly on the ground. He took a bigger swig of whisky. He let the liquor lie in a wet slick on his lips before licking it thoughtfully. Celia watched his mouth, his jaw, the way he swallowed. 'So you'll know how horny she is?'

'Horny?' Celia went red as she said it. In the distance she could hear some more music striking up in the hotel. She crossed her outstretched ankles in a prim little gesture of denial. This bizarre description of her plump, funny, auburn-haired Bess was triggering a confused rush of pleasure inside her and she couldn't keep still. 'No. Not that kind of action. I've never seen her with a man.'

'That's because she doesn't want to shock you. Trust me, she'll be shagging anything in trousers, day and night, if she gets the chance. Like she's on heat.'

Another group of walkers stopped chattering and glanced over the heather. Celia smiled at them and put her hand out to land on his leg. It was so warm beneath the tartan. So firm. She stroked it. The fabric of the kilt wrinkled slightly up his thigh. She waited for him to flick her hand away. He didn't. He was staring, all moody now, out to sea.

Celia got up on her knees so that she was kneeling in front of him. 'She's not like that any more, Stuart. She's not really into – come on, she's your cousin. Perhaps it was all a bit of fun.'

'Oh, yeah. It was fun all right.' His breath rushed on her face as he turned to look at her, surprised how close she was. 'It was wild.'

Celia stayed right where she was, her other hand on his other leg now. Somehow she was now the one in control. But her own legs were shaking with excitement. Talking about Bess was the next best thing to having her here.

'Tell me what she was like back then,' Celia coaxed, pushing her hands further up his legs, pushing the kilt off those tense thighs. 'Did she do it like a bitch?'

'God, asking kinky questions about your friend? You're not such a saint under that demure little dress, are you? I should have guessed by the way you danced.'

He leant forwards and sniffed at her skin. 'You really want to know?'

'Tell me.'

He copied what she was doing to him, ran his fingers under her skirt to lift it up, pausing, not sure. The breeze off the sea rushed up her bare legs, ruffling her pussy. 'Do you like it down there on your knees, Celia?'

Celia couldn't speak, didn't want to speak. Her heart was rattling in her chest now. His fingers were exploring the top of her legs. She pushed her dampening pussy down into the palm of his hand, show him, urge him to go further, get right into her knickers. She slid her hands under his kilt, into the warmth between his legs. How weird. No trousers to grapple with, no buckles or zips. To find a man dressed, yet undressed. How vulnerable that made him. And how sexy to know what she'd been fantasising about all day, that all the time he was, they all were, totally bare under there.

She found his balls first, weighed them lightly in her hand like warm doughnuts. Then she circled the base of his cock with her other finger and thumb, suddenly trapping it tight for a moment. It jumped against her hand. It was already hard.

There was a crunch of boots along the gravelly path. She shifted closer, so that she was pressed up against him. She didn't have to move her hands away. Already the kilt had the advantage. Talk about easy access. She could touch him, hold him, even get her head under there and suck him off in broad daylight, and no one would know.

'I wish these bloody ramblers would all fuck off,' he grunted. His hands were on her buttocks now and he yanked her into him so that their groins were touching.

'Leave them alone. They can't see us,' she murmured, hearing the slick of her sex as his fingers finally pulled at her knickers and the silky fabric stuck briefly to her pubes. 'And even if they could – so what? We could give them a thrill.'

'You're wicked.'

He sounded like he couldn't believe it. Celia laughed. 'Is this what you used to do with Bess, up here on the cliffs, with people walking by? Is this what she liked?'

He groaned. She started to run her curled fist up and down his cock. 'I want to know, Stuart. Did you fuck my friend Bess up here on the cliffs?'

He had her knickers now, ripped them down her legs. She kicked them off, still kneeling, still gripping him.

'Well?'

She opened her legs, but he paused. 'I should get back to the party. Speeches –'

'Fuck the speeches.' She leant forwards and repeated it in his ear. His hair tickled her mouth. She licked his lobe. Her nipples pricked up as they brushed against the front of his jacket. 'You could fuck me, instead. Just like you fucked my Bess.'

'Your Bess?'

His breathing was quick, hot on her neck. He had her skirt right up round her waist now.

'I mean, my friend. Your Bessie.' Celia started to crawl on to his lap, shoving the kilt up. His cock was hard up against his stomach, pinned there by the sporran. She bit back her delight, wishing yet again that Bess was here to share the joke. But the sight of that big cock as she eased it away from his stomach was no joke. It quivered in the stark sea air, looking for a home. Stuart took her buttocks and hoisted her easily astride him. She glanced over his shoulder. Easy to look as if they were having a fully clothed kiss out there on the cliff.

'Yeah, we did it out here. We did it everywhere. Why do you want to know?'

Celia knelt up, keeping her pussy an inch or so away from his cock. Now her breasts were level with his face.

She gyrated a little so they scraped against his chin and the contact kick-started the harsh desire that had been simmering all day. She held his shoulders for balance, watched the lust sparking up in his eyes and a flush spreading through his face. He laid his big hands on her breasts and squeezed them through the fabric of her dress, rubbed the palms of his hand across her nipples and it was as if he was squeezing sighs out of her. She lowered her wet pussy a fraction, savouring the promise.

'You little minx. Butter wouldn't melt. Why do you keep asking about Bess?' he asked again. He glanced past her towards the hotel. She caught his instant of distraction and shoved her damp fanny down on the blunt end of his cock, felt it twitch and nudge upwards.

'You started it.'

'Oh, fuck it.' He groaned again, tipped his hips to push his cock further inside. 'I want it now.'

Celia didn't have the strength to stop him. She let herself sink down on to him, still speaking softly: 'And because it makes me horny. Because I'm here and she isn't. Because she had you, and now I want you.'

He took her hips and pushed her down on to his cock. Celia was wet and ready, and the length slid in easily.

'You girls,' he grunted, nudging further up inside her, her sex splitting open warm and wide for him. 'Always fighting over each other's toys.'

'Just tasting. Only fair.' Celia rocked herself very slightly, enough to send tiny thrills up her body. 'She wouldn't mind. We share everything.'

The urge to laugh out loud sizzled through her. If only he knew. If only Bess knew. Celia's hips jerked. She threw herself at him, rubbing her tits in his face one minute, pulling restlessly away the next, wishing they were in a bedroom somewhere and she could get this dress right off. Her nipples were hard and aching, wishing he could suck on them.

But since he couldn't, at least not now, her pussy needed to be touched and filled instead. A knot of lust was tightening inside her.

'She liked it rough,' he said. 'And she liked to be on her back, down in the grass.'

Celia was barely listening now. She started to sink, her legs really giving way, his cock supporting her. The urge to grind down greedily was overpowering. It had been a long time since she'd felt the smooth flesh of a man's cock inside her. A thumping great dildo, even if a gorgeous woman was wielding it and it was ribbed and called Stallion or Sheik or even Jock, was nothing like the throbbing energy of a real live one. Bess was going to kill her.

'Who would have thought it,' he groaned, seeing the lustful look on her face. 'A whore under that prissy flowery number.'

In answer she let his cock tease her burning clit for a moment, angled herself to rub it till it burnt, to prepare herself, use him like a toy. The smooth surface of him was already wet, slicked with her honey, and she felt wild and abandoned out here on the cliff top, she wanted to be that whore. She wished Bess was here to see. There were people walking past who could see her bouncing on his lap. They could hardly mistake it for a chaste kiss now.

She laughed out loud. The breeze was tugging at her hair, her skirt. Stuart's kilt flapped heavily on his leg. His cock was pulsing as it pushed right up inside until she was impaled, till she could spin on it.

'There's people –' he grunted.

'Let them see – can't stop,' Celia grunted back, starting the stroke up his cock.

She had no choice but to move, already the heat was spreading dangerously through her. His cock was growing, getting bigger, there was no choice even though she could see the group of people approaching, running, hurrying, anyway something different about them, not scruffy old ramblers in sunhats this time. She watched them rushing through the wooden gate from the hotel and along the cliff path but she had no choice but to grip him fast inside her. She was nearly up at the top. She was poised to move, move, graze every inch then slam back down

'They're coming. Out of sight – quick!'

Stuart suddenly wrapped her legs right round his hips and rolled with her down into the longer grass. He was still wedged inside her. She giggled softly, nails scratching under his shirt as she clutched him and rolled, then she was down on her back, a few feet away from the path, nothing between her and the public except a few scrubby bushes of heather.

Now he was crouched over her like some kind of hound and this was even better. His shirt, his tie, his jacket, still impeccable. His kilt like a tent over their arses. Her skirt hoisted round her waist like a cheap tart. They could hear the voices now, names, questions.

'You're going to have it rough, down in the grass,' Stuart panted, pushing at her, scraping the skin of her back. 'That's how your precious Bessie liked it.'

That did it. Streaks of evil excitement ran up her.

'Maybe she did *then*, honey,' she hissed back at him. 'But it's women she likes now.' She reared up to kiss him, pulled at his wet tongue with her teeth. 'Me. It's me she likes now.'

'Oh, really. Oh, really?' He shook his head, then drew his hips back slowly, getting ready. 'So what's her gay lover doing shagging with me?'

'I told you. We share. And you're gorgeous.' Celia kissed him again, then fell back in the grass, flinging her arms open. 'And I never said *I* was gay, did I? Might be bi. Might be straight. Whatever. Just do it to me as rough as you like!'

He said nothing. Just curled that bruised mouth. He

got rough, maybe angry, and started slamming into her, he was back in charge now, and there were voices distracting, plucking at them, close to the heather bush now, her name, definitely her name, the breeze tickling her bare butt for the last time as she lifted it to meet his, her pussy open to the air, both of them curving and arching and humping, and here it came, flooding through her just as someone gasped or screeched above their heads.

'Fuck – it's them. Talk of the devil. It's her.' Stuart was making no sense. His eyes glazed over, glaring only at Celia as he thrust and bucked at her and then his mouth relaxed in a real grin of pleasure as he started to come, pushing her over the little stones and prickles and rough grass with the force of it, her dress must be ripping, totally the whore now, and she failed, dismally, to bite back one last moan of pleasure.

Sound carries differently outdoors. Perhaps the people had gone past. There was only the sea breeze rushing in her ears. Celia's legs flopped sideways as Stuart rested on her for a moment. He rolled off, and his kilt rearranged itself perfectly, covering his subsiding cock.

'What are you doing, Celia? That's my cousin!'

The groom loomed above them. Beside him stood the bride's father. A couple of bridesmaids. Some other women, faces rosy from the dancing and the excitement and their mouths forming an O.

And Bess.

Primula Bond is the author of the Black Lace novels *Country Pleasures* and *Club Crème* and her short stories have appeared in numerous Wicked Words collections. Her new novel, *Behind the Curtain*, is published by Nexus in June 2007.

Public Relations

Mathilde Madden

Miles knows that Laura likes rope. Favours rope bondage above any other kind. Knots no boy scout knows and complicated diagrams, line drawings and photos that she insists Miles copy precisely on to her. Patterns and symbols like a new language. Written on the body.

Like a magic ritual, without the magic.

And after she has persuaded Miles to try every possible arrangement of jute and cotton and twine and her limbs on the ground, she starts talking about suspension. When Miles points out that his flat doesn't have the structure for that (and nor does hers) she tells him she knows the perfect place.

'Here, amongst all this . . . this archive?' Miles stands in the basement of Laura's office building, drifting in an ocean of foolscap and filing drawers.

'Yes, look at the ceiling supports.'

Miles looks up. The ceiling is criss-crossed with metal supports. Above this basement there are four floors of Motif, the weighty PR company where Laura is an account manger. Maybe Motif needs all the extra reinforcement for all its wily, headline-grabbing schemes. Or maybe it was just designed by the god of kink to perfectly fulfil Laura's latest twisted desires.

Laura jumps up and catches one of the grid of iron beams, which supports the ceiling, swinging from it. 'It holds my weight, see, you don't need to worry.' While

Miles watches she swings from beam to beam. Hand over hand. Monkeylike. Childlike. Un-Laura-like.

Miles looks around. The perfect place? Almost, but not quite. Not quite private enough, really. Oh, the building is empty right now, Miles is sure Laura wouldn't risk it otherwise. But he notices a small grimy window in the door to this storeroom and he notes it coolly like he does everything.

Casually, still on surveillance, Miles pulls open a filing drawer. It doesn't make a sound. Clearly Motif favours beautifully made expensive furniture – even in the basement. Miles lifts out a sheaf of paper. 'These files are . . . these are personnel files. Aren't they confidential? This cabinet should be locked.'

'Yep. Whatever. Does it matter?' Laura drops the foot or so to the ground, landing clack-clack on her expensive stiletto heels. 'Anyway, shall we get on? I was thinking a Strappado.'

'I thought you wanted a suspension,' Miles says, not looking at her as he bends over to place the file he's holding down on the floor. Sitting on the floor next to it is a soft leather bag beside his. A bag from which he starts to pull armfuls of bright-white cotton rope.

'I do,' Laura says, a little breathless already. As she speaks she clasps her hands behind her back and then slowly raises them up in the air, bending over automatically as she does so, until her arms are pointing straight up – perfectly vertical and rigid in the air – and her body is parallel to the floor. 'Strappado. Oh yes.'

Miles walks softly up behind her and presses his groin against her smoothly tailored buttocks, leaning across her back to place his lips right by her ear. Very slowly he whispers, 'A Strappado with suspension will dislocate both of your shoulders, you stupid little bitch.'

He knows that little note of hardness in his voice will have got to her. Somewhere inside. He also knows she won't show it. Yet.

But Laura gives him a little, because she catches her breath and wriggles against him, precise and calculated, turning her head so her eyes meet his. Too close to focus; black blurs. 'Just do it, Miles.'

Orders already is it? Silently, Miles straightens and catches Laura's patiently pre-positioned wrists in one hand, flicking the rope he is holding into place with the other; capturing them with bondage-master ease. He knows it feels like lovemaking to Laura when he wraps the ropes around her like this. More intimate than any caress. And he knows she's never known anyone who could give her what she needs – what she hates to admit she needs – like he can.

As Miles works on, throwing the end of the rope around the beam and securing it, Laura says nothing more that is intelligible apart from one single half-gasped 'God, tighter', as he clinches her elbows strictly behind her back.

But a few minutes later, after he's finally managed to re-tie the rope in a way that satisfies Laura's masochistic specifications, and is hitching off the one that holds her wrists high in the air, Laura looks over at him angrily, shuffling her feet. Feet that are still very much on the ground.

'This isn't a suspension.' Her angry lips barely move as she speaks.

Miles finishes tying off the rope and walks back to where she stands. She is bent right over by the way the rope is pulling her arms back and into the air. 'I know,' he says, 'I thought I'd take charge, make an executive decision.'

Her eyes are luminous. He particularly likes that. That fury. It's making him hard. 'But I said I wanted suspension. We came here for suspension.'

Miles smiles and doesn't reply. He has many possible replies in his head – mostly about doing what he wants for a change, or isn't he meant to be the one making the decisions here, or back to the old dislocation of shoulders idea. But he says nothing. Why explain? He knows he doesn't need to. He walks back to his old soft bag. He reaches inside and pulls out a spreader bar about three feet long, and with a lightly padded ankle cuff at each end. He carries it back over to Laura.

Quietly, he fastens each of her ankles to either end of the bar, pulling her legs wide apart. Her feet are still on the floor though. Even with this extra stretch. This is not the suspension she wanted – but pretty uncomfortable nevertheless. Not giving Laura quite what she wants is always part of Miles's best and most deviously twisted plans. This position is every bit as frustrating as being suspended would be. Yet it's safe and restrictive and leaves Laura utterly vulnerable. It's also on Miles's terms. Laura growls low with annoyance, twisting pointlessly.

Miles stands up from where he was checking the ankle cuffs and looks at her for a moment, bending a little to get at eye level and then raising her defiant chin with his index finger.

He scrutinises her eyes. Was she there yet? Every time the same – she basically has to be forced into subspace, fighting tooth and claw all the damn way.

But yes, close now. Her eyes *are* a little glassy. The spreader bar has helped somewhat and in spite of herself she is going under. She is acquiescing. *Finally.*

And Miles smiles. 'You know, you'll enjoy it much more if you just let me do it. I thought you were supposed to be the submissive. How about submitting now and again?' He bends down and gets kiss-close to her lips. 'Or just shutting up?'

She growls again, pulling a little more defiance from somewhere. 'Make me.' She is practically dripping with it, but she doesn't fool Miles. He knows for certain now she is less than a breath away from sub-space. Well, maybe not a breath, maybe something a little more substantial.

Miles has the very thing to tip her over. 'Make you? Oh my pleasure.' He reaches in his pocket and pulls out a ball gag. Holding it up so she could see exactly what it is. Just a rubber ball on leather thong – the exact same thing she has seen a million times before – except that with this one the ball, which is usually red rubber, is sugar pink. Miles had been unable to resist it. Too perfect for her.

Laura looks at the gag and there's a second's delay, as if she's processing the information. 'How many times Miles,' she says eventually, 'how many times do I have to tell you I don't like being gagged?'

Miles's next smile is the one he knows is slow and seductive. Melting. 'Oh, you know I have such a terrible memory,' he says walking slowly towards where she is trussed and helpless, twisting, with her feet scuffling on the polished concrete floor.

'You try it and I'll safe word so fast –' But it's an empty threat.

'No. No you won't,' Miles interrupts and, holding her head still with a hasty handful of hair, he pushes the ball into her mouth. If she has any further complaints about Miles's treatment he's happily ignorant about them now.

Once the thong is tied tightly behind her head and her hair lovingly rearranged, Miles takes a step back. 'You never safe word, sweetheart, you know that,' he says. Then he leans in to peck her on the cheek and whispers, 'And pink is *so* your colour.'

The noises Laura makes after that are pretty loud, but unintelligible, so Miles simply tunes them out. He walks around her a couple of times and then stops behind her and drops his trousers.

He puts his hands on her hips to still her where she

is struggling and squirming. He knows all his knots would hold through any amount of fighting, but he would still rather she calmed down so he could enjoy his handiwork. He slips a hand up her softly expensive skirt and she seems to respond then, moving into his touch. Wanting.

There's no underwear beneath her skirt and she's easily wet enough that he can tell he isn't going to have to bother with any kind of foreplay or lube. He takes his hand away, leaves a beat for her anticipation to build – wait for it – and then he slides inside.

He fucks her very, very gently, rocking on the balls of his feet. He knows what she would be expecting – wanting – at this point: rough treatment. A harsh nasty fucking; leaving her bruised and rope burnt. *Well, guess what you're not getting, baby?*

How long is it going to take her to realise that what he really relishes giving her is a sweet combination of exactly what she wants spiked with just enough of what she doesn't want to give him that feeling of controlling her? Controlling Miss Uncontrollable. For him that's what it's all about.

He keeps his movements light and gentle because he doesn't want her to have a chance of coming. He knows how much that will drive her mad after the planning she's put into this.

But he does give her a little bit of something special. 'You know,' he breathes into her ear, pressing his chest down across her back and twisting around her bound arms, 'I've been thinking, all the time we've been here, about how much fun it would be to leave you like this.'

Laura makes a muffled sound, a moan that could be anything from desperate arousal to frustrated rage.

'Mmm-hmm. It would be so easy. At your place of work. And who'd find you? A cleaner? A boss? A good-looking co-worker? Would they cut you down? Maybe I could leave a sign on your arse, here, inviting anyone who found you to use you for their pleasure.'

Laura's moans get more intense and unreadable than ever. She's moving against him as far has her bondage will allow, but Miles keeps his movements as restrained as she is.

'It would be terrible for you,' Miles continues, 'to be exposed like that. I know you like to keep this wanton side of yourself very private. Ice queen in public, bitch on heat in private. Oh, I know the drill. Ironic, isn't it that you work in public relations, when you like your own relations to be kept so very private.'

Laura moans. She's close to coming. Miles stops talking then. Laura still has a long time to wait before that. And then, when she is standing growling and spluttering frustratedly into his pink gag, with his warm semen gliding down her glass-smooth stockings, he walks away from her, retrieves the files he had slipped into his bag and begins to read.

Her file and Gabriel Blaine's.

It's nearly an hour later when he lets her go. He's found a lot more information in the forgotten drawers of Motif's basement since then. Including the time the late-night cleaners start their shift. Miles spotted the cleaning supplies storeroom next to the basement when they came in and decides to sit tight for the shift starting. He wonders if any of the cleaners look through the basement window as they collect their buckets and baskets of spray cans. He waits until he has listened to them come and go and confused panic lights Laura's eyes.

'I am never playing with you again,' Laura spits as he unhitches the rope that supports her, letting her stiff limbs tumble to the floor.

'Oh, don't pretend you didn't love every minute,' he

says, straddling her as she lies on the floor and tugging loose the knots which hold her wrists.

And then, with her wrists mostly loose but still half-tangled in bits of rope and with the spreader bar still holding her ankles apart, Miles pushes her skirt up and presses his tongue against her wet cunt. She bucks. Fire in his hands. He can't resist pulling away and saying, 'So, you hated every minute, did you?'

'Uh.' Just a desperate noise.

He gives her back his tongue, twirling it around her clit until she screams so loudly that he swears he hears one of the cleaners knock over their bucket upstairs.

Before Laura has recovered, Miles has sorted and stowed all his rope and equipment back in his bag. Along with a couple of Motif's badly stored personnel files.

Later, very late at night, waiting for her to call, Miles flicks open Gabriel Blaine's file. The picture of him on the very first page had already told Miles all he needed to know when he looked at it in the basement. Dark hair, dark smile. This is the guy Laura is thinking of cheating on me with? Miles knows she has been thinking about it for at least a month.

Did you really think I wouldn't notice? Did she really think that, when she had had that expensive haircut, changed her make-up and started dropping a rather distinctive-sounding name into conversation just a little bit *too* often, a man like Miles wouldn't notice?

As he reads through Gabriel's file again, checks the dates, Miles notes that Gabriel started as account manager at Motif just over a month ago. How very unsurprising.

In some ways Miles thinks it's kind of sad. Sad that a sparklingly intelligent woman like Laura could have her head turned by a walking, talking piece of beefcake like Gabriel Blaine, without really knowing if he could meet her very precise sexual needs.

Miles thinks about her then, semi-suspended from the ceiling in Motif's basement, twisting and making muffled noises into the pretty pink gag. Thinks about how wet she was when he fucked her, and how much wetter she was later when he pressed his mouth to her cunt. Wet and angry; always her way. Precise needs, indeed.

But the thing about needs like Laura's – or, indeed, needs like Miles's – is that they couldn't be met by just anyone. Laura needs to understand that. Finding someone who has it in them, who can climb and soar the way she needs them to, isn't something that she can tell by looking.

What people show in public, the way they present themselves to the world, often gives away nothing at all about what they want in bed. In fact, more often than not it's just the opposite. The powerful politician who wants to be tied up and whipped might be a cliché. But it's a cliché Miles has seen walking, talking and moaning with pleasure more times than he can count during his voyages through the sexual underworld.

Just a glance at Gabriel's photograph is enough for Miles to know that is how Laura sees him, though. All that packed muscle and that dark brooding brow.

Miles knows that, when Laura looks at Gabriel, she imagines him slamming her up against the wall, kicking her legs apart, taking her hard, being the brutal beast he looks like. She sees a man who is all built – practically made of coiled power – and thinks that power just can't wait to be unleashed. It doesn't occur to her that it would be far more fitting to see all that urgent muscle bound and contained.

Because Miles knows what makes Gabriel tick. Not

from looking at his public corporate face. Miles knows because Miles has met Gabriel before.

It was at a party. Some night after a club at some anonymous suburban house. Miles was there with a pretty girl on a dog leash whose name and face are now buried by their many successors. Thinking about it now, Miles finds that a bit shameful, but, in some ways, maybe that's what happens when you find the one – all the others are eclipsed by the blinding light, drowned out by the choirs of angels. Not that he thinks of Laura like that. Not really.

But, the party. Gabriel. He remembers Gabriel. Too pretty to go unnoticed. That great hulk was kneeling, handcuffed, kissing the boots of his mistress – or at least his mistress for the night.

Lots of people looked at Gabriel at that party. Even in a room full of tousled blondes badly packed into PVC, Gabriel, with his luminescent dark skin and his big bright eyes, drew the gazes like nothing else in the room. There is something about a big alpha-looking man on his knees that appeals to almost anyone. Miles watched Gabriel for a long time at that party, with the kind of detached fascination he had perfected for events like these. He watched for far longer than he should have done to be fair to his own pretty thing.

He was watching when the seated mistress had lifted her foot from the floor, so Gabriel could bend right down and suck on her stiletto heel like it was a slender cock. And he watched Gabriel's own cock – heavy, hard and barely contained by the white jock he was wearing – twitch and throb as she forced the shaft in and out of his lips.

So Miles knows that when Gabriel looks at Laura he doesn't see what she hopes he sees. He doesn't think about what a delicious sight she'll be, brought down a peg or two, with all the puff taken out of her billowing sails. Oh no. He doesn't see Laura the way Miles sees her. Miles knows that when Gabriel looks at Laura his cock gets hard imagining how that strict, sharp-tongued bitch she presents in the boardroom at Motif would translate her nasty act to his bedroom. And to him, helpless and tormented beneath her sharp heels.

Those higher-than-high heels – the conundrum they embody. Miles knows that Gabriel must think of them as signals of Laura's taste for cruel dominance – pedestals – but he knows that they are really a part of her twisted masochism.

So there's poor Gabriel; like Laura just too young and pretty to realise that a woman who struts like a dominatrix in public might be something rather different between the rubber sheets.

It's while Miles is thinking about this that he notices that Laura still hasn't called. He torments himself by thinking that she's at home, fantasising about Gabriel.

He looks over at Laura's file – he'd taken that from Motif's basement too. He notices her date of birth and he gets an idea. Wouldn't Gabriel Blaine be a perfect way to give Laura exactly what she wanted in exactly the way she didn't want it?

The next morning, Miles calls Gabriel at Motif. He pretends to be talking business for a while, saying he has a new company and needs a public-relations firm. Then he says, 'Your name is familiar, though, Gabriel Blaine?'

Gabriel laughs. A deep boom of a laugh. Miles imagines Laura, sitting only feet away, squeezing her thighs together at that dark sound, casting it as potentially a laugh of sadistic glee. 'It's a name people tend to remember,' Gabriel says.

'Oh, I know,' says Miles. 'But where do I know you from? Hang on . . . Are you a friend of Sabrina?'

'Sabrina?' Gabriel says, the tiniest hitch in his voice.

'Mmm, you know who I mean, don't you?'

'Yes.'

Sabrina is the name of the dominatrix Miles saw Gabriel with at that party. He isn't really up on that kind of thing, but he called around. Finally found someone who remembered that party better than he did. Remembered Gabriel. Remembered who he was with.

It isn't about blackmail with Miles, it's about persuasion. Miles likes being persuasive. Actually revels in it. And Gabriel turns out to be the kind of man who is easily persuaded by the right kind of invitation.

Laura calls Miles in the end. She always does. She let it go a week this time, which was almost her record, but then, one hot night . . .

'Hey, Miles. It's Laura.'

'Laura . . .? I don't . . .?'

'Oh fuck off, Miles, don't give me that fake Laura-who crap. I want to meet up.'

'Oh. *That* Laura.'

'Listen, I was thinking, it's my birthday next week. How about we do something special? I was thinking something long term. Over the whole weekend. A captivity scene. We'd need equipment, but I can go online. Get some new stuff. Maybe metal.'

'Metal, that's new for you. I thought you were all about rope?'

'I can change my mind, can't I?'

'Yeah, OK,' Miles says, trying not to chuckle because, really, this is just too perfect.

'Great!' Laura sounds almost surprised that he agrees to what she wants so easily. But she doesn't sound wary. Even now, Laura still doesn't seem to check for a catch. 'Shall I go online, order some stuff?'

'No, baby, leave it to me.'

* * *

Miles knows that Laura is being impulsive again. Asking for the moon. He knows that the kind of custom-made hardcore metal restraints she's thinking of are crazy expensive and would take months to be delivered if ordered online. But Miles knows about the Mole's House.

Tinkle-tinkle.

'Ah, hello, sir. No lady friend?' The Mole is brisk and small with dark tight eyes like bugle beads. He sits behind the counter working on a wide strip of black leather with a knife easily the length of his own forearm.

'No. Not today.' Miles wonders which lady he's referring to. When had he last been here? Like most of his people he bought so many toys online these days.

'Ah, that's quite the shame, sir.' The Mole glances down, gouges heavily with his knife twice, and then continues, 'So are you still interested in the percussion section?' He gestures towards a wall hung with canes, whips, paddles and crops, and one long bullwhip snaking across the top.

Miles shakes his head. 'No, not today.' He remembers then, the last time. A thin blonde, crazy as a masochist; she was always dragging him here for new toys to hit her with.

But that isn't the requirement today. Today Miles wants restraints. Just as Laura had outlined. Metal. Strong ones. Big ones. Not the cheap leather or tinny handcuffs he knows he would be offered in the normal sexual recreation shops in Soho. And not the single old set of metal handcuffs he has back at home.

Gabriel is a big man. Miles remembers that party again, how Gabriel's thick wrists looked cartoonish in a pair of thin handcuffs. Miles wants the aesthetic to be right. And he wants stuff he can depend on. He needs the Mole's House.

The Mole frowns when he explains what he needs.

'These are very big measurements,' he says in an accent Miles can't place and isn't even sure is real.

Miles nods. He sees the look in the Mole's eyes and decides to let him wonder.

The Mole looks at Miles for a moment more, his little nose wrinkling and his whiskers – because at that moment he really did seem to have whiskers – shaking with a rhythm all of their own. And then he says, 'I think you should step out back, sir.'

The Mole leads the way through a rattling beaded curtain and into a room that is even darker and more groaningly ominous than the shop proper. The room is full of furniture. 'Alternative' furniture.

The shuffling Mole walks over to a wall where a mass of chains, rings, hooks and manacles are tangled and draped together, swooping off ceiling hooks and dangling like forest branches. But as the Mole turns, weighing a great iron ring in his hands and grinning toothily, Miles sees the cage and his idea ratchets up a level.

On Friday evening, Miles picks Laura up. He notices that she is wearing a black dress, which he has often said that he liked, but when she gets into the car he doesn't say anything. Not even 'Happy birthday'.

Laura isn't so quiet. She's full of questions, curiosity, demands. 'You got them, right? Metal restraints. I took Monday off work just in case. I mean, Gabriel can cope without me.'

'I'm sure Gabriel can cope,' Miles says, stressing almost every word in the sentence.

'OK, so what's the plan? You're going to chain me up, what, standing?'

'Why don't you just wait and see?'

'I hate "wait and see". I want to *know. Now.* How do I know that it's something I'll like?'

'Laura, baby. You'll love it. I promise. It's exactly what you want.'

'Oh really? You know exactly what I want now, do you?'

'Oh yeah.' *And I'm going to give it to you.*

Laura bounces up the steps ahead of Miles – his flat is on the third floor. Her excitement is making him feel a little strange. Torn between a desire to turn this all around and give her what she wants and a deep pulse in his cock when he thinks about how twisted everything is going to become when he opens the door.

He arrives at the door to his flat with Laura waiting, hopping from foot to stilettoed foot. Eager. Buzzing. He puts his key in the lock and stands back to let her enter first.

She heads straight in the living room. Probably hoping that's where her new toys will be. Hoping right. Over the clatter of his keys on the hall table he hears her say, 'Oh, why have you got the curtains closed in here?' And then, 'What *is* this?' And then, 'God. What the . . . Oh my God! Gabriel?'

Miles moves to the living-room doorway so he can see her. See her face when she sees her gift – exactly what she wants and yet, not what she wants at all. Gabriel Blaine, her big hard-bodied fantasy dom, trussed in metal manacles and crouching in a cage Miles bought from the Mole's House. The cage isn't that small, but Gabriel is so big that his body inside the cage looks like an optical illusion. His muscles are burnished with sweat as he struggles and shifts position constantly in the small space. He's crouched, his big haunches splayed by his curled chest. His head bowed by the top of the cage. His hands are chained behind his back. His ankles are cuffed together too – albeit rather needlessly. He's naked, but a little scrap of metal glints at his crotch. An impulse buy.

Laura's expression won't stay still. She's shocked, horrified, aroused, confused . . .

Aroused?

Miles never saw that coming.

'Laura?' he says.

Laura turns and pushes past him into the hallway. For a moment Miles thinks she's leaving. Walking out. But she stops by the hall table and picks up Miles's keys. A set of keys that contains a few extra ones tonight. The keys to Gabriel's restraints.

She pockets them and heads back into the living room, pausing only to close the door softly in Miles's face.

Miles is sitting out in the hall, listening to the sounds coming from behind the closed door – familiar sounds of two people making each other very, very happy. He thinks how funny it is that just as what a person shows you in public can hide what they are really like in private, what they show you in private can sometimes be just another mask. Like peeling an onion. Who'd have thought that Laura would pull a switch on him like that?

Just goes to show, you never can tell.

Mathilde Madden is the author of the Black Lace novels *Mad About the Boy*, *Peep Show* and *Equal Opportunities*.

WICKED WORDS ANTHOLOGIES –

THE BEST IN WOMEN'S EROTIC WRITING FROM THE UK AND USA

Really do live up to their title of 'wicked' – Forum

Deliciously sexy and explicitly erotic, *Wicked Words* collections are guaranteed to excite. This immensely popular series is perfect for those who enjoy lust-filled, wildly indulgent sexy stories. The series is a showcase of writing by women at the cutting edge of the genre, pushing the boundaries of unashamed, explicit writing.

The first ten *Wicked Words* collections are now available in eye-catching illustrative covers and, since 2005, we have been publishing themed collections beginning with *Sex in the Office*. If you never got the chance to buy all the books when they were first published, you can now complete your collection and be the envy of your friends! Look out for the colourful covers – guaranteed to stand out from everything else on the erotica shelves – or alternatively order from us direct on our website at www.blacklace-books.co.uk

Full of action and attitude, humour and hedonism, they are a wonderful contribution to any erotic book collection. Each book contains 15–20 stories. Here's a sampler of what's on offer:

Wicked Words

ISBN 0 352 33363 4
£6.99

- In an elegant, exclusive ladies' club, *fin de siècle* fantasies come to life.
- In a dark, primeval forest, a mysterious young woman shapeshifts into a creature of the night.
- In a sleazy midwest motel room, a fetishistic female patrol cop gets dressed for work.

More Wicked Words

ISBN 0 352 33487 8
£6.99

- Tasha's in lust with a celebrity chef – it's his temper that drives her wild.
- Reverend Billy Washburn needs salvation from Sister Julie – a teenage temptress who's set him on fire.
- Pearl doesn't want to get married; she just wants sex and blueberry smoothies on her LA poolside patio.

Wicked Words 3

ISBN 0 352 33522 X
£6.99

- The seductive dentist – Nick's encounter with sexy Dr May turns into a pretty unorthodox check-up.
- The gender-playing journalist – Kat lusts after male strangers whilst cruising as a gay man.
- The submissive PA – Mandy's new job fulfils her fantasies and reveals her boss's fetish for all things leather.

Wicked Words 4

ISBN 0 352 33603 X
£6.99

- Alexia has always fantasised about being Marilyn Monroe. One day a surprise package arrives with a sexy courier.
- Bridget is tired of being a chef. Maybe a little experimentation with a colleague is all she needs to get back her love of food.
- A mysterious woman prowls the back streets of New York, seeking pleasure from the sleaziest corners of the city.

Wicked Words 5

ISBN 0 352 33642 0
£6.99

- Connor the tax auditor gets a shocking surprise when he investigates a client's expenses claim for strap-on sex toys.
- Kate the sexy museum curator allows a buff young graduate to make a thorough excavation of her hidden treasures.
- Melanie the interior designer and porn fan swaps blokes with her best mate and gets up to nasty fun with the builders.

Wicked Words 6

ISBN 0 352 33690 0
£6.99

- Maxine gets turned on selling exquisite lingerie to gentlemen customers.
- Jules is stripped naked and covered in cream when she becomes the birthday cake for her brother's best mate's thirtieth.
- Elle wears handcuffs for an indecent liaison with a stranger in a motel room.

Wicked Words 7

ISBN 0 352 33743 5
£6.99

- An artist's model wants to be more than just painted, and things get pretty steamy in the studio.
- A bride-to-be pays a clandestine visit to the bathroom with her future father-in-law, and gets much more than she bargained for.
- An uptight MP has his mind (and something else!) blown by a charming young woman of devious intentions.

Wicked Words 8

ISBN 0 352 33787 7
£6.99

- Adam the young supermarket assistant cannot believe his luck when a saucy female customer needs his help.
- Lauren's first night at a fetish club brings out the sexy show-off in her when she is required to wear an outrageously daring rubber outfit.
- Cat's fantasies about hunky construction workers come true when they start work opposite her Santa Monica beach house.

Wicked Words 9

ISBN 0 352 33860 1

- Sarah gets a surprise when she and her husband go dogging in the local car park.
- The Wytchfinder interrogates a pagan wild woman and finds himself aroused to bursting point.
- Miss Charmond's charm school relies on old-fashioned discipline to keep wayward girls in line.

Wicked Words 10 – The Best of Wicked Words

- An editor's choice of the best, most original stories of the past five years.

Sex in the Office

ISBN 0 352 33944 6

- A lady boss with a foot fetish
- A security guard who's a CCTV voyeur
- An office cleaner with a crush on the MD

Explores the forbidden – and sometimes blatant – lusts that abound in the workplace where characters get up to something they shouldn't, with someone they shouldn't – someone who works in the office.

Sex on Holiday

ISBN 0 352 33961 6

- Spanking in Prague
- Domination in Switzerland
- Sexy salsa in Cuba

Holidays always bring a certain frisson. There's a naughty holiday fling to suit every taste in this X-rated collection. With a rich sensuality and an eye on the exotic, this makes the perfect beach read!

Sex at the Sports Club

ISBN 0 352 33991 8

- A young cricketer is seduced by his mate's mum
- A couple swap partners on the golf course
- An athletic female polo player sorts out the opposition

Everyone loves a good sport – especially if he has fantastic thighs and a great bod! Whether in the showers after a rugby match, or proving his all at the tennis court, there's something about a man working his body to the limit that really gets a girl going. In this latest themed collection we explore the sexual tensions that go on at various sports clubs.

Sex in Uniform

ISBN 0 352 34002 9

- A tourist meets a mysterious usherette in a Parisian cinema
- A nun seduces an unusual confirmation from a priest
- A chauffeur sees it all via the rear-view mirror

Once again, our writers new and old have risen to the challenge and produced so many steamy and memorable stories for fans of men and women in uniform. Polished buttons and peaked caps will never look the same again.

Sex in the Kitchen

ISBN 0 352 34018 5

- Dusty's got a sweet tooth and the pastry chef is making her mouth water
- Honey's crazy enough about Jamie to be prepared and served as his main course
- Milly is a wine buyer who gets a big surprise in a French cellar

Whether it's a fiery chef cooking up a storm in a Michelin-starred restaurant or the minimal calm of sushi for two, there's nothing like the promise of fine feasting to get in the mood for love. From lavish banquets to a packed lunch at a motorway service station, this Wicked Words collection guarantees to serve up a good portion!

Sex on the Move

ISBN 0 352 34034 7

- Nadia Kasparova sees the earth move from a space station while investigating sex at zero gravity . . .
- Candy likes leather pants, big powerful bikes, miles of open road and the men who ride them . . .
- Penny and Clair run a limousine business guaranteed to STRETCH the expectations of anyone lucky enough to sit in the back . . .

Being on the move can be an escape from convention, the eyes of those we know, and from ourselves. There are few experiences as liberating as travelling. So whether it's planes, trains and automobiles, ships or even a space station, you can count on the Wicked Words authors to capture the exhilaration, freedom and passion of modern women on the move. Original tales of lust and abandon guaranteed to surprise and thrill!

Sex and Shopping

ISBN 0 352 34076 2

- Francesca exchanges the man in her life after an encounter in the men's changing rooms
- Juliet gets a ladder in her stockings, but meeting the mysterious stranger who replaces them hits a few snags
- Adele creates an internet shopping experience with a twist: her new online business launches with only one item for sale: herself

Who says shopping is a sex-substitute? Wicked Words discovers it's just about the best time to make all kinds of deals and special purchases. Transactions of the sensual variety that keep the tills and senses ringing long after the stores have closed. Whether you're shopping for shoes, jeans, a corset, or the guy that delivers it to your door, *Sex and Shopping* is a must-have item.